Conrad Williams

was born in Warrington. appeared in numero magazines including *Panurge, Sunk Island Review, ABeSea, A Book of Two Halves, Last Rites & Resurrections, Blue Motel, Dark Terrors 2* and *3, The Year's Best Horror Stories XXII, Darklands 2* and *Sirens and Other Daemon Lovers*. In 1993 he won the British Fantasy Award for Best Newcomer and was a recipient of a Littlewood Arc prize. *Head Injuries* is his first novel.

'*Conrad Williams is a demon-Spirit, weaving beautiful nests of tight prose, hatching spectacular nightmares out of love, guilt, remorse and unreliable memory. The flights of his fiction are dazzling and dangerous.*'

– Graham Joyce

To Hilary —
You went to so much
trouble... just for me!

Head Injuries

Conrad Williams

Thanks —
love
Conrad
x

FRONTLINES

THE DO-NOT PRESS

First Published in Great Britain in 1998 by
The Do-Not Press
PO Box 4215
London SE23 2QD

A Paperback Original

ISBN 1 899344 36 5

British Library Cataloguing in Publication Data. A catalogue
record for this book is available from the British Library.

Printed and bound in Great Britain by The Guernsey Press Co Ltd.

h g f e d c b a

Picture credit (front cover): Conrad Williams
Photo adjustment& cover design by Angus McGuillicuddy

Acknowledgments

I am indebted to the following for their friendship, encouragement and support: Richard Coady, Mark Morris, Nicholas Royle and Michael Marshall Smith.

Thanks also to: Frank Baguley of the National Caving Association, Suzanne and Richard Barbieri, Michael Blackburn, the British Fantasy Society, Ramsey Campbell, Peter Crowther, Ellen Datlow, Francesca Day, Jim Driver, Les and Val Edwards, Adèle Fielding, Jo Fletcher, Neil Gaiman, Paula Grainger, Annette Green, Mike Harrison, David Hosier, Simon Ings, Liz Jensen, Steve Jones, Graham Joyce, Chris Kenworthy, Robert Kirby, Joel Lane, Paul McAuley, Robin Newby, Kim Newman, John Oakey, Caroline Oakley, David Peak, Amanda Reynolds, Kate Ryan, Seamus Ryan, Anna Scott, Dave Sutton, Karl Edward Wagner, Nel Whatmore, Terri Windling, my sister Nicola and Keri Green.

This novel is for my parents, Leonora and Grenville, with much love.

Death is its own best friend, and our dreams know it.
Derek Raymond, 'How the Dead Live'

Prologue

Sometimes, during his morning walks across the field to school, he would see the cat. It was coffee-coloured, with blue eyes and a kink at the tip of its tail, as if it had been snapped like a green stick. Often, it would approach him and allow its tummy to be stroked while it purred and creased its eyes at him in pleasure. On these occasions, he felt that his day at school would be all right; that the teachers might notice him and praise his work. That the boys would leave him alone.

The cat was there, but it was dead. They had painted its face green and gouged its eyes out, leaving them on a paper plate next to the body. The words YOR BREKFAST, CUNTIE had been scrawled upon it. The smell of piss rose from the bundle that had stretched and vibrated beneath his fingers, like a promise made by the future. He hoped it was the cat's piss. He hoped that it had died quickly.

He felt for the package in his pocket. Still there, as it had been since he left the house that morning. His mother's kiss felt like a scar, cold against his cheek. She didn't understand. She thought that it was every boy's right to get roughed up in the playground. *If it's good for the gorilla, it's good for you*, she'd said. *It's natural*, she'd said, *it's the male genes fighting for dominance. Should be like your dad. He had a spine of iron when he was young.*

He still does, he'd wanted to say, bolted and screwed into his back to halt the progress of multiple sclerosis. His father never said anything. Just stared and sneered at him like a scrunched-up piece of paper wadded into his wheelchair, a spinning thread of silver connecting his lip with his shoulder.

'All right there, Dad,' he whispered, continuing his journey towards the playground. 'No, don't get up.' He barked laughter and had to swallow hard against a stream of bile. Don't bother getting up.

They were waiting for him, as they always did, on the fringe of the teachers' car park. The school behind them was like a theatrical backdrop. Four boys. Blazers framing off-white shirts, collars undone, unfeasibly wide Windsor knots in their ties.

'Has anybody seen my pussy?' called one and a laugh got juggled about between them. It wasn't pleasant laughter. There was a nervousness in it. This one here, with the ginger hair and the invisible eyelashes, he usually started it and he stepped forward now, spitting into the ground in front of his feet to stop the boy going any further.

'Hey, he's got toothpaste round his gob, the scruffy twat!' someone called. Always someone called but he couldn't focus on them any more, he didn't care. He wasn't here. He was somewhere else, in a soft field filled with poppies, chasing a cat to a shaded place where they could sit and curl against each other and be free from anyone.

'Nah, it's not toothpaste. It's spunk. You been sucking your dad off again, you dirty bastard? And him, with his iffy back an' all.'

A place to which the cat would take him, through the trees where the sun always shone and there was food and other cats and the sky filled with purring. Every eye that turned on him would blink with acceptance and love. Every paw that landed on his face would be soft and entreating, claws sheathed. Come and play. Come and look at this tree with me. Let's sleep in the shade. Come and play.

'I had a fuck awful morning,' Ginger spat. 'Bus late. Spilled me Coke all over me fucking lap. Cap it all, I did the wrong cocking homework. I decide to be a good boy, do the exercises, keep Lovesey off my dicking back and what happens? I shitting well do the quadratics instead of the simultaneouses. Not that it really matters, cos I couldn't fucking do them anyway. But the effort, see? All that bastard effort down the shitter. And I want you to know how bad I feel. Which is pretty fucking evil, actually.'

The fur. So deep, so impossibly soft. The heat of an uncomplicated body beneath it. Simple, unconditional love.

He took the canister from his pocket and drenched his head under the spray. His eyes were blinded with the pain and he almost stopped, but somehow it was better now because he couldn't see them. They were making noises; uncertain noises. He imagined them backing off; they knew how desperate he'd become. Surely that time by the gym had warned them. But it was over now.

He struck the wheel of the lighter and his head took off.

Who was screaming? Them or him? He really didn't give a shit.

one
gravitating

We stopped at the wishing well opposite Woolworth's but even though she saw me feed it a coin, Helen didn't kiss me. The tide was rushing in. Across Morecambe Bay the hills of the Lake District were pale and blue; I could just make out villages speckled white in the hollows of land. At night, lights pooled there like scattered new pennies.

I asked Helen if she fancied some tea. She nodded but I couldn't see her eyes to gauge whether she really wanted to shelter from the cold: her hair was wrapped in thin bands across her face. The scar was a white arrow flying from her mouth.

We crossed the road, the wind swiftly dying as we stalked beneath the awnings of shops and guest houses until we found a café; I remembered it from my college days – they even had the same naff plastic tablecloths and paper napkins, chalked menus and a No Smoking section that comprised a single table and one stool under an extractor fan. Inside I nodded towards a table by the window and dithered uncertainly in the aisle where a cross-eyed dog was licking its undercarriage.

'There'll be a waitress along,' said Helen. I sat opposite her, again unsure as to the wisdom of my choice. Maybe she wanted me to sit alongside. It was tiring me out.

When the waitress came over I asked for a piece of toast and two teas.

'Coffee for me, please,' said Helen, after our order had been pencilled. The waitress withdrew, giving me a sour look. The café was empty but for us. It was mid-October and the promenade was host only to a few spent wheelchairs and prams. It felt as though we were the only real people left in the world. I was already starting to get the coastal town blues I'd felt from last time. Home, my family, the few friends that still lived back in Warrington, bloated in my thoughts like something out of a gravy advert – all warmth, sustenance and love. I yearned for it though I'd only been away a couple of days. I was giving it the gold leaf treatment anyway; five minutes at home and I'd be bored rigid, or arguing with everyone, or trying to get the cat down off the hessian wallpaper in the back room. I fantasised for a while, thinking about some colourful clothes to replace my current drab wardrobe – this town needed all the anti-pathos treatment I could feed it.

The café proprietor, a stunted man with a crumpled face, like a used tissue, interrupted our burgeoning misery.

'Getcha?' he gummed, around a bolus of phlegm.

'We've ordered, thanks,' I said, hoping he didn't recognise me. When previously I used to breakfast here, we struck up quite a rapport, if you could call his gritted, nicotian greetings and my non-committal returns anything so grand. He smelled faintly of beef paste and tripe. His name, if memory served, was Ernest. Now, he gave the table a swift once over with his listeria rag before eyeballing Helen's chest.

'Getcha?'

The button on his shirt just above the waistband of his voluminous slacks was missing, inviting a view of a navel well-packed with assorted oddments. I suddenly wanted nothing more substantial than a glass of liver salts.

'We've ordered,' monotoned Helen, in her best Dalek. He caught the dormant violence in her look and retreated sharpish, pointing at me and smiling.

'Know you! Cunt stay way from me kippers, eh? Eh? Ya miss me kippers?'

Once the plastic rainbow streamers which separated his

kitchen from the main body of the café had consumed him, I turned my attention back to Helen. I couldn't blame Ernest, she was rather marvellously packaged. I'd forgotten.

I could tell she was looking at me; there'd be no affection there. Only hate, or pity. Or despair. Five years ago, I often wondered if she was my girlfriend because she was too lazy to find someone else: she'd hinted at as much early on when we talked about relationships during freezing evenings at Seven Arches, how starting out was exciting but somehow false too, as if you needed to tiptoe around and be nice so that in the long run you could find out how much of a bastard you'd ended up with. Wooing was twee and trite she'd said and if it hadn't been for her scowl at the time I might have laughed. Such odd words, almost quaint – doubly so coming from Helen's lips.

Maybe she realised how brusque she was sounding. She rubbed the heel of my hand with a finger. Its tip was purple and ragged from chewing. She dipped it into the torn packet of sugar and I watched its journey back to her mouth. She sucked long after the sugar had dissolved on her tongue.

Through the soapy window (soup, pies, chips, balms) I watched a couple bent into the wind trying to light cigarettes. Like a vampire the woman lifted up a flap of her trench coat while her partner ducked into its shade. An eddy of smoke. She walked on and he fell into a crippled gait behind her, his twisted limbs moving in grotesque yet oddly delicate parabolas. I watched them until they disappeared behind the clock tower. I had seen them before. Morecambe was like the dim, sunken corridors behind a theatre where character actors mope from week to week waiting for two or three lines in a play that has been running for years.

Ernest reappeared with a tray. He had done up the offending button and smoothed his CrispNDry head into something more befitting the Conservative front bench. He still smelled but it had been tamed by the recent application of Hai Karate. The tea was greasy but strong and I disguised its taste with sugar.

'No kipper for you today, uh?'

'No thanks,' I replied, willing him, with every shred of my body to bugger away off.

With another glance at Helen's breasts, he left us, bowing slightly and offering Helen anything she wanted. 'Do you kipper,' he said, hopefully. 'A little bit of sausage? Hot.'

'Oh for Christ's sake, David. Why did we come here?'

'I used to come here when I was at college.' It wasn't a reason but I shrugged when I said it.

I've loved café toast for ever: even Mum was unable to equal it. It always comes hot and crunchy and golden, the butter already melted. It's one of those things, like freshly cut grass or milky drinks or *Match of the Day*, that you find yourself using as a metaphor for life. For good things. I explained all this to Helen once. She said: 'How very Hovis. You stupid twat.' I tend not to wax lyrical in front of her any more.

'Have some,' I said. She just stared at it. 'People who don't eat die, you know. I read that in the newspaper.' It was a weak attempt but it worked. She broke off a corner of toast and chewed, a comma of grease at her lip. My throat grew painful then and I found it hard to swallow my food. Why couldn't it be like it was at college? She looked so vulnerable sitting there with butter on her mouth that I wanted to hug her and nuzzle her hair.

The waitress took my plate away before I'd swallowed the last bite. I wanted to ask if her haste was due to an imminent coachload of tourists, flocking to this gastronomic heaven, but it would have only alienated me further from Helen. She wasn't one for faffing about. I left a small hill of coppers on the table.

A bitter wind, reeking of dead fish, mugged us as we stepped outside.

'We could go back to mine,' I said feebly, knowing she'd refuse. She turned away but not before I saw a look of disgust crease her face. I wish I could let my anger out now and again but I always feel foolish when I shout and I can't keep it up. Helen was wonderfully eloquent when in a rage. It would appear to be part of her natural constitution. She always seems sickly and pathetic when pleasant.

'I haven't walked enough yet,' she said. 'And I need to be at the pub in time for Shay. He'll be here soon.'

My attempts at feigning nonchalance were pitiful; I could feel my features sloping. Shay – Seamus Cope – had been a friend of mine back in our Warrington childhood; the kind you can't wait to leave behind and never get in touch with again. The three of us would tool about the town centre or throw stones at birds by the railway line behind our school. He wormed his way into my life because a teacher had asked me to look out for him. Said he was shy. Like most people one feels a hostility towards, I couldn't pinpoint exact reasons; rather, it was a steady disaffection like the build-up of plaque upon teeth.

'Why?'

'He called me over the summer. He was in a real mess – he *is* in a real mess. I think that whatever I'm suffering… he is too.'

'Look, Helen. What is going on? Have you two got some kind of disease? And why call me about it? Ever since I got here I've felt like someone for you to piss on, someone to make you feel better. Well, it's just –' and here my anger expired. I could feel my mouth stiffening. I felt sad; I wanted to bury my face in a cardigan.

She was smiling, but in a kind of resigned way. It was the most compassionate she'd appeared yet. 'Believe me. You're involved. Do you think I'd have contacted you if you weren't?' She was talking softly but I still felt the blow of that last sentence, deep in my belly. It's an ache we know well.

'David. Shay needs to be here. He needs friends around him.'

I balked. She held up her hand. 'I know he drives you mad but he was fond of you. And he always had time for me. He's nobody else to turn to.'

I wanted her to tell me that the reason she called me was that she wanted us to get closer; she really wanted us to work.

The longer she talked without such an allusion only served to thicken the doubt surrounding my being in Morecambe.

'There's something you're not telling me Helen. I'm not just here to play comfort blanket to you both. I need to know.'

Already I felt unwelcome, even though it was Helen who had instigated my return to the town with her brief phone call. It had come one snowy evening towards the end of September and I recognised her voice immediately.

I'd first met Helen in nursery school. I had been in a race: up a slight incline to the tree at the end of the playground and back. I've seen that tree since, it's no more than twenty feet away from where the starting line had been but it felt like miles back then. On the return leg of the race, Helen had stood up in the sand pit and positioned her spade at my eye level. I was more concerned by the mouth full of grit I received than the cut above my eye. It was how she introduced herself. I had followed her ever since.

Until she rang, her face had developed a softness which blurred her features, as if I was looking at her through a foggy pane of glass. Her surname was as elusive as the last pea on the plate. Talking to her again swept all those cobwebs aside. How could I have forgotten: Soper; the scar; her love of Dime bars; phobias of insects and fungus (she'd once said the scariest thing she could imagine was a spider eating a mushroom).

I realise now how much of what she'd said had been injected with a false bonhomie – I'd been sucked into the affection in her words and hadn't been able to detect the desperation behind them. After all, I'd had a good four years in which to forget how she behaved. It's hard to remember what we talked about; the past, what we were doing with our lives – I can't recall specifics. Apart from her mention of a death in her family and the way that coming winter was disturbing her to the extent that it filled her sleep with terrible images.

'So far I've never remembered any of them, only this awful clenched presence that lingers round me when I wake up. It's only a matter of time. And I don't know what I'll do then.'

I don't know why I capitulated so readily when she asked me to spend some time in Morecambe. I'd like to think it was because Warrington was stale, a town I knew inside out and hadn't been able to shrug away from. More likely, it was because the barely concealed ache of loneliness that she exuded down the line tweaked at something similar in me. We'd shared some close moments in Warrington and later, in Morecambe; maybe its magic could work on us again.

I reluctantly agreed to go over to the pub for Seamus' arrival and left her at the corner so I could go back to my digs and unpack. I'd picked one of the guest houses in a side street off the Marine Road that was less garish and in-your-face than the others. Even so, this one looked like a flower stall in its attempt to brighten the town. The old duffer tooling about on the flags with his trowel and bag of Fisons nodded a hello and went back to his truffling with slow-motion enthusiasm. Through a window poked the profile of his better half, like an inhospitable face of the Eiger.

'Ooroit, Dievid?' she asked, through a mouthful of green teeth and prunes. 'Owzya room? Sorted?'

'Nearly,' I said, and pushed through the front door so I wouldn't get into another interminable pow-wow with her. Yesterday, it had been water content in bacon and shivering poodles, the state of her ribs and Pick 'n' Mix queues at Woolworth's.

These newly painted walls (white and peppermint) were blighted with framed pictures of cars made out of watch pieces. Maureen, the landlady (Eiger's daughter), had positioned a large plastic vase on the first landing. An invitation was taped to its rim:

For Your Umberellas

Through the fire door, I collided with Duncan. Six foot fuck off, Neanderthal forehead, prognathic jaw, bull-shouldered, cow-eyed. His ginger hair was brushed back from his brow like a nest of fuse wire.

'I'm just nipping to the shops. Do you need any milk, or bread? Or lint remover. I'm going for lint remover.'

'No thank you, Duncan.' Inside, I locked my door and stepped over the boxes I had yet to disgorge. There was hardly any room; enough to swing a cat if you didn't mind clouting it open against the walls. I heard Duncan lumber outside, ask Eiger if she wanted any lint remover and her non-sequitur about the discrepancies of Belisha beacons, how they never flashed in tandem. I closed the window and put on some music.

It seemed strange that, despite my not thinking of Seamus other than in the most rudimentary way, he should now dance glass-sharp into my thoughts where Helen had always been wraith-like, smudged by time and my questionable memory into an indistinct figure. Strange too that I should conjure him like this: scooping his beloved thick-cut marmalade into a split pitta, his bespectacled gaze soaking up the obituaries (The Bitch, we called him – 'I'm coming... just let me finish the bitcheries will yer!'), spare hand squirming against the flesh that peeked through the holes in his towelling bathrobe.

Though frequently caustic, he could sometimes be capable of a disarming tenderness – a quality that seemed instinctive rather than pre-meditated; often he would look bewildered when soothing a distressed companion, ostensibly uncertain of his behaviour. He looked like a child that has suddenly discovered how to whistle. His warmth worked, but – because of his more forthright and nervy side – only at a superficial level; comfort rather than cure. I never experienced this softness, only his angles and edges. Habitually late for anything we'd arranged, it would invariably be me who was called upon to encourage his haste, but we didn't mesh too well and would find ourselves growing heated in places that should have been neutral zones. Sudden spats in beer gardens, sneered remarks on the bus home, exasperated plays of hostility in the cinema queue. Remarkably, an audience was essential to precipitate this kind of behaviour. Alone, we would get on fine, tolerating the quirks that irritated us so much.

Like me, Seamus had been mesmerised by Helen's lovely face and the way she made you feel as though you were the only person worth talking to in the world. She had a perspective on things that was totally unlike any other kid I knew. The way she talked had a lot to do with the way we fell absolutely under her spell. I think we probably loved Helen a bit all through our formative years. She was the factor that brought us together and the reason why we would never really get on.

The last time I saw Seamus was on the morning of my final exam. I'd been revising most of the night and felt hollow, ductile as hot wire. Seamus had been pacing about the house while I crammed, his exams completed some time before. Every argument or opinion I studied was corrupted by a creak or the soft click of a closing door. He was getting psyched up for a caving expedition to the Brecon Beacons; he'd decided that caves were the only uncharted territory left on the planet and that he wanted to discover a new pocket in the Earth's crust. He said it was the thrill of knowing his would be the first footstep to ever mark a piece of land that was millions of years old.

Over a bowl of cereal I tried to ignore the clunking of his belaying pins and karabiners, his checking and rechecking of lamps and ropes. I cracked when he finally relaxed, plonking himself down on the kitchen sideboard, virtually raping the newspaper in his desire to get to the bitcheries.

'Fuck me,' he said at last, 'Arlene Farraday's rolled a seven.'

I threw a teacup at him which bounced off his forehead and shattered on the floor. He didn't say a word, merely folded his newspaper and left. I had to strain to hear the front door snick shut. And that was that. No letters, no telephone calls. His sulk had lasted three years.

On the floor with my boxes I gradually succumbed to a light claustrophobia; I wasn't making inroads on the piles of stuff waiting to be put away, simply moving them around. Downstairs in the kitchen, I boiled some water and flicked through a catering magazine that Maureen had left on the table. Now that the summer season was over, the huge range and double oven seemed ridiculously extravagant, especially when I was only boiling an egg. At least I wanted for nothing: the drawers and cupboards were filled with every kind of kitchen paraphernalia, from blenders and electric knives to indulgences such as corn-on-the-cob holders and a carousel for cooking jacket potatoes. I selected a double egg-cup and one of the toast racks, turned the egg-timer over just as the water began to bubble and Terry, the landlord, skimmed out of his adjoining living room decked in overalls and Dunlop tennis shoes. He had a mathematically precise side parting in his hair and a Berkeley hung from the expanse of his bottom lip (the top was non-existent). He was carrying a sander in his hands. And his ubiquitous cuppa, brewed to the colour of a jaundiced person's piss.

'All vight there, sunshine? No vest for the wicked, hey David? Got a job yet?'

I had in fact, but Terry didn't stick around long enough for me to tell him what it was. Maureen stumbled into the light shortly after, her face lined as though it had been used as a cats' scratching post. She was sucking on a cigarette like an asthma sufferer using an inhaler. On seeing me, she pulled the collars of her dressing gown around the speckled waste land of her chest and sat beneath a framed certificate which read:

Sales Person Of The Year (3rd Place): Juicy Fruit Greengrocers (Wolverhampton Branch) awarded to Maureen Wimbush.

'Is yeroom warm enough, Doivid chucky? Ownly, the 'eating's a bit shagged, yer know? Terry's adabashatit but no joy oim afroid. Plenty o blankits if yer cold, luv.' She began picking at the blackish roots of an otherwise strawberry blonde bob. I said the room was fine, after managing to decode her polyglot. Assembling my lunch, I declined her invitation to sit and chat. The last time I did that, she'd told me all about the weepy nature of the cyst in her armpit.

I ate my eggs while watching the local colour scoot in and

out of peeling doors or tap at engines with spanners. Girls who looked young enough to be sitting in the prams they pushed wandered by in twos while a stray pack of dogs had a meeting by the bins across the road.

I thought about Helen. What was wrong? Was it simply that she missed us and wanted to breathe life into the volatile mix the three of us created? I doubted it. For the first time, I dwelt upon her words, the concern that she felt. Although she had yet to flesh out that anxiety, it was already pricking at me with possibilities. She might be pregnant. She might have contracted a life-threatening disease. Whatever it was, was it enough to warrant her summoning of Seamus and myself? I wondered if I would have answered her distress call had I been living further afield, in London, say, or abroad. Probably. If there was the sniff of her being interested in me again, I had to check it out. Oh me. David Munro, aka Sad Bastard.

I managed to get out of the guest house unmolested, slightly peeved that I'd be returning to my cardboard hovel later on. The sky looked mightily pissed off, drawing its colour from the dead bowl of sea. I crashed through the well-oiled doors of The Battery just as the first flecks of rain found dry land and suffered the disapproving looks of the regulars as I shed my greatcoat and muscled into the passive scrum at the bar. Helen was there already, buying her second pint.

We took our drinks over to a far corner where a fruit machine farted tunes at five-minute intervals. A dog curled on an armchair raised its eyebrows at us hopefully, but I hadn't bought any crisps. An old couple sipped halves of bitter and looked into space. But for their infrequent movements, they could have been fashioned from papier-mâché, so grey and listless were they.

Her tongue found the scar. She asked me how I was settling in. She asked me when I started work. And, pleasantries over, she dragged me back into the strange hinterland of ambiguity and evasion we had inhabited at breakfast.

'I'm not altogether sure why I stayed here after we

finished college. Apart from Pol living nearby.' She frowned. 'But I haven't been to see her while I've been here.'

'Who's Pol?' I asked. My pint was disappearing fast – a sure sign that I was uncomfortable.

'My grandmother. You do know about her. I have talked about her in the past.'

I nodded and smiled as though the name had just found some significance.

'Thing with Pol is,' she continued, 'I never really knew her. Still don't. I only ever saw her at Christmas and that was years ago, when I was still at school.'

'Seems like a poor excuse to stay here.' I regretted the words but I was fed up of having to watch what I said. If I remembered correctly Helen liked me because I was honest, sometimes painfully so. I could see no point in stifling my nature just to make things easier for her.

'You're right,' she laughed, surprising me. 'Maybe I wanted to come to the sea again. A place where there's lots of children.'

'Helen. It's winter almost. The season's finished. Some alky TV has-been's turned out all the lights. This place is going to be dead for months now.'

She placed her drink on the table, clinking it against the ashtray. 'I don't know why I'm here. I had to live some-where.' She grew quiet, gazing into a place beyond the diamond patterns in the carpet. 'I can't seem to shake it off.' And then, quickly, she said: 'I'm being followed.'

I waited. Saying something might only knock her out of her rhythm; cause her to snap at me. I wanted to know what was happening. More drinks. I glanced back at her twice while I waited at the bar. She was looking out of the window at the bank of telephones by the bus stop, her face tilted back, awash with weak sunlight. For a second, she didn't seem real; more a celluloid cut-out pasted on to a drab back-ground. Her edges appeared to shimmer. Then normality swooned back into place as clouds stubbed out the fluke light, lending her, in shadow, a new austerity.

'I don't know who it is but he wants me to suffer.' It was all she said before the door swung open and in walked Seamus. His face was hidden partly by a black knitted skullcap, partly by an eyepatch. He nodded in our direction before moving to the bar. Waiting for his drink he seemed desperate to avoid any further contact. Maybe he was psyching himself up for our confrontation or maybe he was rehearsing his first line. He took off the cap as the bartender handed over his change. Seamus had gone for the bald look: his head was divertingly attractive, shorn of its usual red chaos. The plates of his skull were softly angular; they caught and held the light, bled shadow across his face, which, for a moment, looked shockingly wasted, the eyepatch like a hole – something that was eating him away. He placed a copy of the *Guardian* next to his tonic water, curling one foot beneath his bottom as he sat down.

'Ay up,' he said, 'it's Morrissey.'

'Fuck off, Seamus,' I said. 'You've changed.'

'Important to do so. I wanted to kill off all that I was at college, you know, renew myself, get in touch with parts of me that needed to be recognised, that needed release.' He rubbed his scalp. 'What do you think?'

'Very fetching. The eyepatch too.' I thought I was doing pretty well; my voice was bright and friendly, not at all how I felt.

'The eyepatch isn't a fashion accessory. It's for real. I was in a fight in Bristol – you know a pub called The Sugar Loaves? and I was stabbed in the face with a broken bottle. Don't remember all that much about it.' He leered at me and fingered the edges of the fabric, which was biting into his livid flesh, empurpling it. 'Want to see?'

I shook my head. Helen leaned over to kiss him on the cheek. Her eyes closed, tightening as her lips found him. I almost felt her need pass through them both. When she opened her eyes again they seemed bluer. All I could think was: she's shagged the bastard.

'Good to see you both again,' said Seamus, raising his

glass as if to toast us. 'I feel as though I've come home – despite the fact I've never lived here before. You can see why though. What a fucking dump. As my sister would say: "I wouldn't wipe my arse on it".'

He laughed and Helen followed suit although it sounded painfully false.

'So why *are* you here? Why are any of us here?'

Seamus fell silent then and I noticed a tic begin under his good eye. His ear-ring glittered. He was shivering. 'Come on, Davey,' he said, forgetting, as I had done until then, how much I hate that name. 'Give a man chance to settle down. We can talk later.'

All his spirit had flown, his voice bereft of its original edge. He lifted his glass, thought better of it and left the table. I saw him looking at his watch almost hungrily as he headed for the toilet.

'Nice one, David.'

'Oh give it a fucking rest, Helen. Have you heard the way he's speaking? *I want to renew myself.* What a bunch of hairy bollocks.'

'He's here for me. I'm in trouble. We all might –'

'*Then tell me what it is.*' My voice cracked half way through and although it was a relief to get rid of the tension inside I couldn't help but start laughing when I saw Helen's stricken face.

'Oh come here, you,' she said, all smiley and sad at the same time. She hugged my neck with her arm. 'I've been pissing you about a bit. I'm sorry, David. Really. It's just something that needs a little thinking out. I don't want to drop something cold on you. But I know – and here she lifted my face so she could look through her fringe into my eyes – you're a part of this.'

'How?' I asked. 'A part of what?'

She closed her eyes and I saw them roll skyward beneath the delicate flesh of her lids. 'Well, I'm being hunted. I believe I'm being hunted. Sniffed out.'

A spattering of snow on the window made me jump. The

sky was low and sullen. Seamus had crept back to his stool and was watching me, his face wreathed in smoke from a cigarette that shivered between his lips. Helen continued, her eyes still closed, her fingers rubbing my neck.

'I can't describe him; I've never seen his face. But he smells of cinnamon and old things and sweetness. And I often see him when I am at my most vulnerable. When I'm ill. Shitting. Fucking.' A couple on the next table looked at Helen and then at each other. Helen didn't bat an eye. 'Sometimes I glimpse him and I feel a pull, very strong, at a part of me that can almost understand what it is, what drives his fascination with me. Sometimes I think I must know him from years ago and that I'm going to have some Eureka moment when I unravel all the knots in a dream. Mostly though, I feel he's coming at me from my future, that fate has supplied me, us, with a convergence.'

She opened her eyes. Her voice had been level and strong, almost as if the words she'd spoken were rehearsed. Perhaps they were: whatever she was suffering had churned within her for a while; she'd had enough time to try to construct some kind of rationale around it.

'A convergence,' I said.

'Yes.' This was from Seamus. 'It's not just us who have been drawn to Morecambe.'

'You've had this too?'

He dragged deeply on his cigarette and stubbed it out. His words came in erratic blue gusts. 'Not the same kind of thing, but a pressure from inside, like butterflies, only more subtle. I think it might be related to Helen's experiences because I tend to believe I know what's at the foot of it but I can't quite see what it is. It's a who though, as opposed to a what. When we discussed it we found a number of common factors, like the frequency of its appearance. I called Helen the first time it happened to me. This was what, late July? I hadn't spoken to her since college. I don't know why I called Helen, but it felt right to, it just felt right.'

Seamus picked at the sliver of lemon in his drink. Snow

came in vicious, wet flurries. The clouds across the bay were underlit with orange from the villages. Around me, people drank and smoked and talked. A soft clack of billiard balls. The hubbub was peripheral, yet thickening with every beat; the pubs walls closing around us. I became sensitised to the slightest nuance of sound and motion: Seamus' heartbeat bussing the curve of his T-shirt; the hiss of air through Helen's lips; a thin whine in the dog's throat as it yawned from across the room. Sweat sprang on to my forehead in a line, like beads of blood following the route of a knife on flesh.

Seamus' eyebrows arched. I nodded because I didn't know what else to do. 'I'm glad I called Helen,' he said. 'It meant I didn't have time to feel alone. I don't know what I'd have done if I was on my own. I don't know what I'd have done to get away, to get it away from me.'

I sat quietly, taking this in, trying to relax. It was good to get accustomed to the way we worked together again, which hadn't really changed bar a kind of restraining courtesy, something I was sure would dissolve as time went on. All the things I'd fallen in love with Helen for were still there; mannerisms that I'd forgotten about over the years but which now hastened the air in my lungs and filled me with yearning. The way she dabbed her lips with a Body Shop lip balm; took businesslike drags of a cigarette; tied her hair back from her face with a band she wore on her wrist. Such an incredible face, a stunning face. I'd been attracted to her the first time we met, before we'd exchanged words. Her jawbone was strong and square; the cheekbones high yet softened, not so pronounced as to make her look starved or severe. Her mouth protruded due to a slight overbite which I found uncommonly sexy. She had large, soft, friendly brown eyes which sometimes appeared sad but mostly were filled with humour and a deep interest for the person she was focusing them on: Seamus, at the moment.

'Where are you staying?' she asked.

'I've a place in Skerton. Sharing with a couple of people who advertised a room at college. Pretty reasonable.'

'You should have tried to find a place in Morecambe. What if we need to contact you? What if you need us?'

Seamus gestured outside. 'I've got a car. Nowhere's far away if you've got wheels. I can be here in five minutes.'

They turned to me. Seamus looked as though he was going to ask the same question. 'I'm staying at a guest house round the corner,' I said. 'Nice and comfy. Cheap.'

'Doesn't sound very long term,' he said, pulling out a pen and a battered old Filofax with a still of Jane Fonda from *Barbarella* taped to its cover.

'Why should it be?'

He ignored the question and wrote down my address and telephone number. 'You looking for work?'

'I've got some bar work, at The Whistling Clam up the road. Three or four nights a week, some lunchtimes. It's pretty flexible. Not started yet, though. There's some savings if I need to fall back on them.'

'Are you still painting?'

I was taken aback somewhat by that, and touched that he remembered. 'After a fashion. I had a small exhibition in Warrington Museum last summer. Nothing grand.'

'I'd like to see some of your stuff,' he said, packing his Filofax back into the bulky depths of his jacket.

'Me too,' urged Helen, resting her hand lightly on my arm.

My paranoia whispered that they just wanted to give my work a psychological once-over; that their interest would only pay dividends if they found some kind of black theme in the paintings I'd produced over the last six months. I bit down on challenging them about this because I was tired of the friction. Instead, I asked Helen if she'd talked to the police about her pursuer.

'Of course I have. They said that they couldn't do anything unless I knew who it was or could prove that he'd been harassing me. I have to leave my bedroom curtains shut because I'm convinced hell be floating there, twenty feet up, if I open them. My work's starting to go down the toilet.'

Helen had told me about her craft shop in those preliminary phone calls. Partly funded by the demise of a relative or two, she'd rented premises along Heysham Road filled with whatever she was making these days. She didn't make much money, but she supplemented her income by looking after Pol, who helped her pay the rent on the living quarters at the back of the shop. Helen explained how she was unable to concentrate on new projects, how the results were always misshapen or lacking verve.

'So what about you, David?' Helen asked, throwing Seamus a look. I should have felt privileged that they needed to have my input before they could go further. 'Have you noticed anything different lately?'

'What, spooks mooning me outside the window?'

'If you like,' said Seamus, throwing Helen a look this time. Seamus, like me, probably wasn't too enamoured of my being here.

'I don't know. I suppose I might have been feeling a little on edge, almost as if I was expecting something out of the blue – in this case, maybe Helen's phone call. But it might just have been frustration at being stuck in the house with nothing to do.'

The week preceding Helen's call had been gloomy wherever I went. I'd spent much of it walking around Warrington market, hoping to find some decent old paperbacks, or an ornament with which to decorate my desk and take my mind off the painting I was trying to complete. When I was outside I wanted to be back in the warmth of home. Once there, I was stifled; outside seemed to offer so much freshness and opportunity – I felt that I was missing out on so many exciting things. But the friends I had in the town weren't as close as I'd have liked; it wasn't comfortable to drop in on them unannounced. I only ever saw them at weekends when we'd visit noisy pubs and sit around a table and talk about work. No matter how central my position at such times, I always felt as if I was the last one to the table, the one who pulls up a stool and sits just outside the circle, taking manic sips from a pint and trying to look interested. If I was silent it was because I hadn't the energy to compete with the chatter around me; sometimes my reluctance to join in was noticed and I'd be chided for it, or accused of being miserable.

I remembered that I'd watched snow dusting the trees, turning them into twisted structures of bone as Helen spoke. Her voice had been spice-warm. Into the lowering night, streetlamps fizzed in soft coronas of orange. They climbed away into the darkness; pale bricks of flame suspended in the sky. It felt as though my minute body hairs had been brushed against the nap of my skin. I felt electric and very sick; I'd had to vomit as soon as Helen got off the line.

I told them this, the sharpening of my senses, and the nausea. It reminded me that I'd also felt it in the pub, just before Seamus came through the door. 'Funny, it's as if getting together with you two plebs completes some circuit and switches me on,' I finished and took a drink, mildly embarrassed. As a rider I added: 'It doesn't help that in Warrington I've got Seven Arches outside my bedroom window, you know.'

Seamus and Helen looked away from me at my casual mention of the viaduct's name. So much of our history together, the petty arguments, incests, and experiments of youth had taken place there it was hard to divorce it from our lives. It was always going to be important to us, especially when we met. Maybe that was one of the reasons for coming to Morecambe, so that our decisions and movements wouldn't be clouded by the strength of its attraction.

'One thing bothers me,' I said, trying to bring the conversation back on track. 'I haven't had a glimpse of a person like you two have. Just a heightening of my senses. Feels like taking a quarter of E.'

'You might be blocking it,' Helen said, 'subconsciously, or via some kind of activity. Your painting might be distracting you.'

'Or,' Seamus intervened, a forefinger raised, 'you might be accepting whatever is bothering us *through* your painting.

I think we should see your work as soon as possible. How about now?'

'Hey, come on! I protested. It's my work. I should know what it's supposed to be about.'

'Have you painted Seven Arches at all recently? Before Helen called, say?'

'I might have done,' I said, trying not to sound defensive, 'but so what? It's there every day I open the curtains. I might as well. I've also painted Delamere Forest and Helsby Hill and the Runcorn Bridge. Cast your runes for those bastards, High Priest.'

'David!' Helen's reproach was mingled with shocked laughter. 'Don't get so heated. We're only trying to help.'

'I'm sorry,' I said. 'Maybe if Dr Antony Clare here stopped sounding so pompous…'

Seamus wasn't offended by my outburst, which only rankled me more. 'We need to look at this laterally, Davey, if we're going to codify it, give it some solidity. Give us something to target.'

I nodded, grinding my teeth together.

'So, about those paintings?' Helen took my hand.

'Not now. I'm still unpacking. Tomorrow. We'll see about tomorrow. I stood up, anxious to let things lie as they were for the time being. It was a lot to take in. I'm shattered,' I said. Helen looked pained; she always wore her feelings so flagrantly. I wanted to lean over and kiss those thick, pouting lips of hers. 'I think I need a walk.'

'We'll come,' said Helen, then: 'Don't go yet, David.'

'I've really got to get out of here. My head needs clearing. Look, how about we meet later on? Go for a meal in Lancaster, yeah?' I was starting to fidget, a habit I have when I've made up my mind but can't execute the decision. Claustrophobia threatens at times like that. Thankfully, Seamus set me free, telling me he'd pick me up from my guest house at eight. Helen acquiesced; I detected the slightest slump in her broad shoulders.

'See you later then,' I murmured, always useless at goodbyes, no matter how temporary. I didn't wait for a reply. I thought back to the stripped, imploring cast of her voice on the phone when she summoned me from Warrington.

'Please come, David,' she had said. 'You have to come. Something's *unfolding*.'

That word. It threw up so many ugly, shapeless images as I strode out of the pub and headed for the beach that she seemed to have infected me with a new disease.

two
different echoes

I walked back along the promenade, conscious that they'd
be able to watch me from the pub window. I pulled the
collar of my greatcoat up against the solid wall of wind
and wished I had a hat like Seamus' to keep my ears warm.
I'd walked the entire length of this promenade with Helen,
either south to Heysham village or north, where, after a
couple of miles, it gave way to normal pavement opposite
Happy Mount Park. So much of our short history was tied
into its red Tarmac, or the landmarks that lay along it. I aimed
for one now – the lighthouse – and tried to make sense of the
little that had been said. Why they'd been so cryptic was a
mystery in itself – perhaps they just couldn't find the words
to explain. I found myself searching my immediate past for
associated outlandish instances; moments when I'd found
myself shadowed by something that wanted to feed off my
insecurity. None was forthcoming. Maybe I just wasn't as
sensitised to this situation as the others; Warrington could
have quickened the atrophy of my thoughts. I did harbour
some degree of unease over the way certain events had
attained a more intense level of detail on occasion. The first
time I talked to Helen on the telephone, for example, or in the
pub when I'd been intimately conscious of the tics and
twitches of bodies around me. This was a new facet of my
consciousness, or rather, my recognition of it was new. I don't
know how long I'd been attuned to such minutiae but I
suspected it had only been of late. That such a phenomenon

could be associated with what Helen and Seamus were experiencing was both horrifying and heartening. Much as I was sceptical and confused about recent developments, I wanted to be involved, I wanted to be the third point of the triangle, as we had been throughout our childhood, no matter how fraught our points of contact had been. It was important I understood my involvement though, as they seemed to be able. I didn't want to just be a witness. I wanted to be a consultant, an intrinsic part of what lay ahead. Being around Helen and Seamus was not enough. I had to dig for the bad tissue in me that connected us all. I felt my stomach tightening with need: I deserved to be an ingredient; more so than Seamus. The links between myself and Helen ran deeper than those he laid claim to.

Or so I hoped. I turned on to the pier, the Midland Hotel pale and scabrous at my back, and marched into the teeth of the wind towards the lighthouse. At the pier's end it stood, by a café and a building where mussels and the like were cleaned and sorted. It was a short, unimpressive affair, with a static light. It did its job though; you could see the white tip clearly from all points on the promenade at night. The pier itself was deserted; not so the first time I'd been here, early October some years ago. There'd been men night-fishing, their rods tipped with luminous yellow bite indicators which hung in mid-air like fire flies. And cars, their doors open, music and the low muttering of men waiting for something to happen. Alone, it would have been a menacing sight but we were buoyed by bottles of red wine drunk on the armoury of rocks that reached into the sea. Ten days I'd known these people back then: Helen, Seamus and who else? I remember a girl and a couple of blokes whose names escape me. We clattered on to the pier under a sky readying itself for winter. That night was not so cold but we wore heavy coats anyway, as though living by the sea tugged at an innate rule that said we ought to. Helen wore a hat. There'd been some kind of electricity that drew us together in the first week: I was excited to discover we were both reading the same book –

that *had* to count for something. After a day or two, when we went in a group to The Three Mariners, we drifted out in front, holding hands or linking each other as if it were the most natural act in the world. It seemed a pre-ordained matter that we should sleep together.

On the pier. We stood in a semi-circle trying to snatch our breath back from the suck of air above the sea. Helen unscrewed her jar of lip balm and smeared a little over her lips. *Want some?* she'd asked me, stepping up close before I had chance to answer and planting a kiss that tasted of pineapples on my mouth. It was an exciting kiss, perhaps because it was so sticky, because it stands as a signpost in my memory for what was to ensue. I think too it was remarkable because I'd never before kissed a woman who was the same height as me. Not having to lean down, feeling our lips meet vertically – I could look directly into the dark gleam of her eyes – made for a thrilling moment. We flapped and fussed in the wind for a while and I broke away from the group, sidling down the café verandah to a section of fencing beyond which lay pallets emptied of shellfish and a large, oily black tractor which smelled of burned diesel. I was hoping she'd follow me. I heard her heavy boots clomping my way, her hand thrust into the crook of my arm; I could smell the dizzy warmth of her perfume. Her hair brushed against my cheek.

What shall we do now?

I stood at the end of the pier, looking into the grey-green swell of dead water. A boy on a mountain bike skidded to a stop by the railing, spat twice over the edge then pedalled away, shouting at a dog whose lead dragged behind it on the floor as it ran to keep up.

The current roiled under the water, pulling its surface tight like a piece of clingfilm before eddies of foam split it apart again. For a lunatic beat I saw myself leaping to become a part of its mystery: it seemed desperately vital that I consign myself in some way to the lighthouse and what it stood for. Ghosts clung to me, keen as sea spray.

I could see The Whistling Clam from here, one of those homogeneous fun pubs on the front which boast all the enticement of a dogshit flan. I was not looking forward to it. Keith, the manager, when I'd asked him for a job a few days after I'd arrived in Morecambe, had given me a twice-over with gimlet eyes the colour of blood oranges and asked if I had hair on my chest.

'A little,' I'd said.

'Then you'll wear this and unbutton the top of your shirt.' Into my hand he pushed a small phallus made of wood, depending from a thin strap of leather. 'We get a load of old giffers in during the week, coming for a last hurrah before they peg it. Come from all over. Ireland. Denmark. Spain. Penge. If I'm having a bloke on my staff, he's going to fucking well act like one. Black trousers. Tight. I want to see a bulge in there the size of a baby's arm. Put something down there – I don't care what. Banana, Black Mamba, pound of fucking tripe. Not bothered. As long as you're long. See you Wenzdy night. 7 o'clock. You'll be on four quid an hour. Love it or shove it.'

I told him I'd love it and he warned me not to cheek him or he'd 'annihilate' me. I'd found some black pants but they weren't very close fitting. I was considering pushing some socks down the front, or the cap from a can of Lynx deodorant.

I remembered his pub from my student days. We'd used it as a kind of half-way house on the way from Morecambe town to The Battery on interminable pub crawls. Weekends they'd have a charity jar and if it was filled within an hour, Elizabeth, the head barwoman, would take off her blouse and serve in her bra for fifteen minutes. Seamus used to stand and stare first at her chest, then at her face, as if he were trying to assimilate the two features as being under one roof. After the first few minutes, it got boring and we'd fall into a huddle, talking earnestly about complete rubbish such as how it was that you never saw a person with two glass eyes. Apart from Seamus, who would wander back when the quarter of an hour was up and Elizabeth had wormed her way back inside her T-shirt, playing down his interest by saying that he was trying to work out what had caused the scar on her belly.

I moved back under the café's awning. That it was daylight and colder than before mattered not at all. Being here again helped detail the shape of my loss so acutely I thought that I could smell Helen's fruity lips, taste their texture once more. I could almost hear the flighty confidence in her voice, the youth and innocence which had somehow vanished during the years we'd spent apart. There was still an ache for her, something I recognised from the past, a familiar, almost comforting ache which spread like a lazy ripple in a pool of oil. My old optimism had returned; a misplaced, irrational faith that she would gradually warm to me and we could lapse into the past and all it meant to us. God, how we become inured to the pain. Sometimes I think it's the pain we embrace rather than the insecurities of love that precede it. It seems a paradox that a pleasure should be derived from such a torment; that the wrench, the persistent hollowness that follows, is somehow attractive. I suppose it's like waking with a hangover to vow never again. Easy to forget what the pain means and how much it's likely to affect us, until next time. Standing there, with the wind and my memories buffeting me, I was filled with the slow, bemusing shock that I would gladly welcome a reawakening of our relationship despite the threat of another disintegration.

Walking back to the guest house, I saw a man in a gaberdine coat picking his way across the damp sand below me, a metal detector ranging about before him. The footprints he made grew misshapen, were sucked smooth by trapped water; erased. I wondered what he was looking for and what he might find instead. He was like me, seeking a sign, something solid that would make the aimlessness of his search worthwhile. Only I didn't have the luxury of a tool to help. A dread that was child-like in its intensity whipped through my midriff and I almost called out to the man to stop, to go home and forget his treasure hunting. But of course I didn't. I stalked away from him, cursing Helen and Seamus for the way in which they'd rattled me.

Back in my room I realised it was time to unpack my things and turn the place into somewhere in which I could relax. I'd made quite a mess; my suitcase in the corner was like a mouth, its tongue of clothes lolling all over the carpet. My easel I'd leaned against the windowsill. Most of my canvases were back at my parents' house in Warrington; a dozen or so had made the journey north with me, the ones that had affected me most directly upon painting them. Terry had allowed me to store half of them in his pantry – I didn't have enough space up here. I looked at a few of them now, watercolour roughs of the urban aspect to my town. I had chosen to interpret the seamier joints as a conflict to the pastures and farmhouses I'd been concentrating on the previous summer. I'd made the decision consciously, I remembered, for the challenge it would represent and as a cautionary measure, a way of jolting me out of the comforts of landscapes.

I liked the work I'd achieved, the dilapidated shopfronts, the vandalised phone booths and railway sidings choked with litter. I'd painted the mangled remains of the gasometer after the IRA bomb and a night scene outside a dead end pub, sketched on the night of a police raid. But it was this picture, of Seven Arches viaduct – a Liverpool-Manchester Sprinter surging across it – that I liked best. It worried me that Seamus had posited his idea so accurately, although I recalled no bad tidings at the time I had painted it, an afternoon in late August, no sunshine left in the sky, just a few dregs of colour slipping like vividly coloured medicine down the gullet of night.

Sometimes you know when the paint is going to work for you, when the whiteness of the canvas seems filled with an autonomous air; you could almost leave it alone to complete itself. It doesn't happen often, which is probably a good thing, but when it does it's the best high I know. It would be interesting to see if new surroundings influenced my work; gave it a fresh impetus or helped me hone my style. Nice to have some of them placed about the room – something to lose myself in when the view through the window lost its appeal. Which wouldn't take long. All I could see was the house across the way and a tired Ford Escort with a sticker in the window which read MAD BASTARD DRIVING THIS CAR. No trees. The only green to which I had access was in a tube marked *viridian*.

I put an old Pixies cassette in the player and sang along which helped distract me from the dip in my pillow where her head had rested. I caught a whiff of her perfume as I turned the sheets and I felt both angry and weakened by the strength of Helen's presence. It has always distressed me, the way you can miss somebody even when they are still a part of your life. Did she have a clue as to the way I still felt for her? If she did, she was hiding it well.

With everything tidy, the room seemed more like a cell. There was a lounge I could use downstairs but that was even more uninviting: the TV didn't work and the room's ceiling was often obscured by a fug of smoke; I think I was the only person in the building who didn't share the habit.

I wished Helen hadn't stayed with me last night even though it was my fault. I'd assured her it would be on purely platonic terms; that I wouldn't make any move on her. It had been raining and we'd drank quite a lot in Lancaster where we'd gone to see a film – her idea; we'd been going out to quite a few places since I'd landed in Morecambe, possibly because it reduced the time we had to talk about what was going on. After the film we caught a bus, which conveniently stops just round the corner from me. It wasn't that hard to persuade her to sleep over but there was a moment's awkwardness when we'd stripped down to our underwear (I lent Helen a T-shirt). I took the floor but Helen told me not to be stupid. Once the light was out, I was able to relax. I think Helen felt the same way because I heard her sigh. It's not such a big bed, certainly bigger than the one we used to share in our college days, but not exactly a double either. Whenever my foot touched hers she would flinch and I would apologise. Gradually the warmth of our bodies mingled and the bed grew more comfortable. I dozed, wishing I had the guts to turn over and spoon with her as we used to. It just wasn't enough to be lying next to her, listening to the measured ebb and flow of her breathing, watching the moonlight edge her upturned face with silver. It's odd how one's observation of propriety remains activated during these times. In the past, Helen would roll over, deep in slumber, to rest her hand in the waistband of my boxer shorts or plant a kiss on my shoulder. Now her internal midnight watch maintained the distance between us.

I looked at my alarm clock. There was time. The sky outside had dried itself off; the glut of snow-packed cloud staggering north. There was even a suggestion of sunshine mooching about behind the blanket of grey. Sod Seamus, I thought, picking up my sketch book and a few soluble coloured pencils. Gloom and doom my arse. I'd show him that my moods weren't so strong that I couldn't bend them to my will.

A gang of half a dozen kids were playing a game of cricket near the shingles when I returned to the beach. It was a crude, clumsy affair: wickets made out of a tower of rusting soft drink cans, a chunk of rotten driftwood for a bat. They were using a seemingly inexhaustible supply of dead crabs for balls.

'How are you supposed to field that?' I asked, gesturing at the limp ganglia of claws and legs.

'Suck on my fucking knobster, dogwank,' spat the bowler, all of seven years old, as he mock-polished the crab against his off-whites. He took a run up and bowled. What was left of the crab as it arrived hit the batsman – who was creased up thanks to the bowler's not inconsiderable powers of insult – on his shoulder.

'You are *out*!' shouted the bowler-cum-umpire, his middle, as opposed to the customary forefinger, raised. 'AB-twatting-W. My go on the fucking bat, bollockchops.'

I moved off, heading towards the lighthouse which, I thought, would make a nice painting, especially with the angry background colour. Before I reached the pier, however, I saw the car.

It was a burned-out wreck, dumped on the sea front by the pier's access point. All of its windows were gone and the wheels were down to their hubs, the axle showing. A black patch around each of the four corners told of the fate of the tyres. The panelling was scorched and dented; the headlights had exploded with the heat. From here, about two hundred feet away, I could see the interior had been roasted down to its skeleton. Stumps of metal for a headrest, little else. Before taking a closer look, I circled the car – a Renault Fuego – so that the lighthouse would provide an interesting backdrop to this minor tragedy. Once the juxtaposition was sketched, I wetted the pencils and filled in a few sections of the drawing, to get an idea of what the final tone and colouring would be like.

When I looked up from my sketch pad, I saw a figure sitting where the driver's seat had been.

I stuffed my sketch pad into a pocket and walked over. 'Hello,' I said, 'is this your car?'

'Hello yourself. Are you a policeman?' She was eating an apple, taking huge, wolfish mouthfuls out of its green flesh. A roomy bag was slung over her shoulder.

'Do I look like a policeman?'

'Does this look like my car?'

I smiled. She had really beautiful teasing eyes that goaded and sparkled. She had the measure of me immediately but knew where to draw the line. I suddenly realised that I was deeply attracted to her. 'No, it doesn't. It doesn't even look like a car any more. Why are you sitting in it?'

'I don't know. I didn't think about it. I just wanted to sit down while I ate my apple. Want some?' She extended her arm so that the apple eclipsed her face. Her fingernails were clear and almond-shaped; her hands small and elegant. A silver bracelet glittered on her wrist.

I went to take the apple from her but she drew her hand back slightly. As I bent to take a bite, her chest came into view. She was wearing a light V-necked jumper and I saw the top of her breasts move against it, quicker than I was expecting from such a relaxed-looking person. Her other hand rested against her thigh, fingers curled by degree like an opening flower; she wore a silver ring set with an amber stone.

It was a very weird moment.

'Get in,' she said.

'Are you going to take me for a drive?' I asked, around the apple as I perched on the floor of the car.

'If you like. It's a different view from here, isn't it?'

She was right. A tired line of mercury trembling just above the sea wall marked the tide. An oil tanker was a faint shape from an ink stamp on the horizon. The lighthouse dominated, almost leaning over us. Shops behind curved around on either side like a protective barrier.

'I wonder whose car this is?'

'It was a middle-aged man, I think. The ambulance took him away a few days ago. He set fire to himself.'

I recoiled and reached for a door handle that wasn't there.

'Relax,' she said. 'He isn't going to mind us sitting in his property.'

I looked at the denuded dashboard and carbonised roof. I wondered what the strange black shapes on the floor by my feet were and then realised they were the soles of shoes, fused into the base.

'Shit,' I gasped. 'Can't we get out? Wouldn't you rather sit somewhere more comfortable? Like how about a bucket of piranhas?'

She laughed and crammed the stripped core of the apple into her mouth, snipping off the stalk with her teeth and tossing it out through the vanished windscreen.

She turned to me on swallowing; I watched the slow ripple of her throat and then looked at her eyes. She was drinking in every detail of my face, like a child devouring the constituents in a round of Kim's Game.

'Morecambe's a funny place, don't you think?' She edged closer and let her mouth relax, slightly open, a moist smile loitering within a fraction of revealing itself. Her teeth were white edges just beyond the rim of her swollen lips. We were going to end up kissing each other, I knew it.

Flustered, I nodded. A dizzying smell drifted over me, warm and spiced. She put a hand through the thick wodge of brown hair she wore short and unstyled.

'I like you,' I said. 'I don't know you at all, but I just... you are beautiful.'

Her eyebrows arched. I realised how close I was sitting to her and drew away, a sudden gust of cold air fluting throught the wreck. Asleep in the wadded heat of a duvet, I'd just surfaced for fresh air. The restorative breath I took sobered me.

'I'm sorry. I didn't know what –'

'Hush,' she said, and followed the contour of my jaw with a fingernail. I felt the electric trace all the way down to my balls. She pressed her finger gently against her lips, which yielded, impossibly soft, then she got out of the car and walked away. I watched the swing of her hips as she diminished, framed by the charred rhomboid of the window. By the time I'd gathered my senses enough to call after her, she was gone.

I got back to the guest house without consciously following any route. I went straight up to my room and looked in the mirror where she'd touched me. The flesh was tender and scored. In places, the skin had broken. I licked a finger and wiped away the pinheads of blood that had dried there.

Downstairs I fell back on a comfort food from youth to help me relax: peanut butter and apricot jam on toast; a glass of Ribena to follow. Just the ticket. There wasn't that long to go before Seamus picked me up. I did some stretching before lingering over the football reports in a hot bath with Radio 5 Live. I reached up and opened the window. I thought about the girl – her long throat, the smooth swells at the V of her sweater – and felt my penis stir. I thought about masturbating but then a breeze whipped into the bathroom, tightening my skin, and I smelled something sweet and hot; cakes baking. Though it vanished as swiftly as it had arisen, it was enough to put me in mind of the dread I'd known, seeing the man on the beach and, more specifically, the image from my childhood he evoked. It bothered me that I'd never really thought of this episode before. Certainly not in any detailed way. But here it was, developing before me in swift flashes, like a palette knife scraping magic on a canvas, but all of the colours were grim.

I see Seamus and Dando on the bowling green. It's autumn and leaves have stolen the colour from half of the square. Seamus is hacking divots out of the grass with the heel of his DMs. Dando is slicing his name into the centre with a piece of broken glass. I'm sitting with Helen and Kerry on the concrete floor of the pavilion, watching them through the rotting staves of a fence which surrounds the green, designed to protect it. Kerry's my girlfriend. It's October 13th, 1980.

'Stop snogging, Dave. Come and play footy.' Seamus' voice cracks half way through and Helen laughs, something Dando is quick to seize upon.

'Oh yay-hay, Shay! Helen likes you, Seamus. She wants to have your rabies.'

'Fuck off, Dando. At least I've got a snog if I want it. What are you gonna do? Go home and get your mother to toss you off again?'

Dando toe-pokes the ball at Seamus. It cannons off his backside, rolls into the block of shade beneath the trees.

I've been seeing Kerry for three weeks. She bought me a 7-inch single for my 14th birthday by a band called The Beat. The song is 'Mirror in the Bathroom'. I'm worried this is some kind of subtle message that she thinks I'm vain. She lets me hold her hand when we go out at night. When I see her in the school library at lunchtimes I sit so close to her that my shin rubs the soft swell of her calf. We pretend to read books at these times. I read the same line over and over again, hoping nobody can see my heart bashing away under my shirt. Once, when we had to crowd round a table during a biology practical, I stroked a gap of flesh on her back between her skirt and blouse until I felt dizzy. I've not kissed her yet. I get the feeling shes becoming fed up. She's more sophisticated than me. When I asked her, casual as you like, how many boys she'd kissed before, she replied: 'Hundreds.' She's been around. She lived in Crewe before coming to Warrington. She's the only Kerry in the school.

'I *said*, bogbrains, stop snogging the bint and come and have a kick about!' I can see Seamus' eyes, little curls of silver from the sodium lights.

'Seamus, he's not snogged her yet. He's got virgin lips. Or he's a puff.'

I feel Kerry bristling beside me.

'Is that true, Kerry?' asks Helen.

'Course it's fucking true.' Dando saunters over, bored of the football now that there's something more interesting to do. I hate them for this but tomorrow we'll be laughing in the playground, taking the piss out of Alan Bebington's half-mast trousers.

Helen's eyes and mouth make a triangle of Os. 'But you told me –'

'Kerry… you didn't tell everyone that Mr Munro here is a stud, did you? He's only ever done it with Pam.'

Kerry's head snaps up. There's thunder in her brow. I wish I was with the football, deep in the thrashing dark of rhododendron bushes. 'Pam?' she says, her voice thin with shock. If this lot weren't here I could hug her for hours. 'Pam who?'

'Pam of his hand!' Seamus shrieks, pleased the joke worked.

'Ha, ha,' I say, slowly, 'I'm bereft of ribs.'

'*Bereft*? What the fuck's *bereft*?'

'It's a type of hat, isn't it? Speak English, Dave, you daft twat.'

Helen's still gawping. 'You not kissed her yet, Dave? What's up? You frigid or what?'

'So are you gonna kiss her then, Dave?' Seamus asks. 'Go on. Show us you're not chicken.'

'*You* kiss her.' I regret the words even as I speak them. Seamus doesn't need another invitation. He straddles Kerry's knees and cups her face with his hands. Kerry fights him off but not as effectively as she might. She lets him kiss her and for one awful moment I see their tongues squirm together, like slugs mating. I push Seamus away and he wipes his mouth, his eyes blazing with triumph. I grab Kerry's hand and pull her up, leading her round to the back of the pavilion where the cinder five-a-side football pitches glimmer. The dark bulk of Sankey Valley Park sweeps away from us. You can see the black holes of Seven Arches from here. The burned sugar smell of baking cakes from the factory on Delamere Road is there and then gone, swift as breath.

I press Kerry up against the wall. I'm glad they haven't followed us. Somebody wolf-whistles. She's looking at me from beneath her fringe, her eyes both tender and goading. A Mona Lisa smile. I kiss her and she doesn't even seem to mind when our teeth clack against each other. It's good, nowhere near as messy as I expected. When we surface, I try not to let her see how breathless I am.

'At last,' she says, and hugs me.

'There was nothing to stop you from kissing me.'

'I know. But I've been there. It was important you made the move, David. First-timer.' She smiles and I blush. I want to ask her if I was good; if the kiss turned her on. She ducks her head and kisses me this time and she's controlling what happens. Her tongue dabs against mine, her hands crawl up my back and nestle in my hair. When she pulls away, purple spots are swimming behind my eyes.

'It's not against the law to breathe.'

It gets better. Soon, I'm able to think of other things while my mouth works on auto-pilot. I'm thinking of how I should touch her breasts when the shouting starts.

'Why do you hang round with Seamus and Dando? They're a bit rough. Not like you.' We're walking towards the bushes. They slope down to the canal, where the noises are coming from. I can't make out who it is, or what's being said.

'They're okay. Lot of hot air. And it's not like I'm spoilt for choice is it? Our year is full of geeks.' I want to ask her if I kiss better than Seamus. Now I've finally done it, I resent her for letting him get away with what he did.

A couple of feet into the bushes there's a fence. Kerry climbs over first and I follow, realising that my heart is troubled with more than this business of kissing. The shouts, still vague, possess an urgency. Kerry's nails dig into my palm – she senses it too.

'Careful,' I say. 'The bank gets steep here.'

We meet the leading edge of bushes beyond which lies a narrow path forged by fishermen and kids playing truant. Something's going on under the footbridge; four or five figures painted white by the lights are a blur of movement. I'm having to squint to make a sense of it all: it seems like a human knot constantly re-configuring itself.

'Kerry?'

'Oh God,' she says, and lets go of my hand. I run after her.

'What's happening?' I can hear Seamus shouting in that reedy voice of his. And Helen sobbing. Dando I can just see, holding something out in his hands before the knot finds another loop and everything's lost again.

'*Stop it.*' And I'm rattled by the sheer urgency of Kerry's voice. She comes to a sudden halt and I try to look past her. I manage to squeeze by on the path by clinging on to some of the thin branches which overhang. From here I see everything.

I see Seamus circling Dando. I see Kerry with her hands to her face, crouching by the canal. I see Dando. Dando's holding a dog by its hind legs and plunging it into the soft mud on the bank. He's keeping its head submerged until it begins to convulse before pulling it back out again. There's a wet sucking noise as it comes free. The dog is shivering and making odd, weak yelps. Its head is misshapen with mud. Back it goes. Seamus is cheering. Dando's face is half-hidden by shade. The other half blazes. He's got his dick out; a jutting, moonstruck twig.

'*Stop it!*' Kerry screams.

As if only now becoming aware of the people around him, Dando grins and kicks the dog in the stomach. Any noise it might have made is muffled.

'The fucker bit me. No dog gets away with that.' He covers his dick with his hand, giving it a little tweak as he pushes it back into his jeans.

I'm striding over, even though Dando's bigger than me and – if it weren't for Jimmy Price – would be the cock of our year. I aim a punch at his face but he leans away and my fist finds his throat. He loses his footing and falls over, letting go of the dog. Kerry pulls it free of the mud and it runs, blind, straight into the canal. I watch it swim away, its head twitching left and right. At the opposite bank it sprints towards the housing estate. I'm wondering if it will die of shock when Dando wades over and grabs me by the neck.

'I ought to kick your bastard teeth in for that.'

And then… then…

And then what? I sat up in the bath and stared at my hands, which were beginning to prune. My mind wouldn't allow me to drift with the true course of events: how I fell back against a rotten plank and felt the slow heat of a nail sink into my thigh. How I'd gone to casualty where a nurse who smelled of lavender swabbed my wound clean and gave me a tetanus injection. How we went for popcorn and a Coke at the cinema but couldn't get in to see *The Empire Strikes Back* after I'd gone back to the park to rejoin everyone, Dando teasing me that I'd had a prick up my arse. I could think all this, but I couldn't see it. Instead, I saw Dando grab me by my jumper. While he held me, Seamus bound my hands behind my back with a length of twine. Then they upended me and forced me into a hole just wide enough to accommodate my shoulders. My head touched the bottom and the weight of my body above me forced me on to my cheek. The mud, folding around me…

I swallowed thickly. Hands shaking, I pulled out the plug and stood under the shower for a few minutes until the panic was washed clear. But those things hadn't happened. It was like a game in which secrets are passed on and distorted. Dando hadn't tried to kill me.

Scrubbing myself dry, thoughts turned back to Kerry. We'd finished a month or two after that incident. The last time I saw her was a year or two after we'd left school. She was living in Taunton with an Alastair and practising midwifery. I remember thinking – what did I ever see in this girl? Her face was painfully thin, putting me in mind of a teddy bear I once owned whose head was crushed by a prolonged spell down the gap between my bed and the wall. We never talked about that night by the canal. I wonder if that was because of some teenage ability to reject the horrific, or because we consciously stopped it from surfacing? I know I'd blocked it, until tonight. And what of Dando? I gazed into the mirror, the towel around my shoulders; the scratch was a raised whitish worm. We'd spent so much time together it seemed criminal we should lose contact so quickly. How many friends could I boast of now, that meant as much to me as the ones with whom I used to play football until way past a time when the ball was visible in the dark? I found myself mourning Dando – I now realised he meant more to me than most people I'd met since. He'd been a brutal bastard, but he was genuine and honest – with me at least – and immune from any pretentiousness. I hadn't laughed as forcefully in the seven or eight years since our friendship dissolved.

What did I have now? I still held on to Helen and Seamus but only then by the skin of my teeth. How easy it could have been to consign them to the back of my head, dusting them off now and then to massage my need for nostalgia. It would be better for them too, as I'd see them both in a honeyed light; that charitable bent the mind always seems to adopt in moments of reflection. How could I pretend, now they were back in my life? I didn't know the real Seamus any more though he must exist somewhere under all those layers of artifice. And Helen seemed almost self-satisfied with her lot, as if what were happening to her separated her from everyone else, marked her out for a special destiny, no matter how black it proved to be. I felt a prickle of anger when I realised she was exploiting a need for her that I thought (and hoped) I'd beaten over the years. She was probably gloating even now, that she could hold sway over my life after just a few months of tenderness that occurred years ago. But I was probably being unfair to them both. It would have been nice for them to contact me under different circumstances, but at least they'd done it. I hadn't lifted a finger. I should be turning some of this bile on myself, seeing what I was made of for a change, but it was either something I wasn't ready for or something of which I was incapable.

It was just after seven. I was in no mood to continue with the parries and deflections of our first conversation and was in half a mind to contact Helen and call off the evening. There was too much to think about already; I didn't want another bout of ghost stories to keep me awake all night, waiting for something portentous to reveal itself. I wanted to see the girl again. I didn't for a moment believe that I would never see her again. It just wouldn't be up to me; she would reveal herself. She seemed that type of person.

The afternoon's beer had made me sluggish. It would be nice to curl up in bed with something brainless playing on the TV. Instead, I drank a pint and a half of water before deciding to dress against the mood's grain which had developed throughout the day. On went a Daffy Duck T-shirt, improving my temperament enormously. How could the others speak of shadows and danger while I was acting the fool? Hopefully we would talk of lighter things this evening.

True to form, Seamus turned up at the guest house with quarter of an hour to spare. Even his punctuality unnerved me. I felt awkward, tying up my boots while he hovered, flicking through my paperbacks and tapping on the window as he looked into the street. If he asked about my paintings, I'd tell him I'd burned the lot.

'Anyone interesting die today?' I asked him.

He gave me a name but I didn't recognise it. 'She was an economist and a translator. Italian ambassador to Washington too. Leukaemia. Seventy-four.'

I ushered him out of my room. I might have laughed had I tried to say something. Would he think I was ridiculing him if I asked whether or not he kept files on dead public figures? At college it just seemed like a bit of a lark, an idiosyncrasy by which we recognised Seamus or referred to him. He would enter a room, crestfallen, to announce the death of an Australian chef or a joke writer or a stalwart of the Japanese film industry; all unknown to me – and to him, which was where the humour, or his perception of it, lay. It *was* funny at first, so it was probably my fault for laughing because it encouraged him to repeat his performance every morning. By the time we'd forgotten to laugh, or ignored him, he was into the business of tributes in a big way. He would watch TV specials about a celebrity's life and then, if they were cinema stars, he would make sure he caught every one of a season of their films. Biographies began to crop up on his bookcases. Because of his nature, I couldn't help but think he was simply cultivating this image to try to make himself more mysterious and attractive.

He drove well, guiding his black Mini confidently through the night. Lancaster looks almost appealing when you approach it by road. The Ashton Memorial's copper dome looks like the cerulean wash from a Mediterranean watercolour. Impossibly beautiful. In contrast, Lancaster Castle-cum-prison is imposing and dung-black, mottled like the imperfect plumage of grubby pigeons, suitable abode for those languishing in its cells. Though I haven't seen it, I know they have what's called the Drop Room, where condemned criminals waited for the noose. Seamus reached across me and stuck a cassette into the player hanging beneath the glove compartment. Something spare and quirky trickled from the speakers, beefed up after a few seconds by a chunky bass line.

'Qu'est-ce que c'est?'

'PJ Harvey,' he said. 'I love female singers, especially this one. She's got a raunch, a swagger.'

'Really. Where's Helen?' I wiped away condensation on the window in time to see a white neon crucifix hanging in the sky.

'Meeting us there. She's been in town, mooching around for treasure. You know what she's like. Looking for stuff that she can work on for her craft shop.'

'What did you do after I left?'

'Went back to hers for a coffee then I drove her into Lancaster.' Maybe he could sense I was digging for something else. 'She's worried about you, Davey.'

'Come on, Seamus. Like we've been in each other's back pockets for the last four years? The last time I talked to you was on our graduation day. All this concern, it's crap.'

'It's not crap. It's crap that you think it's crap.'

He didn't say anything else for a while. The Ashton Memorial was a bald giant shrugging its shoulders on the skyline. Scarves of mist flapped about the fence separating the road from the river. Every car or bus window that swept by was fogged; filled with smears of shadow which shrank and grew beneath the streetlamps.

'What have you been doing with yourself then, Seamus, these past few years?'

His face clenched in the half-light, as though this was a question he knew was coming but which he dreaded. He steered the car over Skerton Bridge, the new sweep of road casting blue and orange shapes across the famished oval of his head.

'I've been underground for much of it,' he sighed. I readied myself for some tale of clandestine political agitation. 'You might have seen some of my caving gear in the back seat when you got in.'

I glanced round and saw a nylon rope, a carbide lamp and a pair of knee pads.

'So your pot-holing venture took off?' The image of Seamus squeezing himself into dark crevices seemed inexplicably apt.

'Caving, please. Pot-holing is different. To me at least.' He swung the Mini into the car park across from Sainsbury's, cut the engine and sat there, sniffing. The eye-patch gave his face a punched-in look. 'Up until September I was caving most of the time. There are some good wild caves in Britain. I've done them all: Giant's Hole, Lancaster-Easegill, Ogof Craig-a-Ffynnon.'

He kind of trailed off here and I could see something was wrong. I didn't want to push him but then he changed the subject anyway.

'I met someone this afternoon, shortly after dropping Helen off,' he said, carefully. He didn't seem all that certain of what he was telling me. It was as if, in the saying of it, he would somehow firm up what had happened in his own mind. 'On the way back to Lancaster. I was driving along the one-way system in town and I saw this girl. She was in distress.'

I gritted my teeth and shivered; closed the window. *So did I*, I was going to tell him, when I got the chance. *Hey, so did I.*

'She was hurrying along with her hand up, as if warding something off. I thought she was a nutter, but she was cleanly dressed.'

I snorted at this and nodded, aghast at the way Seamus' head worked and about as surprised as a man who has had his surprise gland removed.

'It wasn't raining, but she was clutching her coat closed and she had her hand up in the air, you know how people do when it's pissing down. So I stopped. She came straight over to the car and got in. Said her name was Dawn and could I take her home. When I asked her what was wrong, she said she was having a nightmare.'

'But she was awake?'

'Yeah,' Seamus glanced at me, to see how I was taking it. I must have been wearing a pretty unusual expression because he came back for a second look. 'What do you think of that?' he said.

'Was she sleepwalking?'

'No. She was aware of who she was and where she was and what she was doing. She couldn't stop herself.'

'Was she daydreaming?' I suggested and then thought about it. 'Like, um, daynightmare… dreaming?'

'I don't know. Thing about daydreaming is that you don't know you're doing it until some maths teacher hurls a board rubber at you.'

'You're right there,' I said. 'Maybe she was rehearsing. Maybe she's an actress and she was getting into her part.'

'I don't think so,' said Seamus, hardening his face a little.

'Well, what was she dreaming about?' And I thought about it a little more. 'Seamus, lad. She was taking the piss. Must have been.'

Seamus shook his head. 'I don't think so. She looked pretty flustered. And she was grateful to get in the car. She calmed down instantly.'

'Her nightmare? Did she tell you?'

'Yeah. She said her roof was falling in.'

'What roof?'

Seamus smiled grimly, his lips pressed together. He looked at me again. 'Her head,' he said, searching my face for signs of understanding. I knew then that he'd fallen for her story.

'Her *head*? Is this woman still at large?'

'No, she's back at my place.'

'Bloody hell, Seamus. So what's the story? She suffers from migraines or something?'

He shrugged, staring at the blasted rubble around us. We sat listening to the engine cool down. 'I don't know what she's suffering from. I haven't had a chance to talk to her properly yet. I just gave her the key and told her to make herself at home. She didn't look happy about being left alone, but she was a damn sight happier than when I found her.'

I opened the door and waited till he'd got out before turning to look at him over the roof. I slammed the door shut and told him about Eve. He seemed shocked and he seemed unhappy too, as though I'd trumped him in some way.

'She as weird as mine?' he asked. I liked that possessiveness.

'She was sitting in a knackered car eating an apple. Pretty fucking nuts if you ask me.'

It was a little milder now we'd left the coast behind us. We walked back along Parliament Street to the Indian restaurant, Seamus silent with whatever was uncoiling in his thoughts. I left him to it and watched the bloated river surge by narrow houses on the opposite bank that seemed lifeless and shrunken.

'I would like to talk to you, a little later. About something that happened to me in the summer. Hello Helen!' He waved and strode ahead of me, leaving me to gawp like a fish. Helen was a dim shape against the wall; I suddenly noticed how fragile she appeared, although it could have merely been a trick of the light, and the heavy clothes she wore. Her cheeks were daubed with shade; she looked like a figure from a painting by Munch.

She kissed Seamus lightly on the mouth, the glitter of her eyes never straying from my own. When I was close enough to feel the heat of her breath, she said: 'I met someone today.'

three
lechuguilla

It was a good meal. I was surprised and pleased to find a curry house so far north which served a decent Balti; a dish I usually had to wait for until I visited friends in Birmingham. We shared a bottle of red wine which Helen had brought with her (the restaurant was unlicensed) and, despite my alarm at her earlier words, the evening was thankfully free of anything enigmatic or threatening, as though we'd reached some unspoken agreement for a moratorium on the stuff we'd discussed in the pub. There'd been a subtle change in the way we tip-toed around each other; maybe Helen and Seamus had arranged this deliberately that afternoon, that their persuasions would be made separately in an attempt to eke something out of me that might not be so forthcoming otherwise. I was eager to find out what Seamus wanted to tell me but loath to share my own intrigues with Helen. If this was unfair, then I didn't feel too bad about it: I didn't like the way that they seemed to be cosying up together and leaving me out in the cold, flying auto. Although there was probably something in it, I was reluctant to listen to them appropriate my memories, and the times we shared at Seven Arches and my strange adaptations of them, into something they could use as proof that I was being sucked into their tilted little world.

'So who was it you met earlier?' I asked, trying to sound casual. That the three of us had forged new links at roughly the same time seemed too great a coincidence to be considered as such. But what else could it be? Helen had seemed the least impressed by these events. 'People meet people,' she'd said, at the start of the evening. 'That's what people do.'

Now she lit a cigarette and, through the smoke, said: 'A guy called Jared.'

'Jared?' Seamus and I said, simultaneously. 'What,' (Seamus went on) 'has he got a pint of beer between his shoulders?'

'Not funny, Shay,' Helen sneered. I was impressed by her defence of the stranger. And jealous as fuck. 'Jared. *Jared*. It's a name. It's nice. I like it.'

Seamus scoffed. 'Jared. What's his surname? Amsonjam? Do you get that?'

'Oh fuck off, Shay,' Helen barked. Some diners turned to watch. 'Seamus. What a fucking boring name. Did you know that your name is an anagram of *emu ass*?'

'No. Jesus, is that how you spend your time?'

I chipped in: 'So what's the story?' I was enjoying their tiff, but I could see the waiters getting antsy and I was curious. I wanted to find out how much of a tosspot Jared was so that I could feel better. So that I could get some sleep tonight.

Helen lost her anger and reset her features, scrunching her shoulders up as though she'd just been treated to a warm blast of air. 'He's lovely. But he's a bit odd. He came in the shop and started looking at some of my stuff, then he asked me how I worked, whether I used music or not. Then we started talking about relaxation techniques and he said I should try a sounds of the sea kind of thing. He said that was how he liked to relax.'

'Christ,' said Seamus, 'why doesn't he just have a wank like everyone else?'

Ignoring him, she fixed her gaze on me. Her eyes seemed too liquid, unstable in the candlelight. It was as if some of this water talk he'd charmed her with this afternoon had infected her. 'He told me he had lived by the sea all his life. He says that he's got test tubes in his room filled with water from every ocean in the world, collected by himself. He's working on smaller bodies of water now. He bought some of my water sculptures. He loved them.'

Seamus swigged the last of his wine and beckoned the waiter. 'Would he like a bag of my piss?' he asked.

'He wants to see me again,' she said, ignoring Seamus, but she didn't look massively enamoured of the idea. She chewed her lip. 'He wants to show me his underwater photos.'

'I bet he does. Just before he tries to get a little moisture out of you.'

'Seamus!' Even I was tiring of his act.

Helen said to me: 'Something else happened to you today, didn't it?'

After we'd paid the bill, Helen lingered on the doorstep, obviously wanting to talk to me some more. It was unnerving that she'd been able to read in my countenance the discomfort caused by the dream, but I was half-convincing myself she'd have said what she did regardless. She waved feebly, before crossing the road to the bus stop.

'Why isn't she coming with us?' I asked.

'Because when you went to the toilet I told her I wanted to have you to myself for a while. She can see you some other time. Tomorrow most likely.'

I really loved the sound of that. I don't think. I felt like something that was to be shared between squabbling children. I told him this, and then: 'What if I decide I want to be on my own? What if I'm unavailable tomorrow?'

'Suit yourself,' and he stalked away, capped head bobbing to the rhythm of his gait.

'Where are we going?' I said, trying to keep up without breaking into a trot.

'Somewhere quiet.'

He led me through Market Square. Some wag had polluted the fountain with bubble bath: shivering sud structures lolled over the concrete rim; the roof of the museum was patchy with snow.

He ushered me into the pub so quickly that I didn't get a glimpse of its name.

'I thought you wanted to go somewhere quiet,' I hollered, over the brittle shriek of an electric guitar, but he'd vanished into the pack of bodies at the bar. Sweat leapt from my skin; the pub was like a sauna. Large, ineffectual fans lumbered on the ceiling, windows spawned spreading centres of mist. I shrugged off my coat and pulled the sleeves of my jumper back. Everybody seemed to know everyone else.

Fluorescent green posters told me that this band were called Lettuce: they were a three-man combo – drums, bass, lead – the singer screaming his lyrics out of the side of his mouth while his eyes nursed the fingers on the frets as they shaped the most basic of chords.

'Get this down you,' yelled Seamus, pushing a pint of Guinness into my chest.

'Why are we here?'

'I told you, I wanted to tell you something. Great band, eh? Fucking curvy.'

There was no point in pushing him. I watched the band slog through a series of pseudo Nirvana thrashes that were more cringe than grunge before they finished with a predictable kicking-over of the drumkit and a *Fuck you!* to the audience, who applauded in return.

Seamus was still tapping his foot, even though the only sound from the speakers was a ragged hum. He traced a nail up and down his glass, which was already half empty.

'So what's the news?' I asked, my voice, after the noise, sounding strangely unlike the one I recognised as my own.

He pursed his lips as though searching for a way to begin, or considering whether or not he should tell me after all.

'In the summer – August – me and a friend went to New Mexico for a week. Caving holiday. It's the first time I'd been away. Like I said earlier, we'd done the wild caves in Britain – the ones worth doing anyway – and it was, like, New Challenge Time.' He boomed these last three words and raised his arms for emphasis. Beer slopped down his hand; he ignored it. The lights over the bar grew brighter for a second before dimming. The band were sitting on the dais where they'd performed, affecting slouches, drinking from green-gold bottles, their eyes brimming with shade. It seemed they were all watching me and Seamus.

'Me and Foley, Evan Foley – he's the friend, if you've not worked it out for your fucking self yet – met up with a couple of guys he'd been in touch with who were into caves too. In a big way. One of them, Dale Paris, was a prick. Didn't call himself a caver, he was a speleologist, the cockhole. The other guy was okay. Bob Sinclair, his name. Both came from Colorado. Big caving community in Colorado.'

I could see he was stringing the story out because he didn't want to tell it. I finished my pint and motioned I should get another. He shrugged, then looked over at the band. I went anyway and ordered two more drinks just as the barman rang last orders. The pub had lost about a quarter of its punters though I couldn't remember seeing anybody leave. The lights buzzed above me, sometimes winking to the point of death before flourishing once more. The barman was a pale strip beneath them, red tie like a yawning, Technicolor split in his chest.

When I returned, Seamus had found an empty table. The singer/guitarist from Lettuce was sitting next to him, a cowboy boot covering the stool I might sit on.

'Look out,' I said, my voice suddenly regressing to that of a twelve-year-old. I couldn't keep my eyes off the gold chain which joined an ear-ring to his nose or the shaved part of his head where two small chips from a circuit board had been glued.

'Look out yourself,' he rumbled, but moved his foot away.

I laughed in what I hoped was a jolly all-mates-together kind of way but which probably sounded like I was about to piss my pants. He looked at the drinks as if to say *Where the fuck's mine?* but instead he started rolling a cigarette.

'So you'll come along then?' he asked, watching his fingers work. I started, thinking he was addressing me, but obviously Seamus was his focus.

'Course,' he said. I couldn't tell if he really wanted to go –

wherever it was he'd been invited – or stick around and finish his story. I wondered if he'd told Helen. I wondered who the Yeti sitting next to me was, and how he knew Seamus. It had been a long day; I wanted my bed.

'All right if Davey comes?'

'Davey? Shit. Yeah, I suppose so. You up for it, Davey-*Wavey*?' He rested the roll-up in a mouth that was little more than a slit surrounded by stubble.

'Up for what?'

'We have a party after every gig we play. Sod it, we have a party even if we haven't played a gig.' He looked at my scarf, at my rip-free jeans. 'Think you can handle it?'

I saw myself smashing my pint glass on the edge of the table and swooping its fangs about his face: '*Oi, Yeti, think you can handle this?*'

'Yeah. Could be good.' The fat, white pillow of sleep deflated in my mind. 'What's your name?'

He paused as he rose from his stool. 'Deep Pan,' he said. 'But you can call me Deep Pan.'

I laughed because I felt I ought to but he'd already turned his back on me. The rest of the band followed him outside.

'We should go,' said Seamus.

'I don't know. I'm pretty jiggered.'

'Aw David. Please come. I've got to get all this shit out of my system.' And his face looked so woeful that I could do nothing but smile and nod and wish I was a bastard.

We walked for what seemed like an age. The snow had returned with muscle, liking the taste of this town. It was accompanied by a single thunderclap and a wind which couldn't make up its mind about the direction in which to blow. Swirls of snow attacked us from all sides. The coal of Deep Pan's cigarette was a beacon to follow in the confusion. I heard a short bark of laughter sprint over my head and the hiss of traffic. The smell of burned grease from a chip shop.

We filed into an off-licence where a tired woman wrapped up bottles of cider and my four-pack of cheap bitter. I turned in time to see Deep Pan's friends scrutinising me from outside, their hands leaving stars of white mist on the window.

'What's going on?' I asked Seamus.

He turned the corners of his mouth down by way of reply and walked out of the shop.

I could hear the party before we turned into the road where it was being held. Houses on either side killed the wind to such an extent I could also hear the drummer from Lettuce chewing his gum. I guessed we were pretty close to the railway station though I hadn't been paying much heed to road signs. Deep Pan kicked open the front gate and threw an empty can at the upstairs window through which some-body was mooning. We waited at the front door, which was little more than a rotten frame of wood filled with an opaque plastic oblong of purple bubbles. Deep Pan looked ready to kick that in too but a black guy, naked from the waist up, let us in. The band headed for the kitchen, trading shoulder slaps and insults on the way. I dithered in the hall with Seamus. There was a woman on the stairs who I looked at because she was so still. Her face was half buried in her hands. A small bottle of something clear sat next to her. The tip of a gold tattoo peeked from the V of her T-shirt; I was suddenly desperate to find out what it was. She opened her eyes and looked at me. Only when she moved her arms did I see that it was the girl from the car. She was smiling. My heart spanked against its cage.

'Come on, Davey. We look like a pair of twats standing here.'

I cracked open a can and followed him into a room whose walls danced with candlelight. I couldn't tell how large the room was: its perspective kept swimming in and out of focus with the flame. Vague dark lumps littered the floor, breathing and smoking and drinking. The sweetish odour of dope hung in the air like an awkward question.

'Let's sit here,' he said, crossing his legs before lowering himself into a gap by the television.

'Whose house is this?' I asked.

'Fuck knows. Probably one of Pan's mates.'

'Deep Pan? So you know him then?'

'Course. I met him about a year after we finished college. He was gigging then, but with a different band. Ruptured Gut I think they were called. I saved his life. Rolled him over on to his side when he'd drunk himself stupid. He vomited in his sleep as well. Knows MacCreadle, believe it or not.'

MacCreadle. Everyone seemed to know him. I managed to quell my own thoughts of MacCreadle only by a great effort of will and an even greater swig of lager. 'So how come he's here in Lancaster?'

Seamus offered me that bowed lip again. 'Could be on some pissy little concert tour. Could be visiting mates. I don't know. I just heard he was playing at the pub tonight. Thought it would be good to see him.'

A blast of something raucous fled from a room upstairs, so loud it made my lungs vibrate. I downed the rest of my can, suddenly in a party mood and wishing I'd bought more beer.

'So are you going to finish your story?'

Seamus smiled feebly and nodded. I got the impression he didn't want to talk about it and yet at the same time he seemed desperate for me to egg him on; that he wanted to purge himself of the memory but couldn't without my signal. It must have been on his mind: he picked up the story where he'd left off.

'There's a cave in the Guadalupe Mountains called Lechuguilla. It was my ambition, ever since I found out about it. We were like kids, the four of us, when we got there. I kept expecting someone from my life in England to appear and burst the bubble, you know? As if I wasn't worthy of the moment and I was just hallucinating the whole thing.

'There's a steel tube at the cave's entrance. It stops rock-falls from blocking it. In the morning we kind of stood around the entrance once we'd got our gear together and it was like, *The Moment*. All my needs were wrapped up in what that steel tube signified. We all felt it. It's just that we applied something almost holy to what we felt when the opposite was true. We camped just outside and the wind blew across it during the night – none of us could sleep – and it was like the cave was calling to us. When we opened the lid we got a blast of air that nearly blew us over, must have been 50-60 miles an hour. We crawled through.'

He sighed and drank from his can. I was irritated by his telling of the past; he was so unreliable that I was convinced he was dressing up a part of his history that was dull as double maths.

'It was like being in a sauna. At the bottom of Boulder Falls, Dale got sick and by the time we got to Apricot Pit, which is a deep fucker, let me tell you, about 500 feet in some areas, he was vomiting bad. Bob Sinclair sat him down and tried to get him to control his breathing. Me and Evan were pissing ourselves. The speleologist arsehole wasn't going to make it. These guys were supposed to be experts. Bob said he was going to take Dale back and did we want to call it a day? Evan and me just shook our heads and waved bye-bye.

'It was a hard caving trip. Both of us had heavy gear with us so we took it slowly, both a bit spooked over Dale and hoping it wouldn't hit us, knowing that this was the only way out and that things were going to get tough. At the bottom of Apricot Pit we rested and Evan took some photographs on the way. It was so beautiful inside, David. Heaven carved out of the rock. Great columns of gypsum crystal eight metres long, calcite that looked like it had been sculpted. Everything white. And the names of the chambers on my map. Firefall Hall, Lake of the Blue Giants, Ocean Wave Room. We were abseiling and prussiking all over the shop. My arms were on fire but I couldn't feel a thing. I felt like I was tripping, that these structures couldn't be real unless they were inside my mind.

'We had a big climb ahead of us, up 200 feet to what they call The China Shop. At the top we bivvied for the night – we'd been in the cave for about 18 hours. After a night's sleep we all awoke and had some dried fruit and energy bars. We were shivering with excitement.

'We went fucking wild. Hyperventilating and all that shit. If we saw a black hole we'd swing into it whether it was ten or two hundred metres deep. I was convinced we were going to discover something incredible: a brand new colour or a family of troglodytes or a fucking dinosaur! We took off up a sixty-metre wall of aragonite crystals. Got cut to ribbons. Exhausted at the end of it – humidity was 100 per cent. And then we arrived at a sump.' He'd become more animated, the tendons on his neck sprung like taut cables.

The girl had wandered into the room. She was drinking from a bottle of red wine. I saw her cadge a roll-up from Deep Pan who made space for her on his knee. She lay her head against his chest and looked at me. She said something and Deep Pan laughed, the sound rattling in his chest.

'What's a sump?'

'A flooded passage. You can't help coming across water in the caves. We went in and waded for about twenty metres before the ceiling of the cave started to slope down closer to the water's surface. Soon, we were at a point where we could either chicken out or swim underwater, see if we came out anywhere. We were all for that – the thought we might discover a new cave was too great a pull. Evan went first.

'We were underwater for about half a minute – it was getting to the point where I was ready to turn back – but then we surfaced in a tiny pocket of air. Evan asked me if I wanted to go on. I felt pretty claustrophobic there, we were practically kissing each other. I said we should go on. So I killed him in a way.'

Even though I'd been waiting for a line like that, it still sucked the blood from my cheeks when he said it. I offered some kind of weak encouragement but it was unnecessary; he was going to finish whether I wanted to hear or not.

'We surfaced again not long after. We were in a small passage – you couldn't get two abreast so I followed him. He stopped and took some Vaseline out of a bag, smeared it on his arms. He didn't have to say anything, he just grinned at me because he knew how much I hated crawling through narrow tunnels. Suck your belly in, Shay, he said and vanished into this crack in the wall. I went after him. About ten metres in I mashed my face up against his boots. He was stuck. He started joking about it – he'd been in this mess before, you see – talking about how crap his crash diet had proved to be and what a great view he had from his position. I realised it was serious when I saw blood spreading on the back of his vest. He was pinned fast. I was kind of glad I couldn't see his face, just the back of his head. I tried to pull him towards me but I couldn't gain purchase on anything so I tried pushing and he screamed.'

A shudder racked through Seamus, almost in slow motion, starting at his feet and ending in his shoulders, which he hunched in against his neck. His face was white around the eyepatch. I passed him one of my cans of bitter and he took a drink.

'I said I'd get help and he started shouting at me. Whenever he took in breath a new stream of blood would work its way out of the wound on his back. "What's the fucking point?" he yelled. "What's the fucking point?" And he was right. There was no way you could get more than one person into the tunnel. I said I'd tie a rope round his feet and scramble out backwards, try to pull him out when I could stand up and use some leverage but he said I'd rip his spine out. It was like the part of ceiling that had him was curved forward. he'd been able to slide into it but its hook caught him whenever he moved against it.

'So I stayed with him. I talked to him. I talked to him even when I could hear him weeping. I talked him through the panic when he thrashed about. I stroked his legs. He stopped for a long while and pressed his lips together. When he carried on, it was in a much quieter, calmer voice. I talked. It was strange because he died sooner than I thought he would. I thought he would go from lack of food but no. His body started shaking – he'd been quiet for a long time – and he just went. As if his body had just given up hope. Can you die from sudden depression? Anyway, probably the cold that did it. Just cold.'

Seamus stood up and walked away. I looked into the dark space he'd vacated, my heart beating so loud it was muffling the sound of drums from upstairs. All I could see was my head being lowered into a bank of mud, body in liquid spasm as my lungs filled.

To keep myself from rekindling the horror of my own recollections, I went after Seamus for more of his. All he could say though, out in a garden littered with red napkins from an earlier barbecue, was: 'The poor cunt's still down there for all I know. Buried in his beloved fucking cave. With a camera that's got pictures of me grinning in the Throne Room. Sticking the Vs up at him. I was wrong to say Lechuguilla was what mattered to me. It was Evan Foley. He was my ambition. Not the damn hole in the ground.'

I felt bad that I'd considered his retelling of the tragedy fanciful; a tale of effect rather than bereavement. I put my hand on his shoulder and immediately took it away again, feeling like the worst kind of hypocrite. 'Come inside, Shay,' I said, the first time I'd used his foreshortened name. 'It's cold. You'll catch your death.'

I left him in the garden, wishing – as one does in such situations – that I could impart some simple phrase of wisdom. It was easier to understand the absence of hope here though. It felt as though there was a vacuum drawing us in to a place that was dark yet so familiar it was as if we'd known all its colours and sounds and moods since birth; that it was a destiny of ours, its co-ordinates punched in as we slumbered in the womb, the three of us searching each other out without ever having to use our eyes.

If there had been a Big Bang in our past, only now were we beginning to notice its ripples, feel them assume control over the way our lives were shaped. Though I was in the dark about most things, and blurred because of that night's excesses, I began to believe that if something was developing, then it had its roots in a previous episode, something that we'd managed to bury within ourselves, like a murderer's diary of confessions hidden in the attic.

four
Δ-9-THC

I missed the last bus back to Morecambe and spent the rest of the night accepting bottles from arms that snaked out of the floor. I guess I must have smoked something dodgy too because I wound up in the bathroom, lying flat on my back because I thought my head was going to spin off. I followed the cracks in the ceiling with eyes that felt too dry. The dark against a window free of any net curtain seemed packed in layers, like soil. Its glass bulged inwards the longer I stared. Somebody had replaced the lightbulb with a mist-filled glass pear. The flex hung loose near its housing; brown and blue wires made a brief helix there. Jesus, I was unwell. Somebody knocked on the door three times, then once more after a pause.

'Wrong sequence,' I croaked. 'Do you know today's pass-word? I'm busy. I'm in a meeting.'

Somehow I managed to stand, just in time for a glut of vomit to loose itself from my throat. Eyes watering, but feeling better despite the shock that the violence of being sick awakens in me, I covered my mess with lines of toilet tissue, hoping that whoever rented the house would see the act as something approaching an apology.

I opened the door on a strange beast with two heads.

'You parked that well,' said one, stepping to one side so I could see they belonged to the drummer and bassist from Deep Pan's band. 'Come and have a chatette,' he said, gripping my elbow. I might have thought *uh-oh* if I was in any fit state but I allowed myself to be led downstairs, back to the garden where I'd held Seamus' arm briefly millions of years ago.

'Some joker's swapped your eyes for cherry tomatoes.' This was from the bass player. He shrugged his leather jacket – which was a size too big for him – around on his shoulders as he spoke. The legend on his T-shirt read: *Do I Not Like That*. I noticed one of his eyes was blue, the other green, its pupil dilated stubbornly. I toyed briefly with the thought of asking him what *his* eyes had been swapped for but realised, stoned as I was, that it wouldn't be met with a smile and kind words.

'What can I say?' I slurred. 'All the better for keeping them peeled. That's what I fucking say.'

'Are you taking the rise?'

A distant, sober part of me wagged its finger. I shook my head, waiting for the first blow. 'Have you seen Shay. Mus?'

'Gone home. You're Davey, right?' The drummer's voice was a tight whinge. He was probably from Manchester.

'David technically. And you are?'

'I'm Frank,' said the drummer.

'You are that if nothing else,' I said and fell over, laughing. My fun ended when the edge of a low wall took about a foot of skin from my back. I thought about screaming, realised what time it must be then thought *sod it* and screamed anyway. The pain fled from one end of my spine to the other, as though someone were rolling a ball of flame up and down it.

'And this is Tonka,' he jabbed a thumb at the bass player before lifting me up. 'You all right, you dizzy cunt?'

I knew my back wasn't bleeding, that the wetness was that clear, weeping lymph which lies against the skin. 'Yes,' I said, my voice strangled.

'We've been looking at you all night, David,' Tonka breathed, his voice little more than a husky whisper.

This I knew, but I wasn't expecting a confession. It was hard, getting used to all this brutal honesty and I wasn't at all sure that I liked it that much.

'Trying to work out which planet I'm from, I'll warrant.'

'We think the Bag Lady would like you. We think a meeting would be a good idea.'

'And the Bag Lady is?' Ripples of heat moved slowly across my back. The pain was shifting my drunkenness to a place where it could more easily be coped with. I burped and the thick, flat taste of bad wine filled my mouth.

Frank leaned over me. The whiff of Doublemint fell from his lips along with: 'You've seen her. Name's Eve. You tell me – she's had her beady one on you all night, yeah? She says she's already met you. Had a nice chatette, eh, dans la voiture?'

'I think I know who you mean. She's very nice, but I'm not one for nobbing women cold, you know.' I considered for a moment. 'I'm not one for nobbing women of late full stop.'

'She can help you with your sadness.'

I snapped my head up. Seeds of light popped behind my eyes and the cold, black heel of alcohol's hand pressed down once again. I couldn't see Tonka's face properly. It swam against the darkness as though made from oil; the brilliant light from a bare bulb in the alleyway splintered at his shoulder, dazzling me. I saw the thin shapes his breath made in the cold but I couldn't decode the words carried upon it any more. My T-shirt was fusing with the wetness on my back.

'Come on, friend,' said Frank. 'We'll get you a coffee and walk this shit out of you.'

We didn't stray far from the party. From the bridge overlooking Lancaster train station I watched the twin trails of a jet underline the paling sky. The coffee had warmed me, and cleansed my palate, but the queasiness remained, a fat worm squirming in my belly. I'd returned to the bathroom to wash my face and gaped at the mirror, at the pinkness of my eyes. I drank as much water as I could stomach, hoping that the dehydration would be pushed back by breakfast time. The train station was quiet apart from a soft hum rising from the electric cables. The smell of diesel was oddly comforting –

perhaps because it put me in mind of train journeys I'd taken with my parents. A more civilised time when anything unpleasant lay beyond the fortress walls of family.

'Not so mouthy all of a sudden, hey?' murmured Tonka.

'I'm not sad,' I said. And then again, more quietly: 'I'm not sad,' as if to convince myself.

'I didn't hear nobody say you were. But that said, Davey, you don't half resemble some miserable bastard now.'

'I'm pissed out of my swede. I want my bed. I'm freezing my nads off. I have a right to be fed up.' My back twinged. When the booze wore off I would be in a heap of trouble there. Helen flashed into my thoughts, eyes wild with anger and I almost smiled. A yearning broke open in my chest. With her there I felt a little confidence come back.

'Why are you interested in me? What's so important to you about setting me up with Eve?'

Tonka spread his hands. With his long hair and beard he looked like Christ in a biker jacket. 'Because our lives are so empty we need to get our rocks off by interfering with everyone else's.'

'Because,' said Frank, putting his arm round me, 'Eve is our friend and she's had a bitch of a year and it would be nice if we found her a new friend. She's a wonderful woman. She'll never let you down. She's expressed an interest.'

'I don't think I'll be here very long. I'm passing through really.'

'So is she.' He stuck a piece of paper in my pocket and put his finger in front of my eyes. Its nail was black and long. 'For when you reconsider. When you sober up.'

Then they walked away. I followed at a distance and back at the party stumbled across a room that was being used for storing coats. Somehow I found sleep down amongst the musty jackets and the threadbare carpet. The cold, hard floor seemed to suck the heat from my flesh as I rested so that, by the time I wakened to the sound of the door scraping open, I was shivering violently. A flame floated into the room: a moment later, I focused on the face behind it.

'Something warm for you,' she said, and slid under the coats. She placed the candle on the floor and passed me a mug of tea while her legs knotted with mine and my chest became a pillow for her head.

'I'm David. David Munro.'

'Hello David David Munro. I'm Eve Eve Baguley.'

'Would you like some of this tea?' My back was flaring but I didn't want her to move away. Her warmth was massive, enveloping me like a bubble. Beneath the smoke trapped in her hair I could smell peaches.

Dirty light was sifting through the thin curtains. It was quiet downstairs. 'What time is it?' There was a dead bird on the floor next to Eve. A panicky moment saw me thinking she'd brought it in during the night, like a cat.

'Just after six. You smell nice.'

'Thank you.' The tip of her tattoo was again visible, something fanciful-coloured peeking from her chest. Shadows dipped away beneath the wool. It didn't seem correct to ask her what slept there.

'Did you enjoy the party?' I asked, trying to keep the silence away so that she'd not hear my manic heartbeat.

'I did, yes. I watched you. You didn't look very happy.'

'My friend told me some bad news.'

'The way you look, it's as if you've fallen into a bucket of tits and come out sucking your thumb.'

I nodded, laughing. 'I still enjoyed the party though.'

She placed her hand against my back and I winced. 'Sorry,' she said, 'Frank told me about your gymnastics. Do you want me to have a look at it?'

The thought of Eve looking at my back, even in its raw state, was quite attractive but I shook my head, uncertain that this was the path I really wanted to go down. I was here for a reason, serious matters. It would be stupid to get mixed up with someone and possibly put them at risk.

'It's not too bad,' I said. 'I just need to clean it. I'll be fine.'

'And what about your friend? Is he okay?' She leaned on one arm and drew back from me; her long jumper snagged on the various soft peaks of her body. I really wanted to hold her.

'He's okay. He was telling me about something that happened to him a while ago. A bad accident.'

'Oh dear,' she said, pressing her fingers to her mouth. 'I've been too nosy, haven't I?'

'No,' I said. Silence fell and time seemed to become sticky, gelling around us. Sunlight coated Eve's face in layers, at first polishing and then concealing her skin without blurring the edges of her face. Her eyes were blue suggestions through this. When I could blink and breathe again, I drew away. Her face stole back its form from the sunlight; she was smiling. Her fingers traced the imperfections on the back of my hand. I leaned over to blow out the candle but she stopped me.

'There's a place we can go to, where I can take you, if you need to get away,' she whispered, watching as her fingers measured the mini-bevels of sinews, veins and bones. 'There's a way out.'

I gritted my teeth against an unease that said: *She knows what's going on.* 'I have to go,' I murmured.

She shifted so I could rise. I idled over tying my bootlaces; I wanted time to study her face. Her eyes were closed, which always takes away some of the life in a set of features, but I could tell she was attractive. Not catwalk-attractive; her face was too flawed and interesting for that, unusual enough to keep my attention. The scant impact of the candle flame helped her face lose its structure. I thought, horribly, that it might start sliding off the bone.

'We'll talk soon,' she murmured. 'You have my number.'

I was about to deny this but then I remembered Frank putting something in my pocket. I patted it now and heard it crumple against my thigh. 'Yes. I'll call you.'

'You'll call me.'

'I'll just get rid of breakfast,' I said, picking up the dead bird and flinging it out of the window. She wore the same liquid near-smile I'd seen in the car. As I closed the door I caught her reflection in a mirror. She looked new and unspoiled among the dregs of party, like an overgrown newborn unaware of its limits and enjoying the flex of its body for the first time. Her skin was so pale it seemed transparent.

I popped my head round the corner of the living room, quietly impressed by the volume of empty cans and bottles lying around the place, to say goodbye to anybody who was conscious. There was nobody around. I heard muttered voices in the kitchen. Two guys in vests and baggy track suit bottoms were hunched by the door. I heard the words 'Call the police' and saw one of them cover his face and say, 'Jesus.'

'What's up?' I asked, startling them out of their confab.

'Aw shit, mate,' said the taller of the two, 'you don't want to know.' But even as he was saying this, he was stepping back to allow me through. It felt as though he was handing me a baton in a relay race so that he could forget his part in it.

'What's in there?'

'Have a look. Tell us were imagining things.' This came from the other one, an Australian with blond dreadlocks.

Wishing I'd left when I intended to, I pushed past them, affecting a sigh in the hope that it would conceal the tension I was feeling. There was a girl on the floor with strawberry jam smeared all over her face and breasts. She was naked from the waist up.

'Is she all right?' I asked, concentrating on the steady rise and fall of her chest.

'Is she all right?' the Australian asked, incredulous? 'Is she all *right*?'

'Fuck it, mate,' his partner spat. 'She's fucking *dead*. Look at her.'

The rise and fall of her body had nothing to do with her lungs and everything to do with my own clattering heart. I steadied myself against the wall and edged closer. Her face had been torn from the boss of her skull; the flesh of her chest was macerated. One breast hung free, clinging to the torso by a thick flap of skin. She was looking up at me, sneering a curve of blood-smeared teeth. I stepped back and I think I said, 'Oh.' My foot mashed a piece of mince – a nipple – into the linoleum. After yesterday, with all the omens and demons we'd discussed, I felt partly responsible for her death, as if our words had somehow summoned forth an evil presence intent on making real our fears.

The police came and the ambulance men took her away. We all made statements and gave names of the other party guests. I didn't get away until late but all the while I was there, I didn't see Eve, despite the fact that the police checked all the rooms. She must have slipped out while I was in the kitchen.

On the bus back to Morecambe I tried to remember the colour of Eve's eyes. Though it was a fruitless task, it took my mind off how jaded I felt and the nightmare of that poor girl's face. Her name was Jemima. She was the girlfriend of one of the other guys who had come to the party but who had gone home early because he felt sick. I remembered (but only because I recognised her blue linen skirt) squeezing past her on the hall to get to the toilet.

I closed my eyes tightly, trying to force out the bloody image of her. I tried to think of Helen instead and how claustrophobic I was already feeling. Though I'd only been around my old friends for a short while I was already needful of my own space. The talk we'd had in the pub yesterday seemed distant and unreal; the subject even more so. I wondered if I should just leave, go back to Warrington, anywhere, so that I could claim myself back. Too many weird things were happening here. It was as though this grim, etiolated coastal town was stripping me bare, making me vulnerable to attack from the people it had already defiled with its slow poison. My mind was perceiving a solid world yet it consistently peeked at what was rotten underneath, pulling reality out of true so that I couldn't discern the healthy from the diseased.

The links with my friends didn't appear reduced in any way. If anything, they were stronger than the last time I'd seen them, though I couldn't be sure if this was anything to do with the fact that we'd outgrown our petty phase, or the focus of our conviction had shifted to this new crisis.

A watery sun was doing its best to warm me through the window. I shifted slightly, trying to ignore my back's protest but the pain was too intense. I grunted and felt woozy again, close to fainting. The bus driver's eyes filled his rear-view mirror, black with intent. I felt guilty, like a schoolboy caught defacing the seats.

Somehow I got back to the guest house though I had to stop every few yards and wait for my dizziness to pass. Once inside, I took off my clothes – apart from my T-shirt, which had stuck to my back – and stood under a hot shower until I was able to peel the material away from my skin. My back felt bloated with pain. I washed it gingerly, then rinsed the smoke and beer out of my hair and skin. Uncomfortable as I was, it was heartening to feel cleansed of last night's excesses.

I crumbled some crackers into a mug of instant soup. Duncan walked into the kitchen and showed me his set of socket spanners. 'Got 'em for twenty quid off a bloke round the corner who was about to chuck 'em.' His eyes went waxy. 'I will do great things with these. Let me know if there's anything of yours I can, em, spanner for you. Bike. Or a go-kart. Anything.'

'I will, thanks.'

I sipped my soup lying on my front in bed. Music seemed attractive until I switched on the radio and found a squelchy mass of static. I made do with silence. Towards sleep, I felt her head press gently against me. Her lungs gurgled as she sucked air through the ruin of her chest. Boys bent down to pick crabs from her hair for cricket practice. But I didn't want to see her face. No, not that.

Cricket filled my life when I was small. My father played every Saturday which meant my summer weekends were given to fields by polluted rivers, petrochemical stations, breweries. My immediate horizons were broken by rooftops and chimneys and pylons and pavilions peopled by heavy men dressed in white.

Dad's cricket bag was made from brown canvas and long enough to accommodate his bat. During the closed season, it would reside in the cubby-hole beneath the stairs and I would sometimes crawl under there to open it and smell the summer ghosts it had trapped. There was always a scuffed cricket ball or two, a pair of gloves with their meaty finger shields, a couple of old bails. There was also a box, which was meant to provide protection but felt deeply uncomfortable whenever I tried it on.

As well as the musty smells of canvas and leather, there hung around the bag's pale innards a detergent whiff, of Vosene and astringent soaps, sticking plaster. Although I was too big, I wanted to crawl inside the bag and lie next to the perished rubber grip of the bat and imagine my dad's strong, tanned arms flexing as he used it. I bowled at him once he'd padded up, happy that I could help him practise.

When he was in the field, Helen, Seamus and me would walk the perimeter boundary until we were close enough for him to hand us sticks of JuicyFruit. We'd sit a little distance away and watch rabbits scampering or swallows skimming the pitch.

Dad was the captain, an excellent bowler, very fast and accurate. He raced up to the popping crease, shirt open to his navel, a blur of purpose. We'd cheer when he got a wicket. When the players came in for tea, we'd run up to him and he'd slip us jam and marge sandwiches from the table.

The sideboard at home became cluttered with trophies. His performances became like a history of code to me: 9 for 32, 5 for 2, 5 for 36. I would look through his scoring books, often when the cricket season had finished, and decipher their strange markings, the dots and dashes that represented an entire game. I'd look forward to June when we'd troop out to our Fiat 127 and he'd take me somewhere I'd never been before where I could watch him from the branch of a tree or a bench on the boundary. End of an over – a maiden or a wicket

– he might wave to me and I'd give him the thumbs-up. Pop (with a pulpy paper straw) and crisps in the bar afterwards.

And then he stopped playing. The canvas bag disappeared and he cleared away his trophies. Summers were never so carefree and innocent again. The first year of his retirement from the game, I got pissed with Shay at Seven Arches and met a gang that sat around in the dank shadows necking beer and talking as candles turned the curve around them into an uncertain ceiling, a different kind of night. We were in our early teens and we'd sit a respectful distance from the ringleaders, watching them hungrily when the girls arrived offering kisses that were hot and wet and yielding as freshly laid bitumen. Every woman had a curve and for every curve there was a male hand to cup it.

I once saw a girl, Patti, crouched on the floor in front of a big guy, MacCreadle, sucking at him slowly and deeply while he looked into the mist rising on the canal as if seeing something form there. Her flexed fingers clawed at his thighs with every upstroke, her muffled grunt of pleasure or pain punctuated the limit of her journey down. I dreamed about her for weeks.

Della bore thick ropes of crimson scar tissue on her throat like an extravagant necklace; her father had tried to strangle her with a length of barbed wire when she was a baby. Rifle knew a boy called Pook who had been battered and left to drown in the pond of a nearby pleasure park; the two of them haunted the rides at night. Pepper had driven the sharp end of a claw hammer into his maths teacher's cheek. Pris got drunk and danced topless around the candles.

We watched them and, when MacCreadle was sent to prison for a crime that nobody dared talk about, we spoke to them, especially the quieter, more approachable ones. The low orders. Delicate Freddy, Hangfire, Juckes and Smoac. We wished we knew stories about the dark harlequin figures that capered in the town's underbelly. Instead, we recounted their tales in the playground, gaining the kind of brainless respect that passes for currency at school. Even the nutcases gave us a wide berth. One memorable day, Helen, Shay and me walked into the canteen and the queue dissolved for us. We knew MacCreadle, every child's wardrobe nemesis at bedtime. We were on speaking terms with Sawdust, who had torched a judge's car outside Crown Court.

As summer turned rusty and the weather deteriorated, we started fires under the arch and talked less, concentrating on keeping out the cold. The starts of those evenings were almost magical, despite the deracinated look on everyone's faces, the scarified appearance of the wasteland around us. MacCreadle's bike would suddenly tear a hole in the night somewhere behind the ranks of lock-up garages on the other side of the railway. Its cry would descend from all sides, as if he were flying the machine.

We'd curry favour with them by bringing takeouts. Once, shortly before MacCreadle was put away, he winked at me when I handed him a carton of Chinese. Sometimes, if we stayed out all night wrapped up in sleeping bags, we'd wake up to find everyone gone and a few twists of tin foil, spent syringes at the ash surround of the fire. We didn't know what they got up to when they weren't at Seven Arches, but gradually, over the years, they drifted away, leaving me with the same emptiness I'd felt when Dad's cricketing summers finished. It was as if the focus of my life was constantly being redefined and lost at a crucial point, when the cementing of who I was seemed about to happen. I didn't realise it then, but it wasn't the cricket or the nights under Seven Arches that ratified my character. Helen and Shay were the nucleus of my development, the constants, the positive and negative centres to my universe.

We kept up the visits to Seven Arches, just the three of us now. Exorcised their ghosts, drew a little less menace from the shadows and vandalised brickwork. It became less a place for dormant violence and quick sex and cheap beer than a quiet retreat where I found my thoughts assuming greater clarity. I was able to relax more completely there than at home and acquire a peace that I'd never know elsewhere.

Nobody could get at me here. The traffic and pollution, the people that criss-crossed my life's path were as distant as one of the stars winking through the effluvia piled up over the cooling towers of Fiddlers Ferry power station. Helen and Seamus were a calming restraint on my reveries and a cata-lyst for my energies. We were an equilateral triangle and we knew the measure of each other intimately, holding each other in check: three scorpions clasping claws and dancing in a circle, stings raised high. A lot of talk went on at the arches. We discussed our aspirations. We grew so close that the sepa-rate entities we projected seemed ridiculous; three bodies cleaved into one. Sometimes I would dream of going up on to the tracks with them and lying on the rails, waiting for the tickle and hiss of rails to signify the splitting of our body into its constituent parts.

I remember MacCreadle best like this. Only like this. Jesus, I wish I didn't…

He leaned over Seamus. Spat a wad of Bubblicious on to his cheek.

'Cock-sucking mother-fucking cunt-reaming A-wipe. You fetid scuzz-bag shit-eating cleft-dabbling felcher. Lick my nads, slit-peeler. Fucking scrote-scrubber. Jit-gargling tip-weeping vomit-fart tube-tugging dog-frotting chiselling twatter. Christ. You make me want to throw my ring up. Ream your shaft with a rusty spoon, spunk-guzzling fuck. You… fuck.'

He clomped away, his metal-tipped heels clanging on the fire escape. When they crunched, faintly, on the broken glass of the alleyway behind the detergent factory, Seamus let out a long sigh.

'Don't shit it, Shay,' said Rifle, looming out of the dark, his face haloed by orange light from the spliff in his mouth. 'You might think I'm selling you a bent one here, pal, but…' he drew on the roach, spoke haltingly through his chestful of smoke, '… Mac likes you.'

'*Slit*-peeler?' Shay said. 'Dog-frotting chiselling *twatter*?'

We fell about, laughing.

'Mere expressions of affection, mate,' Rifle went on. 'He's a poetic cunt, granted, when it comes to abuse, but you should see him when he's pissed off with people. Someone shagged his bird, Patti, while he was in clink once. He went down to London, found her, found the bloke who did it.'

'What did he do?'

'Spoilt his face, bad style. Took a blade and opened his mouth from ear to ear. They call the poor bastard Fliptop now.'

Candles sputtered into life as the winterwhite sun was doused by crippled rooftops at the edge of the town. Slowly, bodies became discernible in the gloom, crumpled, spannered out of their gourds thanks to Classic's booze. Classic himself was crouched on a mattress singing John Lee Hooker songs. I couldn't be sure, but I reckoned there were around half a dozen wasted bodies in the squat, many of whom I'd only met last night.

We were sitting in a derelict office building right at the heart of the new town complex. Sardine can factories all over the shop. From the window, the panorama was one of car parks and stylised green areas.

'MacCreadle coming back?' I asked, watching Della as she stroked her choker of scars. They drifted, the women in this group, like unseen ghosts, like partnerless sharks in a dark ocean. Their objectives seemed without concrete shape. Direction meant nothing to them. They drifted, as if, by stopping, it would somehow prove to be their undoing. Della traded places with Pris, who had been tattooing the word HOPE on to Pepper's forearm. Della finished it off. Patti sat with Juckes, neither of them saying a word, but you could see the air between them solidify with meaning, layers of understanding softly forming like the gradual build-up of scale in a kettle. Smoac leaned back into a space that Hangfire unwittingly filled. Their bodies collided and they stayed like that, supporting each other. It was all instinct. There didn't seem to be any room for accidents. Unless you counted Delicate

Freddy, trying to piss into the mouth of a bottle while he held a sandwich.

Rifle kicked off his DMs and lay back on a mattress. 'Yeah, he'll be back. Much as he's with us, he's a loner. If you can understand that. Shit, I can't. Fucking hate being on my tod, I do.'

I did understand MacCreadle's craving for his own space. Sometimes being around other people felt unfathomable, unnatural. I answered more readily to the calls my body made as a singular unit, something that was essentially alone. I knew where MacCreadle would have gone, though, and I stared at Helen and Seamus in the dark. Their polished, straining eyes were enough of a spur. I left them to snack on each other and followed Mac's ghost.

He'd taken his Harley – we'd heard the tubercular rumble of it for long minutes after he'd left – but it was only a twenty-minute walk. It was a cold night and I zipped my leather jacket up around my ears. Lights seem to burn so much more brightly when there's a frost looming; the streetlamps in the distance formed an unbroken chain of wet fire up to a point where they petered out, down by the bottom of the school field where houses were now springing up since its closure, a few years ago. I made it to the canal and bore left, slipping through a rusting fence and following the canal bank west towards the thick black arm of the viaduct clawing across the gulley of the park and into the meat of the railway embankment.

We hadn't been down here for maybe a week, since the weather began to chill over, and I felt the same sickly attraction to the place as I did every time I made this approach. The old school was a low bank of black, with its broken clock-tower and mish-mash of architectural styles ranging from the functional 1930s brick to the pre-fabricated dross of the 1970s. The canteens had been demolished; large, cream chunks of breezeblock lay as a testament to all those hundreds of thousands of ice cream scoops of malty potato, all those water-ridden heaps of cabbage.

'Shagging school dinners,' I muttered, remembering the skill I'd employed, hiding my uneaten, inedible peas under a thin remainder of pie crust, or slipping my semolina – with its wound of raspberry jam – into the pocket of some gobbling idiot sitting next to me.

Up ahead, framed by broken goalposts, I saw a match burst into life and the uncertain appetite of candles as they sucked at the musty air beneath the arch. My heart barrelled around my chest like a pebble in a washing machine. As I neared, I could see that MacCreadle was not alone. He was lying on his back and reaching up to a woman who was standing in the soft swell of light, her upper body swathed in loose bandages. She was passing things down to him from the dark pockets each loop created and he was consuming them, a pained look on his face. Twenty feet away, hugged by the night, I stopped and watched. I was suddenly very frightened. The woman had no eyes, had no top to her head. I could see broad red stains in the bandage, spreading beneath the uppermost layer. MacCreadle was being fed babies, or rather, tiny, barely formed foetuses. The rictus of his mouth was flush with blood. He was crying silently, the prominent nub of his Adam's apple shuttling back and forth along his throat. Still he accepted them, still the woman offered more to him. Until, sensing someone near, she swung my way and made to show me what was moving about beneath her shroud.

MacCreadle launched himself upright, a rope of gore unravelling from his mouth. He shouted – 'No!' – a flat order which bore immediate results. The woman dwindled into a thin streak of light above the candles. Only when she had gone did I realise just how quiet the entire episode had been. A breath of traffic from Lovely Lane whispered across the field. MacCreadle looked at me, tears streaking all the dirt and blood.

I sat down in the dirt and tried to say something but I didn't know what it was I wanted to talk about.

'Leave me alone,' he said, spitting what looked like the skeletal remains of a tiny hand on to the floor.

'Who was she?'

He was coming to his senses now. He wiped his mouth and levered himself upright. 'You fuckin' followed me.'

'I followed you, yes. I just wanted to talk, without everyone else hanging round your arse.'

'You're hanging round my arse now. I don't much like it, friend.' The skin above his beard had grown bluish with shock. I had to lean forward to gauge his eyes, see if any humour lurked in there. They were dead as fish eyes. I wondered how many people MacCreadle had made suffer. I wondered if, as the stories went, he had killed anybody.

'I'm not well,' he said, eyeing me, I was sure, for any disbelief on my features. 'I... am in great pain all the time.'

'Have you been to a doctor?'

'It's nothing they can treat,' he said, flatly. 'You got anything to smoke?'

I shook my head and he kicked at the gravel. A train farted in the distance, approaching from the east. I moved closer and sat down on the edge of a rotting suitcase. The flames shivered, webbing the sooty curve of the arch with sickly light. I withdrew into the paltry shelter of my leather jacket, peeking over the collars, wishing I'd put my track suit bottoms on under these ripped jeans. The train crossed overhead, shedding echoes that engulfed us. Through the thunder, his eyes keen on me, MacCreadle said: 'Atonement.'

'What about it?' I asked, as the train slowed for Warrington Central.

'Do you know why I come here?' his voice was a low burble, irresistible not because of who he was, but because of this sudden show of vulnerability. I didn't mind him trumping my questions if it meant he'd unload a little of his self upon me.

'Because you like being on your own?'

'Fuck off. I can be on my own anywhere. I can be on my own in the middle of a fucking scrum down the Rope and Anchor, mate. Watch me switch off. No, I come here because it's as close to death as I can get without actually doing myself in. Fuck the cem and the crem. I might as well be wandering round a garden centre. There's death in these arches. Some mad fuckers have caused a right old stink here in the past. The Seventies? A couple of rapes and one of the nastiest murders a human being could come up with.'

I think I was going to ask him if he had ever killed anyone then, but the enormity of the question beat me. In that moment I suppose I passed from being a child who thinks that death is just another cartoonish stage in life to something more serious, more personal. That night I went home and cried quietly, my face hot and itchy against the pillow, understanding completely the loss I was going to feel when my parents died. It was a horrible feeling, a feeling that I was missing them already, even though I could have gone downstairs and sat with my mum on the sofa while she watched television or listened to Joni Mitchell with my dad in his den.

'It was a nurse, from the hossie across the road. She was going over the footbridge one night when she was jumped. Knifed, she was. Shredded. Cunt got away. I dream about that woman. Though I never knew her, never clapped eyes on her. I was only ten when she died. It fucked me up at school. I wrote poetry about her. Every picture I drew was of some nurse walking on a bridge. I kept reliving the death, thinking that somehow this time she'd escape. Like watching *Butch Cassidy and The Sundance Kid*. No matter how often I see that film, I keep hoping that *this* time they'll leg it away from all those Bolivian wankers.

'I started getting bad pains in my stomach. I couldn't concentrate on anything else. My mum would have been concerned, I'm sure, if she didn't have her gob either round the end of a bottle of Bells or some new cunt's cock. I started throwing up. I started throwing up stones.'

'Stones?' I could barely utter the word, I was so cold.

'Right.' Some of the colour was returning to his face now, although he still looked shattered, starved, like a badly composed effigy of himself. 'Stones. Black stones, incredibly smooth. I filled a one-pound beetroot jar with them in a week.'

'Did you see a doctor?

'Course I fuckin' did. You've got doctors on the brain, kid. They're all cunts. They did all kinds of tests, gave me a barium meal, but couldn't find anything wrong. GP told me to stop fucking about with his precious time. The chiselling twatter.'

'So what is it? Where are the stones coming from?'

'I don't know. But they comes whenever I start brooding over badstuff. I see a knife fight in a pub in town, someone gets sliced, I choke a stone. Someone in the local rag I'm reading over Ready Brek gets mugged, there's a stone in my Horlicks come bedtime.'

'Jesus, Mac,' I said. 'Stay clear of war reports, won't you?'

'Funny,' he said, deadpan. 'But it don't work like that. It's personal. It's next door stuff. Stuff that hits home. It isn't third-person reportage from some desert. This stuff has a face, a fucking horrible face, and it forces me to have a good old look.'

'What about the woman?'

His lips disappeared into his beard. 'What woman?'

'When I got here, I saw someone with you. Feeding you…'

'We'll never discuss this again, either one on one or in a debating chamber with everyone and his fucking hamster. You've got a problem if you saw anything, kid. You've got a big pile of shit coming your way.'

'What do you mean?'

'I'm making up for… certain things that happened, things that I've done in my past. I did some time for the things I've done, but that matters not one shitty speck in some circles. Sometimes you have to keep on paying. And you'd better keep whatever it is well buried, chum. Or you're going to find yourself spinning like a hanged man between the shit you can see on planet Earth and the shit that nobody deserves to see. Because that shit,' he said, spitting out a fragment, 'is bad shit.'

A blast of cold slammed through the arch, crystallising

the moment. In the years to come, the memories of that evening would fade but I found it easy to recall MacCreadle's face and the pain worked into it. His windswept hair, the scar on his forehead, the beard, collecting flakes of frost. The smears of fat and blood on the back of his hands. I tried not to think about the woman again, because I couldn't believe I'd actually seen it. He sent me away then, and I shifted across the field slowly, my bones seemingly replaced by a gruel of slob ice. I looked back often, watching as his form retreated in the weak candle flame. When it gusted out, it wasn't rekindled. I never saw him again.

It was still light when I wakened. The duvet was tangled between my legs and I was painted with a layer of sweat. My back was stiff; where it had healed I felt the skin crack open as I moved. The mattress was spotted red. I had the dim impression of something fast and formless, shedding smoke as it flashed behind the shelter of my consciousness before the light started bouncing connections inside my head, reminding me of all my discomforts and problems. The voice which had disturbed my slumber came again:

'David? David, are you there?'

I reached over and pulled back the curtain behind the headboard. Helen was standing in the street, arms raised to shoulder level, hands clenched. She looked forsaken; I found it hard to believe that such a frail creature could possess a voice so iron-edged. Guilt and pain turned my smile into a sneer. I couldn't say anything; I tossed my keys to her and sank back into the pillow.

After swearing upon seeing the state of me, she left me alone for a while, returning with a small can and a roll of bandage.

'Relax,' she said, as I made to sit up. 'It's just betadine spray, to stop infection. Bloody hell, David. Can't you look after yourself? How did you do this?'

I told her. The spray was cooling and thankfully didn't sting.

'You were meant to come and see me yesterday. I waited for you.'

'I'm sorry,' I said. 'No I'm not. Who said I was meant to come and see you? We didn't arrange anything. And what do you mean yesterday? You mean today is tomorrow?'

She smiled and began to wrap my body with the bandage. 'You put things so concisely, David. You must have slept all day and all night. Some party, hmm?'

The thought that I'd spent almost twenty-four hours in bed sickened me. No wonder I'd been spared a hangover. I closed my eyes and immediately her face spread all over the darkness, reaching into the creases of my mind and staining them crimson. I could smell the mealy reek of butcher's shops. I retched, dry heaving until I thought I'd faint. A thick rope of bile and saliva hung from my mouth.

Helen placed her hand on my arm and didn't remove it until I'd looked up at her.

'Someone was murdered, Helen. At the party. Some girl called Jemima.'

'What happened?'

I told her what I knew. It didn't take long.

'And the police?'

'They asked questions. They let me go. What, do you think I did it?'

'No, don't be silly. Who do you think did it?'

I shrugged. 'No idea. I was pasted.'

She went quiet for a while, then her face set. 'We have to consider the possibility that this is part of our problem, that you were the target.'

'Oh, don't talk wet. She just met a guy whose wires were crossed, who gatecrashed the party and wouldn't kiss him when he asked her to. Something as shitty as that.'

'The way you describe it, she was systematically butchered. People don't do that just because they can't get someone else's tongue in their mouth.'

'Helen?' I said. 'Are you planning to go back to the mothership soon? Do send me a postcard when you get back to planet Fairy Tale. Tell me all about your sisters: Sweetness and Light.'

'There's more to it than that. We're being stalked. But it's blind at the moment, directionless.' She was chewing the ragged bits of skin around her thumbnail, staring into the middle distance with enough effort to draw her eyebrows together. 'It's like someone playing a game of Battleship. You've got a rough idea of where the target is but you have to lob over a few stray shots to home in.'

'It's not taking long then, is it?' I said, humouring her. She seemed to come back to me but her theory would have been packed away in a little drawer marked *Hmm, nice idea. Re-heat and serve later.*

'I was worried about you, David. I was expecting you to come and see me. I'm sorry if you got the impression that you had no choice in the matter.'

'No, you're right. I did intend to call you yesterday but I flaked out instead. I don't see why there should be all this urgency though.'

She pinned the bandage fast against me. It was tight but had enough give to enable movement. I felt strangely secure wrapped up like that. 'You've just described the reason for urgency,' she said, sounding like an exasperated school-teacher. 'There's a woman dead.'

'Thanks for being Mumsy,' I said and kissed her on the cheek, noticing how she stiffened as I bore down on her. I let that go and said: 'Tell you what. I could do with a walk.'

As I dressed she drew a cup of cold water and pushed it into my hand along with two Neurofen.

Clouds above The Battery were piled up like desert mesas, bellies scooped out where they met the sea. The few people on the promenade were bent before it as if in suppli-cation; the wind was frisky this morning, whipping the fringes of waves white. We turned right and wandered towards the lighthouse. I hoped she might start a conversa-tion with: *God, do you remember that night…* but she wasn't in a chatty mood. The bangs of her red hair were flailing around a face tilted downwards; she was watching her oxblood DMs.

'Have you heard from Seamus? Only he disappeared from the party without saying goodbye.'

'No.'

'I think he was in a bit of a state. He told me about Lechuguilla.'

'He's feeling things press down on him. Can't you? This death, the people we've met…'

'Aw, come on, Helen. Eve hasn't got anything to do with this. She's just someone I bumped into.'

'Was she at the party?'

'Yes. But.'

She sighed. 'But nothing. It doesn't matter.'

'It fucking does. Don't just dismiss me. You think Eve had something to do with that girl's death?'

Helen wiped her mouth with the back of her hand roughly, twice, as if she were scrubbing away an unwanted kiss. 'Yes. Maybe. Funny how she was there at the same time.'

'She was there, yes, but she was lying next to me from the crack of dawn when the party was still going.' If I was hoping Helen would be stung by that revelation, I was a fool. She didn't miss a beat.

'I was kind of waiting for you to tell me. I know you've had a moment.' She gave that last word such stature I was beginning to suspect she was forming her own vocabulary around the episodes affecting her.

'Less a moment, more of a jiffy.' I meant it to be a way of breaking the grey mood which had followed us from my room but she couldn't disguise the hurt in her eyes. 'Sorry,' I said, lamely. Sorry is one of those words that begins to sound stupid if you say it often enough.

'Don't apologise. You don't mean it. Maybe I was wrong to ask for your help. But my life is hell at the moment, David. I can't sleep properly. I'm losing weight.' She'd stopped in front of the Empire nightclub. Window cleaners turned to watch – her voice was gathering pace.

'Helen, please. Let me get you a cup of coffee. I don't want to argue with you in the middle of the street.'

She stamped away before I could finish, so I followed, hoping she'd cool off a little before bringing the subject up again. After a while she crossed the road and sat on one of the benches looking out to sea behind the clocktower. Pigeons clustered nervously at her feet.

'I just don't understand,' I said. 'I feel as though I'm being sucked into something that isn't real, that you and Shay are passing on some of your paranoia. It's contagious, Helen.'

'That's bollocks. You're reducing what's happening to me. You make it sound like it's a Halloween game.'

I'd run out of argument. I strode back across the road and bought two coffees from a stall enveloped by the smells of hot oil and doughnut batter. As I was coming back, the sun chanced through the clouds, striping the hills of Grange-over-Sands. Some of the more distant peaks were still dusted white. Helen looked like a lost character from a French film sitting by herself staring out at the bay; I could almost see her own personal storm cloud fussing at her shoulders. Dissatisfaction radiated from her, evident in her stiff posture, and the way she was shaking her leg. As I approached she lit a cigarette and sucked on it violently until her cheeks hollowed. Her heel tapped against a rugose board daubed with urgent red capitals: GLASS CUTS FLESH.

'Bastard,' she said, all matter-of-fact. She walked away and shrieked 'Fuck off!' when I trotted after her, arms out like a tightrope walker, trying not to spill our drinks. An old woman wearing a head scarf and a Manchester United bomber jacket cackled and winked at me. 'You wanna watch 'em when they're like that. You do! What is it? Girlstuff, eh? Arsenal playing at home, eh?'

I ground down the urge to pour coffee all over her blue fucking rinse and was about to stomp off back to the guest house when I saw that Helen had stopped by the water's edge, just another black mark on the beach.

I trotted over and gave her the coffee then retreated a little.

'Look,' I said, 'I'm working at the Clam tonight. Why don't you and Shay come round and after my shift we'll spend a few hours together, see if anything happens, okay? I just think we need to, I don't know how to describe it… contextualise what's happening to us. Make it solid so we know how to deal with it.'

She nodded, eyes tracking the horizon. 'Come to the shop after work,' she said. 'We'll need some quiet. At least to talk if nothing else.' Her eyes stopped ranging, as if they'd found what they were looking for but the horizon was as featureless as the gutted arcades behind us. 'It would be a real shame,' she said, 'if something happened to either me or Seamus. How would you feel then? Hey?'

In the end, I stumped for one of those sausage balloons, lightly inflated and inserted part way down the left leg of my black slacks. In the mirror it looked unnatural but Keith wanted it that way: like Desert Orchid with a semi on. I placed the wooden phallus around my neck and buttoned the shirt so it couldn't be seen before concealing myself in a greatcoat. God forbid anyone here should get an eyeful of my manifold penises.

Eiger trundled out of her bedroom as I closed the door, much like a ruined mechanical angel being vomited from a clocktower to ring the hour. 'Ooroit, Dievid?' she said. 'You look loik a flasher in that git up! Gunnah show us what yav got?'

I hurried outside and rushed along the front until I reached The Whistling Clam. By the door a sign read: *No Drugs or Nuclear Weapons Allowed Inside.* It was already pretty busy. Six or seven Reservoir Puppies smoked Marlboros and fed a quiz machine with coins, scanning the pub to see who was impressed by their black suits. Clearasil lotion served to emphasise their sebaceous glands: they looked like apprentice hearse loaders, fresh from nosedive results in this year's GCSEs.

A pack of white blouses clustered around halves of

Guinness and blackcurrant: all dewlap and bifocals. 'All right, ladies?' I asked as I shrugged off my coat and headed towards Keith, sausage balloon squeaking lightly against my thigh.

'David, isn't it?' said Keith. 'On time. Nice one. Good dong effect. Like it. Meet the others. That one there, the bird pulling on the Boddingtons? That's Carole, with an e. Bloke playing pocket billiards? Julian. Sharon's talking to Pam. Pam's the one with the black eyeliner and the gold hotpants. Right. Optics up there. Self-explanatory. Beer. Ditto. If there's any overspill, I want it used in the next pint you pour. If I see you chucking any of it away I'll have your knackers for maracas. Anyone spends over fifty quid, they get a Whistling Clam snowstorm. Tips are shared out at the end of the evening. Don't get coy if the punters flirt with you. And undo that top button. I want to see your chest hair. You're on.'

The night became a screaming distortion of music and light and sweaty bodies crushed against the bar: people who worked and lived in the town who couldn't go away when the holiday season ended. Every order was suffixed by a lewd suggestion. I felt as though I was in a *Carry On* movie, but then, *Carry On* movies were subtle compared to this. 'Half a lager and lime and a bloody good seeing to, please love and I can't pay for this, mind if I suck you off instead?' and 'One for yourself and the missus wants to know if that throbber in your pants is for sale.' The balloon had trapped some of my thigh hairs. It was getting extremely uncomfortable.

'You've moved up in the world. I'll have a bottle of Dog please. And a pint of bitter for Shay.' Helen was standing at the bar. Flanked by pancake faces, she looked shockingly pale. Just who I needed to see, dressed up like a cabaret act, I don't think.

'Thought we were scheduled for your place, later on,' I said, trying hard not to excite a bottle of Snowball as my colleagues hurried around me.

'Look, I'm sorry about the way I flounced off this afternoon,' she said. 'What's that down your trousers?'

'I was about to tell you something when you did. You never gave me a chance.' I took my shirt out of the waistband and let it drape across my crotch. 'Nothing. I'm massively aroused at seeing you, that's all.'

'Yo! Pint of Scrumpy.' A Reservoir mutt, nose littered with blackheads. It looked like an unripe strawberry. I ignored him.

Helen poured her brown ale and shrugged. She seemed unaffected by the swarm around her, as if an invisible shield were protecting her from being jostled. 'So tell me now. I'm listening. I was just a bit insecure today.' She lit a cigarette and mouthed the filter hungrily. 'I'm all ears.'

I told her about my dream in the bath and the way I sometimes felt as if my awareness were heightened. As she listened, Helen's eyebrows moved further away from her eyes with interest. The drags on her cigarette became more shallow but fussy as ever, the way I imagined a wasp might smoke.

'There was also something this morning, just as you woke me up. Like a remnant of a dream – but I can't remember what the dream was about.'

'What was it?'

'I couldn't make out what it was. But it was coming towards me, really fast. Then when I opened my eyes I forgot about it. Till now.'

'Do you remember *anything* about your dream?' she asked, leaning back and crumpling her cigarette end into the ashtray.

'I was relaxed. I thought about when we all used to go with my dad on Saturdays to cricket. I was reminiscing, and then I started thinking about Seven Arches.'

'Oi Chief? I said pint of Scrumpy.'

Helen drew her coat around her even though it wasn't cold in the pub. I reached out and touched her hand and the question leapt from my throat before I'd considered the wisdom of its asking. 'Did you sleep with Seamus?' I couldn't sustain eye contact any longer.

'What's it to you?' she asked. It would have been easier to take if there were any anger in her voice but she was calm. My eager, negative half alerted me to what sounded like a mocking tone.

'You know Helen, considering you're supposed to be such a fucking expert on people, on reading situations, you're being pretty dense where I'm involved.'

'And since when have you been *involved*?' She said the word slowly.

'I am involved. I'm here aren't I? Didn't I jump to attention when you called?'

'Only because you thought you had a chance of getting back inside my knickers.' A couple waiting to get served stopped talking and slyly turned our way. Helen's eyes were wide and glassy.

'Are you going to do some work tonight, new boy?' asked Pam. I waved her away and she clucked her tongue against her Pearl Drop teeth with a volume that challenged the Coolio track thundering from the speakers.

I was finding it hard to speak; my throat was dwindling to a point where I was in danger of squeaking if I attempted to protest. Helen had stolen the initiative from me again.

'That's not fair, Helen.' And I hated myself for the weak, plaintive way I uttered her name. 'I care for you.'

'I did sleep with Shay,' she said, sadly. 'We were fucking while I was fucking you. At least he had the decency to recognise it for what it was. I never gave you any reason to think I wanted anything more than physical closeness to you. You were my friend. You could never be anything else.'

My anger couldn't rise above the sick feeling that I'd been duped all this time. I remember with such clarity the depth of sadness to which I sank when she said we couldn't carry on the way we had been. She was sitting on her bed and I'd lain alongside her, gently squeezing the back of her thighs. The neutrality of her face had provoked me to ask what was the matter. When she told me, all I wanted to do was make a big cinematic exit but I dithered, holding a brown paper bag of fruit, pathetically hoping she'd see how crushed I was and that she'd change her mind on the spot. Funny, but I always experience these situations out-of-body, looking down at myself from a corner of the room.

It was like that now, although I felt betrayed too; fooled by the pretence with which she'd protected herself when we were together. I thought I'd been privy to the important, passionate side of her, the intimacies we shared like nothing else she'd known. I remember those silly little ways of speaking, usually in the afterglow, when her head was in the crook of my arm. *How much do you like me?* she'd ask.

Twenty-three, I'd reply.

Out of what?

And I'd say *six*.

Blimey, that's a lot. But it was all empty, all dust.

'Oi! Buggerlugs! A fucking pint of fucking Scrumpy. Stop trying to post your pork through her letterbox. Get your mind on the job.'

I turned on him. 'Got any ID, Mr Green?' I snapped.

'You what? Fuckin' – here… he showed me his plate-sized fist. Here's my ID. Do you want me to cunting well rubber stamp you with it?'

Helen shook her head, slowly. 'Look, we're going. See you later, yes? You know the address?' I nodded. I was getting used to the sight of her back. Seamus was by the doors dressed in black so that it seemed only his bulbous head was present, floating around with that black dent of eyepatch. He did one of those waveless waves, his palm flipping up then down again.

'Bitch,' I hissed when they'd gone, and flung a pint glass against the cold shelf. I wanted to tell Helen about Eve, really rub her nose in it, but that was unfair to all of us, especially the woman whose eye colour I couldn't remember, whose tattoo I'd never seen. To mention her was to underline what Helen had said about me. I was angry that she was right. I was angry that I was so transparent and pliable and I was angry that I danced to Helen's tune. So I did what I usually did with my anger and bottled it up inside where it would stew and keep me awake in the night, knotting my belly as I thought of hurtful rejoinders and counter thrusts.

'David!' It was Keith. 'Go directly to Hell. Do not pass Go, do not collect your wages and do not darken my door again. Oh and give me my wooden dick back. Hey, Boggo? Flynn? One for the pavement!'

The bouncers picked me up like I was a matchstick model and turfed me into the road. They watched me as I dusted myself down and sniffed imperiously, clinging on to my pride, even as the air from my surrogate manhood squealed into the night.

five
actual harm

I caught a taxi to Heysham once I'd changed into something a little less lounge lizardish. The sea peeked through the gaps between houses like small wads of molten tar designed to shore up fractures in the streets. I didn't know what I was going to do now I'd lost my job. Maybe I could sell some paintings. If Helen was living off the shells she sold to tourists then why not me? How hard could it be? I was thinking about how many paintings of the local scenery I'd have to get through – and becoming more and more disenchanted with the idea – when the cab drew up outside a row of terraces.

It had become colder in the hour or two since I'd seen Helen and Seamus. I watched the taxi pull away and scanned the street. It led up to a car park and a wide expanse of grass. A squat public toilet sat like a pill-box, its inner lights spilling out through thin oblongs of window, creamy or sharply splintered depending on whether the glass was broken. To its right, a disused train station hunkered down like a boxer in the sixth round of an ill-advised comeback fight. All of its windows and part of the roof were punched in. Razor wire and new steel fencing gave its archway entrance a gritted, glittering smile. The terraces were painfully thin, not far off the point where you'd have to walk in sideways. Helen's shop seemed like an afterthought, mashed in between two dour, pebble-dashed houses with lights on in the top-floor windows. A group of kids were kicking a punctured football around the street. I thought somebody had drawn a face on its peeled leather but it must have been the pattern of dirt. The sky burned with a strange subdued pallor, like light shining through a thick blanket. A cat appeared, moving against one of the windows, casting its shadow, curved and fluid, across the pavement. I couldn't feel any threat in the air. This village seemed as sleepy as the pensioners cosied up in their beds.

Was nobody up and around now, save the cats? Another of the little hipswingers was sashaying along the wall towards me, its eyes narrowing, tail erect. It looked at me and then turned round, eyeing me again over its shoulder.

'Yeah, gorgeous arse,' I said. 'How much?'

'David!' Helen was watching me from her own upstairs window. I looked up at her and smiled. She was framed by darkness but I could see the white glint of her teeth.

'Well,' I said, 'she's giving me one hell of a come on. I haven't been propositioned like this for years.'

She tossed me a key. 'Bring Vanilla in while you're at it,' she said, her voice a trifle manic. 'And no funny stuff. She's a lady.'

'Your cat? Why doesn't that surprise me? She's probably learned all her tricks from you.'

She'd closed the window on that but I still heard her laughing, a muffled, slightly frangible sound. It set me on edge a little; I didn't want Helen pretending to be in a benevolent mood if she really wanted to rant and swear at us.

I opened the door and Vanilla shot in before me; a tendril of mist disappearing into the dark. As I closed the door behind me I thought I heard a low moan, as of a person struggling with heavy shopping, or wind softly fluting through gutters.

I was standing in the centre of Helen's shop. Diffused light from the stairwell behind the counter settled on the shelves and plinths upon which Helen's wares were strategically placed. She'd used sheet metal, battered into submission to create watery scenes. Here was a pond surrounded by metallic reeds; a seashore shivering white beneath a maw of frothing brine; a glass river underpinned by dense bunches of green wire. Slivers of colour were suspended in these reeds: fish fashioned from darts of foil.

I stepped through the counter and pushed back a curtain that led on to a small kitchen with coir matting covering the floor. On a table was her work in progress, a curtain of thin steel cables and chains merged to resemble a waterfall. I shook my head; it was really quite beautiful stuff.

Vanilla sat on the stairs watching me. She tensed as I ascended and took off again, pausing at the top – where I could see a restless shadow bloating and diminishing within a gloomy orange corona – to look back at me again. Her tail flicked twice and she was gone.

'Shop!' I called, as I reached the top of the staircase.

'In here,' Helen called, although there was really no point; only one room existed other than the bathroom. I ducked into a hanging mass of wooden beads and emerged into a tiny living room.

Helen kissed me: a cold smear on my cheek.

'Anal fudge,' said Seamus, his voice husky and thin, as though spent by its journey. 'Air Commodore Roger 'Rodge' Ronson died in Brighton yesterday. Stroke. Eighty. I'm gutted, it has to be said.'

Seamus was squinting into the murk, as if trying to establish me as fact. Helen was pacing up and down as though she was measuring the dimensions of the room and being constantly disappointed that they added up to just two and a half steps. Her left arm was wedged underneath her breasts, pushing them up into the V of her jumper. Her other hand made jerky movements, the cigarette she was holding creating spastic blue points of reference in the air.

'Helen, relax,' I said. 'You look like a game of fucking ping-pong.'

'Funny,' Helen said, sitting down. 'Really funny. In the way that tit cancer is funny. How was your first night behind the bar?'

'It was my last night thanks to you,' I said. 'And I've got a rash where the rubber pinched my thigh.'

'Charming,' said Seamus, pressing his fingers against the patch on his face. I had an uncomfortable conviction that they'd disappear into it. 'What happened? They sack you for having a cashew nut instead of a chieftain tank down your knickers?'

'No. I lost my rag.'

'What are you going to do now?' Helen said, suddenly concerned. She was right to be.

'Going home,' I said.

'But you *can't*. We haven't finished here.'

'There's nothing to finish, Helen. All we've been doing is arguing and rubbing each other up the wrong way. I'd rather we kept hold of any good memories we have of each other and leave it at that.'

'Not good enough,' Helen snapped, coldly. 'He... it won't leave it at that.'

'Helen was attacked tonight, on the way here,' Seamus said, flat as the beer in the bottle he was sucking on.

'Who attacked you?' I said. 'What happened?'

'I don't know who attacked me,' Helen replied, pulling on her cigarette as if it were a nebuliser and she an asthmatic taking her last gasp. 'I was waiting for Shay outside a chip shop up the road from you. I heard someone over the road shouting a name and saying, "Don't fuck around, get out of the water." He sounded in distress. I thought someone might be having difficulty, a father whose daughter had fallen in the sea or something. So I ran across and looked over the barrier and there was a bloke on the beach, naked, his... he had an erection and he was wanking. But I couldn't see his head. It was... it was like his head had bled into the night, as though the darkness had been teased out in one position and become the shape of a man. I was so shocked by what I was seeing that when he started for me, I stayed put, trying to see his eyes. His hand had become a blur and I smelled him when he got nearer. He smelled like sex. He said: "Four hundred million sperm. One life." And then he came but… it was all water. I'm not fucking kidding. Gallons of water, dirty and stinking like shit. Then some weed spat out and it started sputtering and then his dick swelled up and I could see hair coming out of the end of it and a head and… its face was grey and baggy, the eyes puffed shut…'

She broke off, breathless. The speed and panic of her recollection had shocked me.

'You've called the police?' I said, knowing the answer.

'No.'

Seamus leaned forward and paused a moment before speaking. I felt like someone who had asked a twattish question of a particularly patronising politician.

'David,' he said and licked his lips, 'have you been having any dreams? Dreams of suffocation?'

I blinked at him.

'I didn't tell you about that.' I said, wishing my lips weren't so dry or the chunk of meat in my ribcage wasn't trying so hard to get out.

'No,' he said, spreading his hands. The liquid in the bottle trapped between his thumb and forefinger made a treacly journey around the glass neck. In the thick light, I clearly saw his fingerprints smearing its surface. 'I had a guess. See, Helen's been having dreams of fire and thick smoke.'

'Me too. Well, smoke at least,' I said, thinking of the fumes that had chased me out of sleep before Helen showed up to put the pieces of my back together.

'So why?' asked Helen. 'Why are we having the same dreams, or if not the same dreams, then how come were sharing the same elements?'

'It's like…' Seamus began, 'we've opened up our heads and nailed them together so that we're all sharing the same Widescreen movie.'

'Hmm,' I intoned, gravely. 'Can I have a bottle of that meths you're drinking, Shay? I'm fed up with reality too.'

'Look,' he said, 'we're sharing too much. We've all met someone. Some weird figure –'

'There are some pretty weird figures right in front of my face, mate,' I spluttered, feeling that I should defend Eve.

He held up his hand. 'Fair enough, but it's happened. We've met people. And there's some common land in our dreams. We're plugged in to each other, David. It's like we were back at Seven Arches again, isn't it? Don't you feel it too?'

He was right. If I took the time to relax into the evening, before long I'd notice that we were breathing in time and mirroring each other in posture, expression. Our heart rates would be synchronous. We'd be new-born kittens in a basket.

'Yeah. But I could still murder a beer.'

He clumped downstairs to the kitchen and Helen sat down in his place. I felt like a shrink accepting his next appointment.

'We're going to bait it, David. Tonight.' She smiled and breathed in deeply.

'Does Seamus know?' I asked.

She nodded. 'He's brought a stack of beer with him. And some voddie. More than enough.'

'More than enough for what? Are we going to invite it in for a piss-up? Whatever the shuddering fuck it is.'

She rubbed my hand with her finger and a tube of ash dropped on to my knuckles. 'It'll be okay.'

'How will it be okay? How do you mean, bait it? What do we have to do?'

'Nothing. Remember I said that it came for me when I was at my most vulnerable? We get vulnerable.'

'Helen, if you think I'm going to spend the evening on the bog with my keks round my ankles –'

She laughed, though I was only half-joking. 'There are alternatives,' she said.

'What, we hump each other?'

She pursed her lips and rolled her eyes but that didn't exactly pass as a denial in my book.

'You've had stuff happen to you while you've been asleep, or pissed? So that's how we approach things tonight.

We see how it goes. What matters, what seems to be the catalyst, is us being together.'

'I feel bloody foolish,' I said.

'This from a bloke who spent the best part of his evening with a balloon down his trollies.'

Seamus shivered through the bead curtain and tossed me a bottle. He'd brought the vodka up too.

'What happens if... something happens?' I said.

It seemed that nobody had thought of that. I wish I hadn't bothered to ask. Any warmth that was being generated between us seemed to evaporate. We returned to being the edgy creatures of half an hour ago.

We drank. And Helen put some music on. And we drank. Bottles piled up, empty glasses were refilled. We played drinking games. We wandered around Helen's shop on our own in the dark, drinking all the time. We only stopped drinking to breathe and sometimes we'd snort beer or vodka when we screwed up even that simplest of actions. Sometimes I'd see Vanilla in the dark, curled up on a windowsill or winding like greased mist through the legs of a table. The music grew moodier. I was so pissed, I thought my left eye was trying to slide out of its socket, my vision on that side was so fucked up.

'Hey, if my left-hand vision is screwed, does that mean the right side of my brain is buggered too? Right, Shay?' I said, laughing, but Shay was keeping himself to himself, staring out of the window towards the lighthouse, the pulse of which was discernible as a pale flicker over the roofs. If he acknowledged me at all, it was as a vague hunching of the shoulders. I heard his breath, thick and glottal, catching in his throat. I smelled petrol.

'I am hammered,' I said, lurching towards him and knocking over one of Helen's waterworks. 'Shit.' I scrabbled around on the floor for the various rivets and associated machinery, hoping Helen hadn't heard me wrecking her shop.

Seamus was coming round, turning towards me every so

often and favouring me with a look that was none too pleasant. He sported a big liquid smile, a slick of saliva coating his chin, like a wrapping of cellophane. The top half of his head was pitch black, cut out by the shade provided by a stack of shelves.

'Cock off looking at me like that, Shay,' I said, and banged my head getting up as someone shouted at me from upstairs.

'David! Da-vid!' she called, but her voice had slowed down in my befuddled state so that she sounded male. But then another call, definitely female this time: 'David!'

The figure was rising to its feet. I cut my hand on one of the metal angles, I was gripping it so hard. Sobering quickly now, I whispered to my self.

'All right… it's all right.' I backed into the counter and edged along until I fell backwards through the gap. He was outlined against the window, the scattered, misty pulse of the lighthouse powdering the tip of his head.

He wasn't going anywhere. But the smell of petrol was more intense. It was as I turned to crash out through the back window that I saw the powdering effect of the granular light wasn't down to the lighthouse after all – it was smoke. He'd opened his great wet mouth and his voice was the rasp of a match on sandpaper.

'Heaven marching,' it breathed.

It was hard to read Frank's handwriting; the blue ink had run slightly on the paper so that his eight looked like a six. The note beneath the number was legible enough though: DO THE RITE THING. YOU'LL SEE US AGAIN. STAY TITE, FRANK AND TONKA.

I didn't much care for the part which read *you'll see us again*, but I had to stop being so judgmental; Frank and Tonka were all right, if a little coarse. I imagined them shaven and sweet-smelling, dressed in retiring fashions, drinking Ribena – much easier to control. I rested the paper against the telephone and placed a couple of ten pence pieces within easy reach.

I thought of Helen, quenching my early morning thirsts with water passed from her mouth to mine.

'Oh God,' I whispered. What she'd said had been so underhand yet she expected me to swallow it in the name of liberty. I fuck, you fuck, he fucks, she fucks, we fuck. I was annoyed and embarrassed at the way I'd let myself get swept along. She'd seen my interest in her but instead of curbing it she was happy to let me pant away like a dog expecting his treat. And she'd lost me my job. Not that I was bothered. After last night's fun and games, I was desperate for a different face, a respite from the pressure and the panic.

I dialled the number, got a kebab house. I apologised, tried the six after all and a female voice said: 'David?'

Warning signs flashed in my head but I'd already offered a hello. 'Good guess or do you call everyone David?' I was pleased with the confidence I was displaying. Usually, in situations like this, I get so flustered it's as though I'm aphasic.

'I knew it would be you. It's that time of the night – people get lonely and like to chat. I'm glad you called.' Her voice was tease-slow, I could tell the words were being spoken through a smile. In that instant I saw her on a canvas, her face a broad sweep of blue acrylic. And of course, her eyes were closed.

'I'm glad you answered. It's kind of strange, the way this has come about? Don't you think?'

'Not really. Would you rather have cornered me in some bar and asked me what's a nice girl et cetera? I talked to Deep Pan. He sorted it out for me.'

'So,' I said, my nerve beginning to flag – why did I always shit it when women were direct with me? 'Let's have a drink... or... something.'

She was laughing, the sound deep and throaty. Her face smeared and yawned, the blackness of her mouth spoiling the bright colour around it. Her lips were too red: I must tone that down a little. The fun slipping from her throat looked like orange feathers – I liked that.

'I find you really attractive, David. When you were sitting

with that friend of yours – Seamus is it? I watched the way you kept pursing your mouth. It was like you were getting ready for a snog. Nice mouth. You keep it in good nick, I can tell. Bet you use lip balm.'

I was kind of taken aback with this machine-gun delivery but her honesty, although disorienting, I didn't find a threat, which made for a refreshing change.

'You aren't ready to see me, are you?' she added.

'I'm not sure,' I said, thinking, *How the hell?*

'Let's give it a week. I'll meet you at two o'clock next Saturday, yeah? Half Moon Bay.'

'Half Moon Bay,' I said, thinking, *where the hell?* Then the line went dead.

The next morning I packed a small bag and caught the bus into Lancaster. It felt like I was running away, but Eve was playing some kind of anchor now, so that it was reasonable to assume I would allow myself to return once I'd been able to shake off Helen's grasp: her fingers had reached deep into my flesh and melded there; they'd be difficult to pull free. I thought of how our evening had drawn to a close, the way the night had been bleached by the reluctant dawn while we huddled nervously in side streets listening to something screaming and tearing up and down the village like a minia-ture hurricane. Helen had soothed me while I vomited and cried into a steel bucket once we'd gathered the nerve to return to Helen's shop and check it out. All I could think of as I retched was what she might fashion out of the bucket once I'd finished with it. I wondered if it might get a price tag and a place on her display shelf. *Morecambe Bay*, she could call it.

The shop had been empty, of course. Vanilla had been torn apart on the counter where he'd settled down to sleep last night. I couldn't believe how much blood was contained in a cat.

I could smell scorched phosphor, by the window, and there was a small pool of something clear that I didn't want to dabble my fingers in.

'Must have been someone who wanted to torch the place,' I said, hopefully.

'No, David. It was contact,' Helen said, sobbing over the remains of her pet. 'We didn't have any luck upstairs.'

What, I felt like asking, in a bitter flood that had me tasting last night's sick, *Shay couldn't get it up? Trying too hard to be vulnerable?*

I left them, astonished that they were considering breakfast after what had happened. I agreed to come back but pleaded exhaustion and a need to reclaim a little sanity back home. 'I need to consider what I'll do for work, anyway,' I said. 'Bar jobs don't seem to be a good idea.'

On the way back to the train station in Lancaster, I found myself on a street I recognised – dimly – from the night of the party. On a whim, I decided to see if any of the members of Lettuce were still around and if there'd been any developments regarding the murder. I heard a thin, scratchy piece of music as I turned a corner and knew I'd stumbled across the party's locus. The vocals for the piece stitched into the noise after a second or two but were unable to smooth its rough edges. I saw the pimpled purple door just before it crashed open and a person my age flew on to the path. He picked himself up and stood looking into the hallway, weaving about like a weighted rubber toy that was designed never to be knocked over. He must have thought better of taking umbrage with the person who'd launched him, choosing instead to totter away and make gestures towards the door, which had already closed.

I was oddly happy to see that the party was still going, albeit in an understandably listless manner, as though they were partying for the girl's sake, as a tribute to her. Perhaps it was because I had contributed to it and breathed its excesses – had been a victim of them, in fact – that I found it so appealing, like owning a ticket to an early concert by The Police before they became massive. The house seemed much smaller in the daylight, prompting me to wonder how it could have accommodated so many people at once. There must have been over a hundred sweaty bodies causing that clamour. It was shocking that nobody had seen anything. Maybe they had and had been so eckied up that they thought it had been kind of cool and, when you thought about it, a human, a really charitable act really. Jesus.

I knocked and waited, though the door swung in under the weight of my knuckles. A man wearing sunglasses ducked into the hallway, his arms bent upwards from the elbow like I'd just pulled a gun on him. 'Yes mate?'

I heard a female voice call, 'Come back,' from deeper inside the house. It sounded like Eve – which set off a chain of feelings inside me which began with excitement and ended on a downbeat note, a sadness the origin of which I couldn't trace. Disconcerting too, considering I'd just talked to her on the phone at what I'd guessed was her house.

'Who you after?' he asked, coming into the light. His chin was furred and I noticed he was younger than I'd first estimated.

'Any of Deep Pan's band around?'

'No. Well, I don't know. Come and have a look for yourself.'

He left me on the doorstep wondering if he was the object of the voice's call.

For a moment the thud of drums was replaced by something frail, a pizzicato calm fronting a melody which came and went in delicate loops. A booing came from the stragglers and, before it ended, the music fell into its blunt rut once more.

There was a smell of spilled beer, stale and malty and the ubiquitous stink of dead cigarettes. Mixing with that were recent odours, of fried breakfasts and the sour whiff of vomit, which reminded me of the deposit I'd made in the bathroom. I stood in the hallway, looking at the wall upon which hung a print of The Green Chinaman. An arc of red bisected it, and much of its background Anaglypta, like a spray of arterial blood or, more plausibly, the result of a ketchup fight. Whatever, it was a stark colour in the midst of so much brownish monotony, and something about the way it glistened made me nervous. I was suddenly thinking of the man on the beach with his metal detector and of blurred faces bearing down on me from behind opaque glass doors. And creatures made of smoke.

'You all right?'

He followed me into the kitchen. There was no body there now, of course, but it didn't stop me from skirting the area over which she'd been spilled.

'Who was the girl? Did you know her?'

'Nah,' he said. 'She gatecrashed.'

The way he said it made it sound like she'd deserved what had happened to her. I gave him a look and drew a glass of cold water, sipped it. 'I want to speak to Eve,' I said, desperate for a friendly face.

'Eve went home yesterday. I just checked upstairs and there's only me and Jeff and The Shrike Twins – can you hear 'em playing upstairs? They're on at the Alex tonight. You want to come? Get you tickets?'

'No, no,' I managed, concentrating on my shoes. 'I just wanted to talk to, um... never mind.'

'My bet is they've fucked off down town for some decent grub – there's only a packet of Ritz crackers in the cupboard. Shall I tell 'em you came if I see 'em – whoever you are?'

'I'm David. And it doesn't matter. Really. Thanks.'

Come back. Come back. Come back.

As the broad, mud-streaked snout of the Intercity glided into the station it began to rain. The sky was that live shade of grey you get with thunderstorms, where the clouds seem to possess their own core of light. I pressed myself back against the wall – I've long had a fear of being pushed into the path of an oncoming train – until it stilled, and checked the destination stickers on its windows before boarding a non-smoking carriage where I tossed my bag on to an overhead shelf. It was nice not to have to search for a seat; my travelling companions numbered just three: a man deep in slumber, breathing through a mouth barred with saliva, and two young women who had turned their seats and table into a campsite. They talked to each other over a mass of Sunday newspapers and empty coffee cartons. Somehow they'd managed to curl their legs up on the narrow seats. Coats and cardigans swaddled them.

Outside Preston, one of them leaned over and passed me a camera; asked me to take a picture. As I was about to depress the shutter button, the bank of cloud shifted, allowing a spear of light to pierce the train. The girls smiled and I saw mouths full of fire. They thanked me and told me they were from Canada visiting relatives. I spent the rest of the short journey trying to convince myself that the flames weren't real, that all I'd witnessed was the sunlight reflecting off their dental braces.

Warrington seemed to have contracted since I'd last been here. I didn't know why this was. Perhaps it had something to do with the space Morecambe provided once you were confronted with its bay and the range of hills across the water. The roads and buildings there were, if anything, more tightly packed than the streets I now navigated as I aimed for the town centre. One advantage in being here was that the weight of threat piling against my heart was lifted to such an extent that it was as if the events in Morecambe had never taken place; I was viewing them through a haze that was more usually found around ancient memories. The thought that I would have to go back did not fill me with as much apprehension as it probably should.

The rain grew unpleasant, fine yet heavy – a wetting rain, as my dad might say – trickling down the gap between neck and collar. Because it was Sunday I didn't know how long I would have to wait for a bus so I had no choice but to trudge all the way to the bus station. By the time I arrived, the hand which held my bag was stiffening and my fringe was plastered flat, dripping water into my eyes. I found out that bus journeys were disrupted because someone had started a fire at the company's depot the previous night, damaging some of their fleet. I wasn't going to hang around the bus station for two hours: coffee was the only option. From a café on Bridge Street I drank gritty Kenco while a whimpering radiator did its best to dry my coat at a temperature barely rising above zero. Fat black bins sat squatly in the middle of the pedestrianised thoroughfare – bombproof jobs that looked so mean they might conceal defensive weaponry of their own. Pigeons scuffing about the shoes of teenagers outside McDonald's put me in mind of Helen and I turned her away quickly, but not before I conjured a smirk for her lips.

Warmth from my cup seeped through the damp wool of gloves I couldn't bear to peel from my fingers. I saw a girl I knew from school walk past the window, which helped cement the feeling I'd returned home – things hadn't seemed real up until that point. Everything moves on. Images from school flashed through my head; here were the first heroes I'd known, more vibrant than anything our local Odeon could offer. But even into these safe, solid memories, abominations threatened to tread. Bleak glimpses, like that time by the canal or an incident in my second year when I saw Pete Spearo, one of the seniors, walk up to Glenn Snelson, the Deputy Head Boy and punch him in the face. Snelson went down really quickly, not like the dazed swoon you find in boxing rings. His eyes had rolled into his head and he was leaking blood from his mouth, twitching all over. *Spastic paralysis* were the words whispered by staff for a few days after, when it became clear that Snelson had suffered brain damage. I don't know what happened to Spearo, other than his expulsion.

I tried to dig for sweeter things: Clare Walsh sitting on the edge of a desk in English Lit and stretching gorgeously, the smooth mounds of her breasts rising and separating like proving dough; sharing coconut cake with Barnesy and Rolo after they'd raided the canteens; Gozzo spilling copper sulphate over his shoes in a chemistry class when we asked him the time. But these thoughts failed to obscure my tainted memories. I finished my drink and ordered another and then I was surprised out of my funk. The low bank of cloud passed over, taking the rain with it, and the street became uncomfortable to look at thanks to a blaze of reflected gold from the sun. The people outside seemed to change from thin, decrepit phantoms into beefy characters, bursting with zip. A feeling of goodwill and contentment swelled from my centre and I was newly excited about seeing my parents and the cat. I swigged my coffee and paid at the till. Forget the bus. Though it was still chilly, it was pleasant enough to walk the mile home.

Mum was at the window, in a stance I had seen her in a thousand times before. Left hand on hip, right hand buried in her wheat-blonde hair, twisting it through her fingers. Loot saw me first; mid-wash he looked up at me, superior as you like. His face said: 'Who the *hell* are you?' I laughed and Mum waved, her eyebrows disappearing into her fringe.

That Munro smell greeted me as the door opened. A smell from childhood, it was comprised of Dad's stamp albums, Silvikrin hairspray, vinyl, suede and that smell peculiar to very old teddy bears. I breathed it in and gave Mum a hug.

'Had to come home,' I said, to quash any burrowing questions Mum might have about the reasons for my return. 'Cat-withdrawal symptoms. Where is the little bugger?'

I lost myself for half an hour in Loot's belly, the throb in his throat. Now and again, he'd make a little noise. *Pert*, he'd say. Or *Marie*? I picked him up and his soft, warm weight drifted into me, relaxing the bunches of tension which I'd been unaware of until now. After a while he got bored and stared into the corners of the ceiling where things dwelled that only cats can see.

Dad arrived then and we talked about Morecambe. He told me about the Ferris wheel and the piers that once bracketed the bay. I tried to imagine them but Morecambe was too flat in my mind, almost trodden into the ground. I gave them a sanitised and diluted version of events in the town and they sympathised with my feelings of alienation. Then they offered me my bed for the night. I accepted, but I was upset that the offer had to have been made at all. A distance had developed here too it seemed. So be it. I couldn't expect to just flit in and out of my parents' life when it suited me.

I asked if Kim, my sister, would be around later but Mum told me she was going into town for a meal with her colleagues from work.

'Good,' I said. 'I'll give her a surprise.'

It would be nice to have a drink with her; I'd not seen her for ages. She had spent much of the year either abroad visiting clients or trying to find a house to suit both herself and Will, her fiancé. Chances were, she'd pop into the Barley Mow for an aperitif. If she didn't, it was okay. I'd drunk on my own before.

Later, I showered and shaved then spent some time looking out of my bedroom window at the view of my old school, which was being demolished, and the spread of Sankey Valley Park beyond. I saw two figures standing close together by Seven Arches. One was wearing a long skirt, the other, a black skull cap. A thin, grey haze, like net curtain, hung in the air over the brook, softening them to the point where they looked featureless and fused at the hip, like plasticine people pressed against each other. Gradually the mist thickened, blotting them out. I dressed quickly, one eye on the gathering night where they'd been, worrying that the mist hadn't thickened at all; that they had simply dwindled to nothing. But no, there they were again, shifting in the mist like fish under water: suggestions of bulk, shadows. I pulled on my boots and slipped outside, moved to the back of my parents' garden and climbed over the fence, trying to keep track of the figures wadded in grey by the viaduct. I jogged along the sliproad that had once fed the school and cut across the fields where, as a kid, I'd scored goals and chased girls in the hope of kisses that never came. The skeletons of houses reared up, unfinished estates that had fallen foul of the recession: either the building company had gone bust or nobody could afford to buy them, I didn't know which. Up ahead, the mist had thickened, threatening to consume the couple, who were moving parallel to the canal, towards the Arches. I hesitated, my fingers hooked into the links of a wire fence that had failed to keep out the local vandals, and wondered if I should simply go home and contact Helen in the morning, find out what she was playing at. It was not a place at ease with our ghosts; not a good locus for any kind of fond reminiscence.

A bloom of orange, smudged into the lowest band of mist, drew my eye away from their movement. The area around the colour shivered and pulled back, creating a pocket of light. Directly above, the mist churned, turning dirty as smoke from the fire mingled and drew its mischief into the sky. Maybe it was that plain promise of warmth, that remarkable smear of colour, couched in such a derelict setting that decided me, pulled me on as though appealing to the primal root in me, the part that recognised the bleak glimpses of other worlds that seemed to be breaking into my everyday regimes.

Nearing the arch – our arch – I could smell a mix of wood and damp paper, of reeds and polythene bags. We'd once thrown the carcass of a large rat on one of our arch fires, found squashed on the road outside the hospital, and we'd marvelled at the speed at which it cooked and the smoke as it funnelled out of its eyes.

The couple seemed to come apart in the mist within the arch, shredding as though their inner bodies had caught some of the fun which the mist was having with its corporeal surroundings. It was only as I stepped beneath the curve of sandstone, scattering echoes as easily as a careless foot scatters the ashes of a dead fire, that I realised I'd been wrong all along. It wasn't Shay and Helen. And it wasn't the mist that was making this figure seem less than whole. I watched, my breathing becoming increasingly ragged, as the figure struggled with its inner desire to disintegrate. Slowly, it solidified, drawing some of the substance from the brickwork behind it so that at one point it seemed to be wearing a slice of yellow graffiti across its piecemeal face. It was wearing little more than a pair of ripped Y-fronts and a school tie strung loosely at the throat, knotted ridiculously large – the way we'd worn them at school, as a tiny act of rebellion. I backed away, as if in a dream, drugged into soporific calm. I didn't feel threatened, although I could sense it was smelling the air and tensing, a red tear appearing in the pink, wet cloud of its head. There seemed to be teeth there, broken and misshapen, like chunks of opaque glass set into the coping stones of a wall for security.

It reached for me and I stepped back, watching the eddies in the mist its too-sharp fingernails had created. I heard a clotted murmur – it could have been its voice slurring my name – and then it reared and attacked, or at least lunged towards me, perhaps more from unsteadiness than design. In the instance I ducked and lurched back, I saw one eye swim out of the confusion of liquefied flesh: bruised and niggardly, shining with the glutinous lustre of a raisin. I ran backwards, stumbling through the rubble, until I'd put some distance, and some smoke, between myself and its directionless thrashing. I was torn between wanting to help and wanting to run away, to shake the visions from my head and blame it on the excesses of Morecambe. I took a step towards it, holding out my hand as if I might calm it with gestures alone. It sensed my movement and loosed a stream of bilious abuse my way. Some of the sputum touched my skin and burned there. It smelled thinly of petrol. A milky image spanked me hard behind the eyes. There was the detail of action and nothing else; his features were lost to the shock of recall. I was holding a cricket ball to a boy's mouth, forcing it between his lips while the torpid sound of Sunday afternoon clapping from the pavilion filled the air like the cry of strange insects. His eyes rolling up, red-rimmed, his skin drenched in sweat, muscles in spasm as he breathed in nothing but scorching vapours. The corky finally breached the portcullis of his teeth as the hinges of his jaw sheared apart.

It was still dark when I came to some time later. My hands were balled into fists, each gripping a divot of grass, my chin flooded with pain where it had carved a rut in the ground. The mist had receded somewhat and I could no longer hear the violence of the creature I'd stumbled upon. I remained still for a while, until I was sure it wouldn't be there when I turned my head to look.

I think Mum was a bit peeved that I was choosing to go out on my first night back but I was in no mood for conversation, especially when I knew in which direction it was likely to travel. Mid-week in the town centre: not a lot going on – which was fine by me. I bumped into Kim just as she was leaving the Barley Mow. She performed a monster double-take and squealed before wrapping me in her arms. We've always got on. I smiled at her colleagues as she steered me towards a flashier pub on the corner of the main road. Linking my arm, she told me how dissatisfied she was, how frustrating her search for a house had been. We had a drink and she left soon after – a table at the restaurant had been booked – but not before I'd spotted Daniel Hoth leaning against the wall, talking to one of the bouncers.

After Kim had gone, I took my glass over. Having talked to my sister, I was hungry for more company; the episode earlier had rattled me and I didn't want to be alone in case I was targeted again.

It was nice to be recognised after such a long time.

'Dave,' he said.

'Dando,' I said.

My earlier memories of him still fresh in my mind, I bought him a drink and we stood at the window, watching couples as they ducked into pubs or argued in the street. Our friendship at school had taken a while to develop. We'd turned out for the football trials but for some reason, maybe because we realised deep down how similar we might be, we maintained a distance before any exchanges were made. We'd been pretty thick after that. Fridays we'd walk into town and have a few Cokes at the pool hall, stick Prince's 'Girls and Boys' on the juke box, talk absolute bollocks. And then, like in all my friendships, there evolved a disaffection. At every point of change for me, I have left corpses on the wayside. It pains me, the degree of civility erstwhile companions show each other. So it was with us. We traded poor, stale gossip. The drinks helped strip away the years. Our talk grew laddish and immature, cheering me more than it deserved to. When he asked me if I wanted to go on to a club I nodded and told him to lead the way.

Maybe it was because I knew the town and felt newly comfortable with Dando that the nightclub appeared unthreatening though I'm not a nightclub kind of chap. I felt good about the way the evening was going: our conversation was suitably mindless, consisting of references to Liverpool Football Club's steady recovery of form, girls mutually fancied at school and films we wanted to see. It was good to talk without the feeling I was being monitored all the time. When I laughed, my cheeks ached – it had been that long. We drank lager, but switched to doubles when we realised – if we were going to get smashed, we might as well do it properly. Sometimes, when a song came on that made me feel good, something driven by a thick backbeat and leavened by melodious voices, such as Curve or Lush or Garbage, I felt myself swell and my trips to the bar would fall in with the rhythm of the song. Absurd, but it improved my confidence to the point where I smiled at the barmaid and began chatting to her whenever I bought a drink. Bodies on the dancefloor either slumped to the music under syrupy-red light or appeared to jerk about once the strobes were activated. Everything white: tee-shirts, socks, bras beneath thin tops – even teeth – glowed in an ultra-violet wash from tubes in the ceiling. Men cruised the dancefloors, immaculately pressed or strategically crumpled. The air was drenched with sweat and Obsession.

Morecambe was like a scene from a film so old it was deteriorating before my eyes. Even the events of only a few hours ago took on the opulent sham of cinema. The thought that I would have to restore those scenes was thankfully numbed by vodkas and orange that were rapidly losing their potency – this was dangerous; too much like drinking something soft. I told Dando and he laughed and called me a fanny. I laughed too, agreed, and sank another double to celebrate my newfound fannydom.

And then things started to go odd.

I knew my light-headedness was due to all this alcohol, but there was a deeper imbalance; the kind of thick, inflated sensation you might feel when you've spent all morning in a closed room painting walls. Dando was watching me intently and I was horrified to see his hair start to churn about like anemones in a strong current. His eyes seemed too vivid: his green irises slipping into purple realms for a moment before fluxing yellow and blue then green once more. His pupils dilated and shrank separately like the cartoon eyes of some character clouted by a frying pan.

It was like a dream I'd suffered when I was six or seven. Mum told me I'd almost died from pneumonia, and one particular night I'd been lying in bed listening out for the music from the TV that I liked to hear (I only found out about three years later – when I was allowed to stay up until after nine oclock – that it was the theme tune from *M*A*S*H**). I felt a diabolical heat swoon upon me, pressing me into my mattress and wringing sweat from my body so that I was drenched within seconds. I couldn't lift my arm for the water at my bedside; my lungs were suddenly frothy, unable to suck in enough air for the single syllable I wanted to call out. I'd drifted into exhausted sleep and it seemed all my discomfort had gathered and funnelled itself into that part of my brain that made dreams. It was like being trapped beneath an airless canopy of purple/black canvas that was slowly being drawn closer to the ground with each breath. And something hungry clattered around its heights, flashing its teeth and claws, waiting for the moment we'd be forced together by the collapse around us.

I went to the bar and waited until the girl I liked was free to serve me. As she poured vodka, I saw my vampiric face in the mirror, which began to warp and melt. Close eyes. *Breathe*. She asked me if I was all right. I nodded, said 'pissed', and watched her hands ripple: the veins so clearly embossed against the skin she might be inside out. I watched the journey of her blood for a while, frightened to look at her face, then paid and hacked my way back through the jungle of limbs which blocked my path. Dando was kissing some woman so deeply it looked like he was trying to suck the lower part of her face into his mouth. The colours beyond them had grown more vivid and I seemed able to track each ray as it splashed against the nightclub's limits – as if the speed of light was suddenly no more than ten miles an hour. I ducked when it seemed the errant droplets of light must hit me – an act which drew stares from the people nearby. I was now sure that everybody was clued up about my stupidity: at any moment the DJ would stop spinning discs to call out: 'And that was the latest by Dubstar. No more fly sounds for now I'm afraid, till everyone of you calls David Munro – that's him in the spotlight – a *dizzy sad fuck*.'

My heart had cultivated a heavily knuckled fist which it rapped against my ribcage. Its irregular rhythm horrified me. I placed my drink on a narrow ledge and stumbled for the toilet, noticing that the thin bones beneath the skin of my hand looked more and more like the faces of babies trapped there, screaming soundlessly. The people dancing were losing their basic human form. Traces of their movements hung in the air, commas and curlicues of flesh, like ghosts trapped in a double exposure.

Beneath the brittle light in a Gents thankfully unoccupied, I shuffled into a cubicle and considered making myself sick. My stomach still ached from the last bout of vomiting; I oscillated between feelings of shame and self-despisal. Dando had spiked my drink with something, the bastard. I tried to get a grip, to not let whatever was freaking me out gain deeper access. I closed my eyes and the colours there grew sullen and fractured, peeling away from the veins like layers of paint from wire: new colours, it seemed, alongside a sickly combination of peppermint green and strawberry milk. When I opened them again, and focused on the window above the urinals, I saw a creature made of mist clinging to its lattice pattern, mouth open in pain or rage, its eyes ovine and black.

Gradually, I came down. I was shivering and my back was filmed with sweat. I must have been sitting on the toilet lid for a full two hours, trying to tether the beast, wondering when my eyes were going to burst and spill my head across the pissy tiles. I rose and turned around. I lifted the toilet seat, in need of relief. I unzipped. The boltless door swung open on its hinges, creaking massively. I looked round, waiting for my bladder to relax. Nobody had entered the toilets. The music from the club throbbed through my feet. I watched the tip of my penis and the horseshoe curve of plastic below me. Urine arced in a sudden steaming jet. I thought of Mum and Dad tucked up in bed, utterly numb to what was going on. It was almost funny.

A coldness swept through my midriff, as though I'd just been injected with ice-water. In the next breath it had become unbearable heat, wrapping itself around my innards like sauna towels. My piss turned red.

Turning hurt so much I was close to blacking out. Blood was gushing from a rent above my waistband, creeping through the cloth of my shirt. Pointlessly I went down, because all the stab victims I'd seen in films did just that. Trying to staunch the wound with my hand, I screamed but still the thump of music vibrated in my lungs. Whatever was tripping through my body made the spreading pool of blood look deep and beautiful, like liquid marble.

I wondered how and I wondered who as flashes of white light sparked across the spaces in my head – like shorts in a circuit that has begun to blacken and die.

six
cherry-coloured funk

When I realised I could, I wondered why.

Did there have to be a reason? I knew what the club was like; its licence had been in jeopardy due to violence before – pages were devoted each week in the local press to new incidents. One smart reporter had totted up the number of sutures the victims of the Club of Chaos had accreted: it had beaten the thousand barrier.

Bleary-eyed, I regarded the ward. People lying in beds, so motionless it seemed they were all dead, gazed up at a grey ceiling (I hadn't tried to move for fear of waking up my sleeping back and must have looked the same). I was at such an ebb. My back must have been a real sight: sliced and stitched and scabbed over, though it seemed I'd not been as badly wounded as I'd first believed. I must have hallucinated the blood in my water; the spray from my back.

This starchy hospital bed trapped my legs and made me hot. I was suffering from a hangover that nailed me to the sheets. My mum and dad were probably settling down to a jolly breakfast now, Mum deciding to let me sleep on for a while before taking up a cup of tea.

A nurse walked into my line of vision; I lifted a hand. That's the thing about nurses – unlike, say, some people who wait on you at restaurants – they won't try to ignore your pleas, they want to help you, even though a tip isn't expected for their service. This nurse, all smiles and a faint whiff of Imperial Leather and peppermint, brushed a lock of hair from my eye before reading my mind.

'Water, hmm? I'm not surprised. Whatever you were on last night stripped you dry as a bone.' She checked my drip, told me her name was Olwen and said I couldn't have anything to drink for a while. 'I could let you have an ice-cube to suck on for the time being.'

I nodded. 'And my parents. They should be called.'

'They have already. They're in the waiting room. We told them it would be best if you came round before they saw you.'

The thought that I'd left them worrying for any length of time disgusted me. One day home and I'd disrupted their lives. I was helped to sit up and then she left me. It was important to try to look nonchalant about the whole affair, as if this type of thing happened to me all the time. Ridiculous, I know, but it occurred to me that I must not look as though I had lost control and needed their emotional support. I was an adult who had stumbled across something bad. Right person, wrong place, wrong time, that was all. Once it had been all right to seek comfort in my mother's cardigan; all right to rejoice in the sanctuary she and my father provided. And though I wanted dearly to reach for that now, to create that triangle of comfort, I knew I should not, for their sakes more than anything else. Smiles and confidence would reassure them.

When Mum walked into the ward I burst into tears.

I felt their arms around me, and the heat of the eyes of those who were able to lever themselves up in bed enough to ensure a good view. All of the times I'd broken down under the weight of their devotion – at the resolution of some petty crime or minor injury – came back to me now. I'd never been able to keep my eyes dry when my dad told me he loved me; perhaps because he didn't say it that often. I just let it go, and after a while it was obvious to me that I was shedding more than tears. I felt lighter, as though I'd sloughed off the burden of days spent in Morecambe. I felt I could return there now and be completely guileless and fresh.

Mum asked me if she could bring me anything; Dad was

more interested in statements to the police. He kept asking me who had stabbed me. 'I don't know,' I said. 'It was too dark. I was drunk. I didn't see anybody.'

A look in his eye said he thought I was holding something back, that I was protecting the offender. Then it passed and he sighed.

'Doctor says the cut wasn't that deep. Twelve stitches. Said it was difficult to sew you up because of the mess your back was in already. Bloody hell, David, why can't you be careful?'

I apologised around the knot in my throat. I felt ten years old. 'When can I leave?'

'Day or two, love,' said Mum, smoothing the same lock of hair touched by the nurse. I could see she was fighting against the wobble in her voice which only made me feel worse.

I was managing to regain some control. Wiping my eyes, I coughed and brought some spine back to my voice. 'It would be best if you go. Don't worry about me. I don't feel as bad as I should.' I squeezed Mum's hand. 'I'll make a statement soon as possible. They'll probably visit me soon, the police. I'll tell them what I remember.'

Although this didn't exactly assuage my father, I could see him soften a little. I could tell he wanted to say something else but I suppose it was like locking the gate after the horse has bolted. Nothing he could impart now would be of any use.

'I'm sorry,' I said. For a change.

I stared out those patients who had managed to watch these proceedings until once again we were a ward of ceiling-admirers. Despite my reservations and the circumstances, I felt much better for Mum and Dad's visit and became more chipper by the minute, and was even able to tolerate the appalling hospital radio service. The nurse eventually returned with a cup of tea and a few Jammy Dodgers; the newspaper. 'I could get used to this,' I said as she left.

I watched the day's colours fade over Sankey Valley Park.

The sky became banded with purple and blue, even a pale green smudge at the horizon. Over the headphones came something surging and strong, the sudden antithesis to all that afternoon's banality. I was reminded of the sea; its lips of foam, the scoops of gunmetal blue. I imagined myself standing on its scummy shore on a calm, windless morning and taking the first roll of water between my fingers and peeling it back from what should have been its secret depth and acreage but all that lay beneath was the dull sand, broken now and again by a pleading, desiccated arm or a girder of steel; a jumble of plastic; oil blooms. The sea was one molecule thick in my hand, coming away from its shores like cellophane. Nothing moved in the dusty, fetid bowl beneath. The wind took charge, gusting this mirage sheet from my grasp and sailing it into the sky where it hung like a cloud of glass. Something was striding towards me from the newly uncovered skyline, distorted by distance and the great shoulders of land beyond it. Something large and pale. It moved with a purpose which was upsetting; my fear crowded me like a sneeze's threat. It had a noise, this gaining presence: a buzzing, like that of many flies or wasps. Or the hiss of summer rain. I couldn't quite work out which and while I was working on the different nuances I woke up.

There was a parity between the disorientation I felt at that moment and the times I'd wakened to alien ceilings after one-night stands. A sickening ripple of dread mixed with the compulsion to rise and make good an escape. And a fear of looking to see what kind of creature you've woken up to. Thankfully the panic ended and I slipped my headphones off (the white noise filling the earpieces must have been what I carried into my dream with me) and listened to the somnolent burble of the hospital: the dim rattle of porters' lifts; a *schuss* of slippered feet on linoleum; the unpleasant, whispery suck of ill people on this ward as they skipped the thin line between sleep and something deeper. If I shifted my head (the pain in my back was strangely disconnected now, as if it too had succumbed to slumber) I could see – painted with a barley glow from a desklamp – the duty nurse for the night shift. A book lay open before her; her head rocked back and to. I could hear the hiss of her nails as they worried a scab on her forearm.

Someone over in the corner of the ward, untouched by the soft cone of light, sat up sharply in his bed. The lower half of his body, hidden by blankets but offering a little more in the way of illumination, thrashed about as if his bed were full of insects. I knew that he was looking at me; could even see twin crescents of light where the curve of his eyes bulged.

'Are you in trouble?' I whispered. 'Shall I call the nurse?'

He raised an arm and pointed at me. Something slipped from beneath the blankets and hit the tiles with a wet smack where it jerked around like a torched worm. A blackness more profound than this mask of night spread across his face and I realised his mouth was yawning silently. It stretched to what must be anatomy's limit then went beyond so that his eyes became concealed. I thought the top of his head must fall away. More objects slid on to the floor. A frothing noise began in his throat. I scrabbled above my head for the emergency alarm button set into the wall and bashed it with my fist. A bell rang and the nurse looked up.

'Help,' I gasped, as a tide of dark fluid rose placidly from the man's throat and welled over his face.

Just before he crashed back into his pillow, his body arcing as if a million volts had been passed through it, he gargled my name and then: 'She'll do for you.'

Bodies stirred around him. Nurses descended. The curtains were pulled around his bed. I listened to the rattling he made and the hushed, urgent voices until dawn brought a pink, strangely safe tinge to the ward. The screens were streaked with blood; I was sure a message was daubed there for my benefit but the light was not potent enough to pick it out. I couldn't keep my eyes away from the hem which brushed at the floor, shivering as bodies moved against it. I was sure something pale and organ-like was going to slither into view, spasming like a slug sprinkled with salt.

And then the curtains were drawn back and the nurses were sedate and businesslike, taking away bundles of soiled bedding. One of them even managed a smile for me, though her face was grey with fatigue. The man who had suffered the fit was nowhere to be seen.

'What,' I asked Olwen, later, 'happened to that bloke over there? I didn't see him leave.'

I was able to sit up in bed and spoon Bran Flakes without my back twingeing. All down to the anaesthetics and painkillers, of course, but it was nice to delude myself that I was on the mend.

She looked at the freshly made bed. The curtains had been whisked away, the floor newly scrubbed and all before breakfast. If she'd told me that nothing at all had happened, and that I must have imagined it all, I would have half-believed her, so pristine did the ward now seem. But I'd seen something – not all of which I felt was actual – and I knew some of my neighbours had caught the tail end of this morning's action so I was ready to call foul if she tried to fob me off.

'Mr Demmings. He had a stroke. I'd like to say it was a good job you were awake to raise the alarm but it was too late – not that we could have helped him anyway. He went like that…' She clicked her fingers.

'It didn't seem that way to me,' I countered. I didn't tell her about the writhing pieces of him (at least, I thought they were parts of him) or the way his body had appeared to unfold, or the words I heard him say.

'Well excuse *me*, Dr Munro. Perhaps you could do the rounds for us this morning.' She said this not without humour. I let it lie, knowing that my mind was likely to be up to mischief thanks to the cocktail of painkillers I'd downed the night before.

'Sorry. It was just a scary moment, you know?' I thought about the words he'd uttered (or I thought he'd uttered) before all hell broke loose. 'I didn't see him go.'

'Well, we wheeled him out of here pdq. Even I miss things

sometimes.' She gestured to the bowl. 'Finished? Only there's somebody here to see you.'

'The police?' I asked, trying to get my story right in my head.

'No. A friend of yours.'

'Fine.' It would be Dando, come to apologise for the shabby trick he pulled in the night club.

'Hello David. How are you?'

'I feel good, funnily enough. Like a spangly Cocteau Twins song.'

Olwen left, but not before raising her eyebrows at me from behind Helen's back. Clearly she was impressed, and so was I, despite my reluctance to have anything to do with her on her terms. Helen's hair was tied savagely into a ponytail, accentuating her square jaw and plump, neat lips. She looked super-real, like an actress. One of my hands she clasped between hers. The skin was cold but soft and generous with its grip. I noticed something was wrong with it though – one of the fingers on her left hand was heavily bandaged.

'Looks like we've both been in the wars, hey?'

'Shay too. He went walking in Heysham while he was bazzed out of his gourd on booze and God knows what. Walked over the edge of a sheer drop near Half Moon Bay –'

'Where?' I sat up and my back had something to say about that.

'Half Moon Bay. A dingy bit of shoreline. You can see the power plant from there. Why so interested?'

How could I tell her about Eve? The heartless bastard in me wanted to divulge all, partially because I wanted to hurt her – if she still had any vulnerability regarding me left in her bones. Knowing Helen though, her reaction would involve a hearty congratulations. And she'd ask me if Eve was a good shag. So I kept quiet about her.

'I'm interested because of Seamus, not the geography.' And that was mostly true, though once upon a time I'd have cared more about the coarseness of the grains of sand rather than Seamus' well being. 'How is he?'

'Suffering. He bashed his head in and now he can't see in colour. Seamus and his eyes. Poor dear.'

'Jesus Christ,' I said. 'And you?'

'Trapped my finger in the door of a taxi. They had to lop the tip of it off in casualty.'

She related this so impassively that for a second or two I was numb to the gravity of her news. She might have been telling me she had to buy spinach because Asda didn't have any cabbage left.

'You've had your *finger* amputated?'

'Ssh, David. Yes. Just the tip – I've still got my nail. You can hardly tell.'

'Oh, that's okay then.'

'Look, David, what's the problem? There's no point in being pissed off after the fact. At least I can still walk around, unlike you and Shay. I'd be really pissed off if I were in your pyjamas.' She smiled and rubbed my hand. 'What happened?'

I told her.

'So you escaped Morecambe for this?' Her face changed a degree: the slightest relaxation of muscles took her from happiness to an expression of anguish. 'We need you to come back, David. I need you to come back.'

'And what does that mean exactly?'

'It means I want you to come back. I want us to be friends. I'm sorry about the way it went the other day.' Her lips snapped shut and flattened as though she'd gone too far, which she had, for her. Those weren't the words I wanted to hear but it was nice that Helen apologised: not a common phenomenon.

Suddenly I was blurting out the incident concerning Mr Demmings and Helen's face became scarred with shock though whether from the urgency of my narrative or the story's content, I couldn't be sure. I knew it would be playing into her hands – all this business of ambiguity and threat she was enveloped in – but it was as if the unconscious part of me that was sympathetic to her beliefs was surfacing, actively

seeking a reciprocity of thought with the person I seeme͜
loggerheads with so often. I declared all – even the parts ı
could not trust concretely: the colloid ooze of what I'd
perceived as dissolved portions of him; the blood's intent on
its soft plastic page; his implausibly swift and invisible exit.

'You'll do yourself a mischief, bottling all of this up.'
Victorious, she took my hand. 'Why didn't you tell me you
were sensitive? You stubborn fool. It might have saved us a
lot of grief.'

'Oh I doubt it. This doesn't mean I've been cured of my
scepticism you know. There are explanations.'

'Such as?'

'Well, the drug, the acid or whatever Dando sneaked into
my drink. It could still be in my circulation. It could have
enhanced this morning's incident.'

'But you don't wholly believe it did, do you?'

She was right. There had been a marked reduction in the
drug's efficacy since Saturday night and though I still felt
groggy, I knew this was more to do with the clean, purpose-
ful medication rather than the bitter dregs of Dando's
surprise. 'I suppose not. I'm worried. Even though the nightclub is infamous for this kind of thing I can't help thinking
that whoever stabbed me is going to attack me again.'

. 'It's getting closer. It knows us now. It's got our blood in its
nostrils. Its attacks are going to be more focused. There aren't
going to be any more mistakes, any more innocent
bystanders taking shrapnel.'

I squeezed her hand, then put it against my cheek. She
appeared a little embarrassed but humoured the liberty I'd
taken. She smelled of woodlands.

'The other day,' I said, inspecting the fluted beauty of her
fingers, 'Saturday afternoon – not long after I arrived here, I
was looking out of my bedroom window and I saw two
figures standing by Seven Arches in the park. I thought it was
you and Seamus.' Her slender knuckles waxed as she moved
her hand against mine: its wrinkles disappeared, the skin
yellowed, her grip tightened. Her face was serene – more so

than the way it came to me in dreams when she would allow my mouth to eclipse hers. It surprised me a little, because I'd injected the name of our old haunt with some theatre, in the masochistic hope that it might inspire some kind of reaction in her. That it might cause in her the same resonances that were troubling me so much.

'No,' she said. 'No. Seamus is in traction and I arrived here this afternoon. Maybe you were projecting what you really wanted to be true. They could be echoes of times past.'

'Or times to be?'

In the nod of her head I saw her satisfaction in the way I was assimilating my thoughts with hers. To continue in this vein, though not entirely comfortable to me, might produce a greater understanding of the forces that drove her and Seamus. At least it would deflect any bickering; energy that could be used to more fertile ends.

She steered the conversation towards safer waters: the state of my back ('Can I see your stitches?'), the health of my family, events in Morecambe.

'I was walking along Marine Road, near Bubbles leisure centre and a man came out of Woolworth's with his wife and two kids. "Thirty-two pee for a fucking jellied snake!" he was shouting. "Thirty-fucking-two fucking pee. The robbing bastards!" And he started kicking the windows of Woolworth's in. And the poor kids! They were just waiting for Dad to break this snake in half, calm as you like as if they were used to his tantrums.'

'Helen. Are you and Seamus still… God, I didn't know how to phrase this… being followed?' I hoped that was okay. With the vocabulary she'd given to this sequence of strange events, I was worried I might have weakened the effect with something so commonly used. Maybe I should have ended the sentence with… *suffering an Oppression?* but then she'd have accused me of taking the piss.

'Yes. You?'

'After I saw you… after I thought I saw you and Seamus by the Arches, I jogged over to have a look. There was something there. I don't remember much, I was scared. But there were a few details. A school tie. A cricket ball. And I could smell petrol. It's a smell that's been following me around for a while, now I think about it.'

Helen looked lost but at the same time hopeful, like someone who has misplaced a purse and is standing still, trying to remember the last instance she'd seen it.

'What do we do about it, Helen?'

'I don't know,' she said. 'We tackle it, I suppose. We face it again. It's getting stronger, bearing down on us with more frequency. It keeps me awake at nights. It's as much from within as without. In fact, I'm pretty sure that it's entirely internalised and we're unconsciously providing visuals to enable us to cope with it. Prevent us from going mad.'

'If we haven't gone mad already. I think you're right. We're dealing with ripples from the past, something we've collectively blocked.'

She considered this for a moment before nodding. 'For what other reason could the three of us be involved? Our time together was intense – we got hideously drunk, we screwed each other, we grew close due to events outside our cosy little zone but important to each of us as individuals. For example,' she stopped and thought for a while. 'Back when we were kids, do you remember that night we went out to Sankey Valley and we were on the bowling green? You were with Kerry Losh. Daniel Hoth was there. You remember Dando? And Shay. God, I was only thinking about this the other night. You were off with Kerry, kissing her. And I went with the lads down to the edge of the canal. There was a dog –'

'I remember,' I said. 'I thought about it too. Our heads are letting things through. Stuff they've trapped for years. But the memories are unstable, my mind is being unreliable. It was me I imagined being rammed into the mud by those arseholes, not the poor dog. It's as if my memories are trying to impose some final check, even as they become clear to me. It's as if I'm subconsciously punishing myself. I flailed for a reason but couldn't find one. Why is that?'

'Because whatever it is we've been blocking, the main thing, it's bad, David.' There were tears in her eyes. So much had happened that we hadn't had time to be frightened. But I felt fear now. I didn't know where this was going to end. Were we all going mental? Were these fouled memories some indication of the decay of our minds and would they continue for ever, even if we managed to discover their root cause?

I held her hand. 'It's like eating a packet of Tunes when you have a stuffed nose, Morecambe, isn't it?'

She smiled. 'It's not Morecambe,' she said. 'It's us.'

Olwen stood by a trolley of wet towels and indicated to us that it was time for Helen to leave.

Helen let go of my hand (I had to resist the urge to check the hot skin there for a secret sign she might have left). 'Come back with me,' she murmured.

'I'll come back soon. Before this week's out. And then we'll all talk together. Tell Seamus... tell Seamus he's a prick.'

She left then, gliding between the bars of light and shade so slowly that it was as if time was decelerating, that at any moment it would stop and trap her in the block of darkness between windows and I'd never be able to set her free.

seven
designs

I spent the days leading up to Friday afternoon flanked by magazines and mugs of tea. My meals were brought to me on a tray adorned with a single flower in a stoneware vase. Loot slept with me and played the tart whenever there was a hot plate around. I hugged my mother more in that week than I had done in years and swapped shoulder slaps with Dad like a madman. Kim stopped by often, to drop off a recommended paperback or hand me a warm paper bag filled with croissants. Helen called a few times to check on my recovery and report on Seamus' rehabilitation. Both were swift: I was regaining the suppleness in my back and Seamus was on crutches though his was still a monochrome world. I received a letter from him on the day before my departure.

'The bones in my leg are crazy-paving,' he wrote. 'And Helen looks like a misty actress in some old film. My few waking moments are filled with brief recognitions of people I do not know, or rather, cannot see – which makes my recognition of them all the more illogical and annoying. My bed resembles a coffin more and more. I swear I can feel my spine crumbling. I've been imagining how my bitchery would read. Pretty small column, I expect. Seamus Cope, twat, died. End of fucking story. I've had two hours' sleep since my accident. And yesterday dear old Jean Crance died, committing suicide at the age of 90. The world of crossword puzzle compilers will miss her greatly.'

Whether or not Seamus' letter infected me with its depression, my last hours of sleep in Warrington borrowed heavily from its content and tone. I dreamed of walking back from town, laden with shopping, looking forward to an evening in front of a television boasting some Cup Final or other: I had bought a six-pack of lager and a pillow-sized bag of tortilla chips to share with everyone else while the match was playing. Into this vapid scenario stepped a woman of my own invention. If she was a collage of everything I found attractive in a person, she wasn't so perfectly blended that I couldn't identify some of her constituent parts. Here were Helen's tidy bee-stung lips; Eve's filmy complexion; the caramel eyes of Stephanie, my first girlfriend. This woman's hair I couldn't attribute to anyone: it was a dirty blonde pile falling to her shoulders. Errant strands bracketed a wide face free of any cosmetic. A spray of freckles banded her nose, muscovado dark. Her name would have been something warm and clotted that caught in the throat: Claire, say; or something rude and rich, full of obstacles for the lips and tongue: Lydia, Rachel, Charlotte.

She pulled her beaten leather jacket more comfortably around her shoulders and fell into step beside me. Her suede cowboy boots scraped and clicked. She had a comeliness about her that was not so profound that it made my mouth dry; rather, her rough appeal latched on to me like meshing Velcro surfaces and persuaded a more sedate exchange, as of people well known to each other. Or so my dreamscape suggested. As we reached my front gate she cupped my elbow with her hand and swung me into a kiss. Our mouths were so perfectly matched it was as if this was their natural disposition and we'd been cruelly separated at some former time.

When I wakened I felt instantly bereaved; a yearning I had never felt before, even for the living. The pillow was her softly submitting body. As the day impinged itself more forcibly upon my groggy senses I was aware of her lingering scent and the fact that I could not remember the peculiar assemblage of features I knew so well in others.

Mum stood on the doorstep, arms folded, entreating me

to take care while her expression patently pleaded for me not to go. Dad was all bluster: 'Leave him to it Liz, if he wants to tear off like that. You can't talk to the lad. You can't.' At the last moment, as I closed the front gate, he pressed his lips together – which passed for a smile – and raised a finger. 'Be well,' he said. 'And don't lark about else you want your tripes spilled all over the shop. Give your body time to heal itself. Think on, David.'

I promised I would, marvelling at the way he could make me feel like an infant.

When I arrived back in Morecambe and smelled the sea – or the shit soup which passed for it these days – the fact that the journey had taken just two hours was something of a comfort; I felt close to my parents and, irrational though it was, enjoyed a sense of security in the zone they created for me – as if their protection could reach across the county border and envelop me here on the battered coast. It couldn't buoy me with regard to the mordant, irrepressible greyness of everything and the weight of expectation – a sense that work had to be done, or finished. I dropped my bag off at the guest house and chatted to my landlady about how things were bad for them in the closed season until I saw she was ferreting for rent. Outside, pale sunlight could do little against the grumbling clouds building up over the bay. I walked streets whitened by salt, strangling on bin sacks which slumped out of alleys like drunken threats. Much of the architecture of the 19th century had fallen foul of the sea's breath; corners of buildings were becoming rounded, sandstone crumbling in its ambition to return to the beach. Scaffolding clung to surfaces like arcane dental braces; orange plastic fencing and shivering green brick-nets abounded – the only nod to colour beyond the tawdry prostitution of Morecambe's front.

Turning on to the promenade, I felt sure I was going to bump into Helen, or any of the acquaintances I'd made in the past few weeks. This I didn't want. I checked my watch; the meeting with Eve at Half Moon Bay was to take place in less than three hours; I didn't want to spend all that time locked up in my fusty room, work pending or no. I drifted towards The Battery, then beyond when I realised facing Eve drunk might not be appreciated. I passed a couple in the bus shelter huddled into each other as though trying to negate their individuality. The woman's eyes were hooded. They watched me as their invisible hands rummaged under thick clothing like burrowing animals. I caught a strong, momentary whiff of bladderwrack, its black saltiness reaming my nostrils as efficiently as a snort of ammonia.

Pol, Helen's grandma, lived around here – had done, according to Helen, all her life and had known the town before it became engulfed by the penny-pinchers who sniffed profit in the dubious marriage between sunbathing and one-armed bandits.

I picked up my pace; Pol would be able to fill in the gap (I hoped) between leaving University and more recent events. I didn't know her exact address but I remembered Helen letting on that her grandmother lived alone above a florist's just off Heysham Road. This was no guarantee of me finding it, of course, but it would pass the time. I checked along the first few streets that led off the arterial road but all I could see were banks of houses and tired cars. Clouds swarmed in windows like oil and water pressed between panes of glass. The gabled roof of The Battery pinned the glowering sky into place – my beacon – like some Gothic rampart from a Hammer film. I oughtn't rove too far from that if I didn't want to get lost.

And then I realised I was being followed, if followed was the right word for what was happening. I noticed a figure walking the parallel street to this one at the same pace as me. I would lose sight of him as a block of houses came between us but at the next junction he would reappear, keeping step. At first I thought it was mere coincidence; the post-trauma jitters advising me of anything vaguely awry. But when I tried mixing up my pace – dawdling one moment, eating up the ground with great strides the next – he stepped into the connecting road at exactly the same time as I did. It was as if a vast mirror had been erected at the opposite end of the street, so minutely copied were the figure's movements. I didn't let it worry me. *Go through it*, I told myself, *it will have to stop*. Rather than stop, though, the figure turned sharply left and began sprinting towards me. Its head was a nimbus of frothing pink, like a face on a canvas of mine treated with too much water. Smears of it seemed to hang in the air as though snagged.

I took off, my momentum threatening to send me into a poorly trimmed wall of shrubbery. I managed to stay upright and pelted to the next junction where I at last saw a florist's set back from the road. I swung into the street, casting a glance back: he still hadn't emerged. Feeling threatened, yet somehow calm, as though floating, I checked names next to the various bellpushes. Here was a P MacFarlane – surely it was Pol? I rang it. Her voice came through the metal grille, coated in static. I knew then it was her; she sounded exactly like Helen – the tone was questioning but it was treated with an enamel which was all: *what the fuck do you want?*

Sensing something awful gathering at my shoulders I said: 'I'm David. Helen's friend. Can I talk to you?'

Expecting to be interrogated over the reasons for my visit, I chanced another look back over my shoulder. He was standing at the corner of the road watching me – I supposed – through the pink and red blur of his head. He looked like a Polaroid print that has been smeared by an errant thumb before the chemical fixers have had time to fasten the picture. His arms opened as if to embrace me. I took in his ragged shirt, the charred mess of his blazer, the scuffed comfort of his shoes before the buzzing of the door release rescued me and I tumbled into a hallway filled with masks.

Nothing Helen had told me about Pol prepared me for what I was to encounter. She appeared at the top of the stairs, wreathed in the thin light coming from the back of the house.

'Hello David,' she said, her voice both arch and welcoming. 'I thought we might have met before now, considering how long you've known Helen. But…' and she was sloping off, her shadow contracting like a water stain on a hot pavement. I bounded up to the landing, uncomfortably aware of the masks which glared at me, head height, as I ascended. At the top of the stairs I detected a vegetable tang coming in pulses from the wallpaper as though it were a breathing skin. She was already ensconced in a large chair tucked in the corner of her living room between two windows that were heavily curtained. Motes swarmed in the chinks of light available; a sliver painted her eye livid blue – the rest of her seethed beneath shadow.

'Take a sip of something with me if you please,' she said. 'You'll find the makings of a cup of scaldy in the cupboard behind the kitchen door. There's some fancy Darjeeling I pick up now and again for visitors that never come but I'm for a normal. You help yourself.'

I made a pot, feeling oddly detached from this scene, as if I was viewing it from elsewhere. I hadn't spoken a word yet and already I was acting the skivvy.

'How do you like it?' I asked, appalled at the scratchiness of my voice. I peered through the window; he was still there, blots of red staining his hands like stigmata. *Go away*, I thought, wincing at the nubs of flesh that puckered along my spine. His face was like something Francis Bacon might have created. *Go away*, I thought, and then: *What are you?*

'I have it any way you choose so long as it's hot and wet.' Music filtered from the room, its vinyl-warm crackle helping to work the stress from me. I turned my back on the window and poured tea into two white mugs. 'There'll be a bourbon cream or three I've no doubt. A brandy snap even, if you're lucky.'

'I'm not hungry.'

'Right you are.' She dipped into the light to take her mug. Her lips were astonishingly like Helen's; I was tempted to call her bluff, persuaded that it really was Helen playing a trick on me. Instead I sipped my tea and read the sleeve notes of the Jeri Southern album Pol had slipped on to the turntable.

'Summer music,' she commented, looking at me. I nodded and smiled.

'It's nice.'

'What do you want?'

'Oh, nothing really,' I lied, trying to sound casual and instead achieving the nervy status of a schoolboy accused of shoplifting. 'Just thought I'd call round and say hello. Heard so much about you that –'

'Crap,' she croaked. 'What have you heard about me?' Her hands snaked into the blade of light like lizards sunning themselves: still and leathery but with a latent capacity for blinding speed. One of her nails had grown inexplicably long; it was beginning to curl under her finger. The flesh beneath the cuticle was blackened.

'Okay, nothing. Apart from you living here and being Helen's grandma.'

She seemed pleased with this; perhaps because she felt she'd ground the truth from me. 'So what's the rumpus?'

'I just wanted to come and talk to you. About Helen.'

'Ahh, now there's a tone I recognise. Lovesick dog, aren't you?'

I bristled at this. Not least because I knew it to be untrue. What I felt for Helen these days was frustration; anger even. And sometimes a yearning that had nothing to do with love. Not love. Surely not love.

'I'm worried about her. I've not seen her for so long, I thought maybe you could tell me what she's been like since she graduated.' I thought about what I said for a while and added: 'She seems different. Folded into herself.'

Pol dappled the surface of her tea with those tapered twig-fingers of hers.

'Folded into herself? What is it you're suspicious of?'

'Have you seen her lately?' I couldn't keep the edge from my voice.

Pol must have caught the concern; suddenly, her playfulness receded.

'No,' she said. 'Is she in trouble?'

'Not really. Not yet. But I've a feeling she has the capacity to harm herself. Without even realising it.'

Pol's face collapsed into a sneer. 'Perhaps we can jettison the riddles, hey David? What is going on?'

'I don't know. I think maybe Helen's upset about something that happened in the past. It's really starting to get under her skin.'

'What something?' Her top lip quested over the rim of her tea cup, tapir-like.

'I couldn't tell you. I don't remember.' I sipped my tea. It tasted faintly of washing-up liquid. For a time the quiet in the room was punctuated by Pol's inhalation of tea and the listless tick of a clock I couldn't locate. I wanted badly to look into the street for my pursuer but I was worried that Pol would interpret my covert ways as being directly related to Helen and, specifically, the trouble she now saw her to be in. Pol was wadded into her armchair like a trapped cushion. Scimitars of hair curved from beneath her beret, tangling with her eyelashes so that whenever she blinked, her fringe twitched. She wore a CND pin in the knot of a silk scarf at her throat. On the wall above the three glaring orange bars of the fire hung a photograph of a woman by a pond. The woman was crouched alongside a dog that seemed to be grinning. A pigeon in the background was just taking off, wings blurred to such an extent they resembled a loop of smoke.

Pol replaced her cup in its saucer and steadied its rattling with a finger, the rest of her hand splayed out like a badly drawn asterisk. 'Don't presume to tell me the state of *my* family. I know what's what. Even if I haven't seen Helen for years –' (it was something of a shock hearing her name after so long, as though we'd been discussing someone else) '– I know what that girl has buzzing around in her mind. She was in no state for anyone after that girl drowned. She spent days in her room staring out of the window in the direction of the sea. I was worried sick that she'd just go walking off one night to the bay and keep walking till the water took her.'

'Drowned? What girl? I don't understand.' I might have

felt some emotion at this revelation if it hadn't all been driven out of me over the past weeks.

Pol's hand had drifted to her chest where it lightly massaged. Her face had lost much of its aggression but the features sported the lines and shadows that, when joined, hinted at the fury that could take flight there.

'I lost sleep. She took to wandering around the flat, so dazed that I thought she was sleepwalking but able to speak clearly so that I wasn't sure. I kept talking to her. She began to use a word frequently. "Atonement," she'd say. "There is a need for atonement."'

The dim ticking was subsumed by a tortuous meshing of tired cogs and springs: three chimes sounded. That I had an hour left before meeting Eve (my blood quickened upon recalling her – the tattoo! And what colour eyes?) relaxed me, until I remembered that I didn't know where Half Moon Bay was to be found. My panic rose like seawater to the plimsoll line of my throat.

'I was convinced she was going to kill herself, that her atonement for the drowning of that girl would come with Helen opening a vein in her arm or swallowing pills but she eventually came out of it and it was like she was normal again. But hard with it.'

'Miss MacFarlane,' I said. 'Pol –'

'She was so confused when she was in that state. I remember her voice, so reedy. "There must be atonement. I killed the girl. I killed her." I don't want to be a part of anything like that again.'

I edged forward in my seat. 'I don't know about this drowning. Helen never told me about a dead girl. What happened?'

'I don't know for sure, lad. I wasn't there. But Helen liked to walk along the towpath on the Lune. She liked the barges; sometimes she'd feed the mallards and moorhens. I'd walked with her now and again but it was clear she preferred to make the journey alone so I stopped. She'd happened upon a girl who had fallen into the water. Without a thought

Helen entered the water and fished the girl out. Helen had remembered her First Aid well but the girl did not revive.

'Helen was counselled by therapists at college and on visits home but it was her stubborn view that she was to blame. She took to wondering about the girl – how she spoke or laughed, how she chewed or held her pen. Ridiculous details that she grieved over as though the girl had been her own daughter. I'd catch her writing the name *Samantha* on file paper or staring at blonde girls in catalogues. Helen was excused from having to take first-year exams and returned after summer looking healthy, determined and happier than in previous months. I remember thinking she looked, not so much older, as hardened. She never walked the towpath again. And I haven't seen her since. End of story.'

Pol looked blank, her eyes yolky with age and the effort of recalling Helen's tragedy. She rubbed at her jowls and an insectile rasp – like the pattern of a cricket's call – filled the room. I half-expected a swarm of chittering shells to pour in from the ventilation duct on the wall.

'Does she see much of that dandiprat Seamus? Is he still on the scene?'

'He hasn't been for a while, like me, but he's around now.'

'Course he is. You all diddled each other. There's your magic triangle. You've all smelled and tasted each other. Ball and socket. Key and lock. Fucking brings out the worst in us, David. And it also releases demons.'

'Really?' I said, trying not to appear shocked by her tirade. It was hard to believe that six hours earlier I'd been tickling Loot's chin, eating Rice Krispies and listening to Dad hum along to Neil Young on the radio. 'I must go. Thanks for the tea.' I was trying not to laugh at the phrases that had crept into her invective. *Diddling* for God's sake. *Ball and socket*! And she looked so serious.

I descended the stairwell and her shadow engulfed me as she stepped on to the landing at my back. The masks – papier-mâché, plaster, wood – gurned at me, blackness churning in the holes where the eyes ought to be.

'You're worried about *her*, you say? Worry for yourself. You're all sick bastards. She's the only one with any spunk. Why don't you fuck away and leave her alone?'

On the threshold I stopped as I realised what might still be waiting for me outside. My upper body jerked back as my feet tried bovinely to carry me onward. It was 50/50 as to which of the horrors I'd rather face. In the moment of my remembering him, though, the air shimmered at the street corner where he'd previously stood. I closed the door on Pol's rantings and sensed her face at the window as I reached the main road. I didn't give her the satisfaction of meeting her gaze. Like heat vapour in the coming of dusk, the ripple in the air diminished and I felt safe to continue. I crossed the main road and cut through between buildings to the promenade where the dirty flat seabed stretched away into a distance cut short by a thin line of light like a cross section of glass: the tide's fresh limit. Because the hills beyond were packed in a cladding of mist, this liquid skyline seemed the outermost reaches of geography; beyond I could believe there was little more than a sheer drop.

A keen wind buffeted me as I strode towards Heysham. I reckoned Half Moon Bay was to be found in or around the village. The headland quested towards the sea, like the brow of a Neanderthal giant whose remaining features were buried in the earth. A ruin – what must have been St Patrick's Chapel – clung grimly to the hill. Clustered trees set back from the coastline seemed braced by the wind, swept back like a thickly coiffured mane, their trunks shaped by the incessant breath gusting in from the bay. The light was failing and even the thought of meeting Eve was unable to assuage my lethargy. It had been an error to track down Pol – in a purely physical sense at least. Eking out the news regarding Helen had been hard work. I wanted to please Eve. Turning up couched in this fug of apathy was hardly likely to impress her. I foundered under the need of a lively gambit.

At the promenade's terminus I remembered being here with Helen years ago. It had been a sunny day, a quiet day –

Heysham's nuclear power plant had been audible, a dry hum in the background. Her bangs had been flattened against her cheeks by the wind; the sun had darkened her face and left the shrivelled slash of scar tissue pale above her lip. She'd sucked my tongue deep into her mouth and we'd stood like that, pressing and yielding, eye to eye until her hand found the bulb of my sex as it thickened along the top of my thigh. The rat-tat-tat of claws had us parted in a moment, a thread of connective saliva spinning between us. The woman walking her dog had given us a knowing smile and I remember feeling convinced my hard-on was in perfect bas-relief against my jeans.

'We can walk to Half Moon Bay across the sand from here,' she'd said, any embarrassment already forgotten. 'Half a mile, that's all.'

I could feel blood strumming my glans.

'I'd rather just sit down here with you,' I'd said, which is what we did. Frustrating each other through our clothing until it became dark enough for us to relieve each other with impunity.

Just about here, it was, where a path branched off from the promenade, leading to the main road. I stopped and looked at the spot, trying to identify any chinks in the rock that would fasten the exact space to its historical counterpart. I wanted something of our ghosts to have remained and waited for a smell or a stain of warmth to suggest itself. Vain hope, when I couldn't even remember the clothes she'd worn.

It mattered not at all that my choice to go with Helen to Half Moon Bay (although I didn't know its name then) had been negated by lust; I was gladdened by it now. Of course, in retrospect I could have no idea of the ramifications of such a decision but had I visited that locale with Helen, anything that happened today would be tainted with her which would be unfair to Eve, more so if I was to talk to her in this current state of indifference. I wanted Half Moon bay to *be* Eve.

Though the tide was retiring, it had not done so sufficiently to allow me access to the bay via the sands. Instead, I had to trust to instinct and hope I didn't get lost. As it turned out I needn't have worried; one of the villagers pointed out the quickest way: over the hill by the ruin. As I walked, the incline and trees meshed around me, filling the sky with pockets of grey and leaf-black, I watched Morecambe Bay broaden where the sea curved out to the horizon. An oil tanker cleaved to the dullish background like a template for a child's picture.

From somewhere – I couldn't see a break in the ceiling of haze – gold coins of light dappled the surface of the sea. Plodding down the other side of the hill, the ruined chapel impossibly solid against the brunt of wind, I edged toward the immaculate lip of green, wondering if this was the drop Seamus had suffered. I imagined him scuffing around, hands deep in his pockets, now and again casting a glance at the hulking power station further along the coast. Sniffing madly against the cold. Watching the slow bend of a gull in the sky.

She was sitting on one of the slabs of rock, looking out to the power plant which was slowly misting the sky above with lights nestled into its roof. A large velvet bag slumped at her side, a tablecloth tongue protruding. A brown section of her back – shadowed with the soft swell of her shoulder blades – was visible above the black singlet she wore. I thought about creeping up on her and planting a kiss at her nape but she swung round as soon as my boot connected with the gravel at the top of the beach.

'Hello David David Munro.'

Her eyes… blue. Of course. 'Hello Eve Eve Baguley. Aren't you cold?'

She shrugged herself into an oatmeal cardigan. 'I am now you've mentioned it. Have something to eat.'

She pulled fruit, sandwiches and a bottle of red wine from the bag. I uncorked and raised it to my mouth.

'Heathen,' she said, staying my arm. A fluted glass was slotted into the underside of the bag's covering flap.

'And what about you?'

'We can share it – everything tastes so much better when it's shared.'

'Oh I don't know about that.'

She tilted her head: a wedge of hair dipped into the space on her forehead. 'Meaning?'

'Forget it – I was just trying to be mysterious.'

She poured a glass of wine and offered it to me. Through the curve of glass, the wine itself, I saw half her face swell to grotesque proportions. Her eye was a melting ball of wax, spreading sedately across her skin. A safe illusion – maybe because I didn't sense a threat in her. It was a beautiful day.

'What are you doing later on?' she asked. I watched her, in profile, as she worked her mouth into a peach. Teeth having pared away a little flesh, her tongue fattened against the hollow, staunching any juice. Giddy, I concentrated on more wine, wondering if I should tell her of my intention to visit Seamus that evening or wait to gauge the quality of her alternative. It didn't take long.

'Nothing, why?'

'Come and see The Front Bottoms with me. They're playing at The Garage for a select audience.'

'The Front Bottoms?'

'Lettuce, technically. They changed their name – you know, rock stars.' She leaned over and licked my lips. A glaze of peach juice clung to her mouth. 'Come with me?'

'Yes,' I said.

After we had eaten and finished the wine, we walked back to St Patrick's Chapel and stood in the arch of the South Doorway; enjoyed the spank of air channelling through the tired *voussoir* above us. The sea moved against itself, a weakened tide coming up against the rebound from the rocky shoreline. The resultant motion created shimmers that looked like a vast, dense net settled just above the surface. Eve's hand rubbed at the curve of my shoulder-blade: a single movement, base to crown, but when I looked at her she was leaning against the arch, her hands folded neatly into each other like sleeping birds. Behind me, greensward dipped away into a gulley where life was represented by a listless dog and an old man wrenched into himself by a faltering spine. I was conscious of something else though, something pregnant in the still acreage of turf though I was aware that the sheer mass of the land was enough to disorient. Not one to fall prey to bouts of agoraphobia, I was nevertheless shocked by great, exposed tracts of land. Perhaps it's the wealth of silence, of seeming imminence nestled into spaces like that; or the concealed histories soaked into the ground: any number of deaths, bonfires, conceptions and robberies. Eve dipped her hand into my back pocket and lay her head against my chest.

'Penny for your thoughts.'

'Make it a pound and I'll kiss you instead.'

She slapped my bottom lightly and stood on tiptoe. The outer edge of her iris, and the part immediately next to the pupil, were a blue not unlike this sea; the moat between filled with a milkier hue, like opaque glass. Her mouth was hungry upon mine, yet controlled. When we parted, the light was failing rapidly and night was pushing a chill before it.

'How was Warrington?'

'Grim. How did you know I'd gone home?'

'Word gets round. Did you think of me?'

'Of course.'

'Liar.' Her smile flattened her eyes into cat-slits. I wanted to tell her how sexy, how *new* she seemed.

We walked back to The Battery. On the way, we said little. The banks of land to our left cradled puddles of shadow in between remarkable litter (a naked plastic doll, the cathode tube from a television, a pair of blue corduroy trousers, a sodden, unopened box of tissues) and old dog turds furred with mould. We saw the ashes of a long-dead fire, a single Wellington boot and a black cat watching us imperiously from atop a cairn of magazines stacked inexplicably in the centre of a footpath. Eve kissed me again once we'd drawn level with a camper van, the sunscreen of which was emblazoned with the names CALAMITY and TEX. Her tongue danced around mine; her thigh pushed between my legs and nestled there, spreading its glorious heat.

'I'll come for you,' she said at the gate to the guest house. 'It's a late gig. Two am, they're on. Be ready for me around one.'

I waved her off. After a shower, I went into the kitchen and emptied a tin of soup into a saucepan. Deadened canned laughter crept beneath the door of my landlord's living quarters, accompanied by his phlegmy chortle and the whinny of his wife. As the darkness condensed around me, and the soup warmed, I leaned back against the twin sinks and closed my eyes. So much information jabbered there, collated from the previous weeks, that I had to fight just to relax for a few minutes. I allowed Eve through, and licked my lips to see if she'd left any of her peach juice behind. When I opened my eyes again, the soup was boiling but I found my gaze drawn to the shelves above the cooker where the egg timer was losing sand through its impossibly narrow waist.

I noticed Eve's bag when I entered my room. I must have brought it in with me but I couldn't remember carrying it for her. But then, I couldn't remember fiddling with the egg timer either, so no need to be fazed. I ate my soup and tried to watch a little television but the colours were too busy. When I picked Eve's bag up, the glass we'd been sharing dropped out on to my duvet. As it fell I caught my reflection in the flat spin it described. And caught the reflection of another, standing at my shoulder. His eyes were varnished moonstones and I knew him but a name refused to cement that certainty. When I looked behind me I knew there'd be nothing but empty space between me and the florid wallpaper; I was even deconstructing my initial gut belief: I'd simply seen myself replicated in the opposite curve of glass.

I picked it up. Eve's bottom lip was elaborately delineated against the rim; in its bounty I could make out flaws – nubs and pleats and crinkles – and recall the slick, sticky smear of it against mine.

I fell back upon the bed, closed my eyes and pressed the edge of the glass against my bottom lip.

I struggled out of sleep, upset about something but unable to pin it down until I realised my smoke ghost was capering behind this wall of real vision, winking at me with its ember eyes. The duvet had become wedged under my pelvis, curving my body unnaturally, but it was somehow comfortable, to be supported like that. It was 11.30pm. I had a while before Eve turned up. I rose and went to my door, opened it a crack. The landing was filled with dense black grains; through them I could make out the soft, orange borders of Duncan's door. He was listening to the radio; I also heard the thin clamour of his spanners as he placed them in and retrieved them from his special toolbox. My ears felt as though they were yawning for input, so I listened to the sounds of the hotel softly volley against each other in the dark: coolant in the giant fridges kicking in when the temperatures dropped below their programmed threshold; the drip of the leaking hot water tap in the upper floor bathroom; the sign over the door breathing rustily as the breeze tongued its worn hinges. I thought about my litre of orange juice in the fridge and decided I wanted some so I grabbed my bathrobe, left the door on the latch and slipped downstairs. I bypassed the bathroom, with its frosted slab of glass. It was backlit by some far off streetlamp: a bright, powdery lozenge hung in the centre. To its right, a black, waxy jacket was hanging – probably Terry's; he had been out fishing a lot recently and liked the weathered look of the landed gentry. I skipped down the last flight and ducked under the counter, being careful not to ring the service bell. In the kitchen I halted, because I could hear Maureen beyond the door which led into their downstairs living quarters. I stood with my forehead almost touching the glass, mouth dry, as I heard them making love.

'Ooohm yes, Terry, that'ssssss nicccccce. Uh uh uh uhnnnn...'

I couldn't hear Terry at all until the end, when he hit his vinegar strokes and grunted a couple of times.

Feeling a little faint from holding my breath and being turned on (Jesus... Terry and his isosceles side parting? Turned on by that?) I grabbed the OJ carton and slunk back to the stairs. I was on the third riser when a bolt of blue light flashed in through the window in the main door and striped the hallway, picking the colour from everything. There was the suggestion of smoke in the air now and I heard the bark of a man: 'Jump.'

Gently pulling the door open, I stepped out on to the porch and drank some juice, eyes fast upon the swarms of people gathering around the corner. Most were in night-dresses and pyjamas so I walked towards them, checking once over my shoulder to see if anyone had shared my concern. No sign from downstairs, where Terry and Maureen were still presumably glued together in a soporific trance. Düncan's curtains were moving, but the light was now out. As for Eiger, she and her husband were on the other side of the house anyway.

I turned back and muscled through the knot of people. A beautiful column of flame was spinning around the top floor of one of the guest houses, punched from beneath by frequent fists of black smoke. Somebody else shouted, a woman in a track suit top with a hood. Her legs were concealed by a black nightdress.

'Jump! Come on now. Jump! We'll catch you. It's okay.'

The roar from the fire made it hard for me to hear her cries, so I imagined it must be impossible for the person for which they were intended. I peered into the smoke, wondering why the fire brigade hadn't arrived yet. I could see a figure leaning out of a narrow window. Flames were lashing the space behind her. Thick coils of smoke, like tarred ropes flung to the heavens, churned around the figure. Another pulse of blue light split the road and I saw that the fire brigade *were* here, they just couldn't get to the blaze. Someone had double-parked a Vauxhall Nova, blocking access to the street. A police car pulled up and the occupants started banging on doors to try to track down the arsehole.

Pushing his way through the growing crowd and ignoring the entreaties to do something, the raised fingers, jabbing at what must now be a corpse, a firefighter in breathing apparatus kicked in a pane on the front door and sank through a wall of smoke.

I had crushed the carton of orange juice in my fist. My feet were soaking. When I looked up, I caught a glimpse of Eve as she passed the cluster of terraced houses opposite, before turning north into a street parallel with the bay.

The firefighter had not yet returned. His colleagues were arguing outside as to whether they should go in after him. A gang of men had gathered around the double-parked car and were rocking it violently, trying to get it on to its side.

Suddenly, the person dangling from the window toppled out and crashed on to a sun-lounger, silencing everyone. Her legs had been cooked completely off the bone of her pelvis. I staggered back, smelling burned meat, and dropped the carton of juice. It was a crazy moment. I thought the policeman by my side would caution me for littering.

'Eve,' I croaked, and jogged after her.

I had been shuffling around for half an hour or so when I realised I wasn't making any progress; merely turning blindly into any street, alley or ginnel that offered itself to me. My movements had nothing to do with finding Eve.

I surfaced on the Marine Road. The sea was a cold slab. From here it looked as if it had accrued a layer of dust; I couldn't see a reflection on it anywhere. Exhausted, I sloped back to the guest house. There had been some dispersal but the fire engine remained, dead and quiet. A blanket concealed a form on a stretcher but I couldn't tell who it might be. I hoped the firefighter had made it out alive.

I took the smell of smoke inside with me and felt instantly nauseous. I traipsed up the stairs and saw that the coat in the bathroom had disappeared. I went in and turned on the bath taps, poured some cheap and nasty salts in from a box that had had its brand name bleached out of sight by age and the sun. There was no hook on the back of the door, nothing to hang a coat on. I left the bath running and trotted up to my room. A door snicked shut as I approached the last few risers. Not mine: it was still on the latch. I saw a shadow shift fluidly along the bar of returned light under Duncan's door, like the slow bleed of mercury in a thermometer.

I considered knocking, to tell him about the drama outside, but at the last moment I pulled my hand away from the door and went back to the bathroom, where I failed to wash the stink of death from my skin.

I lay in a sweat of blankets while the vision of the dead woman revisited me. I heard leisurely footsteps pacing up and down the street and at one point I thought I heard a voice ask, in a quiet voice: 'Alex?' but when I looked, I couldn't see anyone. Just before one, I heard the gate squeal open and Eve's footsteps on the path. She didn't knock, which I found endearing. She'd wait for me. As I dressed I heard the fire engine move away, vibrating my bed with its snarling engine. With the window open, the cold air reeked of ash. I slammed it shut.

eight
imago

On the doorstep, my landlady – wrapped in a pink dressing gown with fur collar – hailed me and pushed a scrap of paper into my hand. She was holding a spatula and tapping its broad end against her neck, which was sullied by a lovebite.

'Dint hear you come in earlier, chuck,' she said, through the lipless puncture she sported instead of a mouth. 'But then there was a hell of a to do over the rowd, wasn't there?' She wagged a piece of paper. 'This un cowled et abort foivish. Oi envy yow yongsters gowin out at this toim onoit.' It took a while, and I wasn't sure I'd translated all of it, but I thanked her anyway and closed the door, hushing Eve who was trying not to laugh.

'What did she say?'

I opened my eyes. 'Wasn't it obvious? She said: "The hermaphrodites have invaded Upton-upon-Severn – quick, divest the guinea-fowl of their cutlasses".'

Through her laughter she pointed at the piece of paper. 'Telephone message. From your girlfriend.'

'She's not my girlfriend.'

'Who's not your girlfriend?' Her eyes were egg-large, smug with the knowledge that she'd tricked me.

'Helen. You thought this was from Helen.'

We walked to her car, a dun-coloured Golf parked half-way down the street. All laughter gone from her voice now: 'Helen's poisonous. You're so blind. If you'd stayed clear of her you wouldn't be so sad, so threatened.' This last was accompanied by a squeeze of my hand.

'Well I think I've got the measure of Helen. The balance of power is shifting.' Was it the guarded play of light from cracked streetlamps that made her look so pitiful as she ducked into the driver's seat? I buckled myself in alongside her.

'I saw you last night, after you'd gone,' I said. 'You saw the fire? It was horrible.'

'I did,' said Eve, 'although I didn't really pay much attention.'

'I don't believe you,' I said, stunned. 'It was a terrible fire. How could you not pay attention? People died.'

'I was in a daze. I felt I had to be near you. But I didn't know where to look for you. I can't explain. It was like I was trying to find you by means other than sight. I felt manipulated, forced to move in the dark.'

I held her leg; the muscles responded and I stroked her, moving my hand under the hem of her skirt, between her thighs where she was sweating up.

'I tried to find you, afterwards,' I said. 'But you'd gone.'

'I'd gone, yes.' She moved her legs so I could reach down and curl my hand beneath her thigh. Her skin was soft and smooth, tight against its cargo of flesh. 'I felt very distant. It's happened before. At the party. While you were lying right next to me, I was trying to find you. I felt sick and dreamy and lethal. I felt like a beacon, calling danger towards me. And yet, at the same time, I wanted to protect you. I knew you were in my arms, but I was blind, snuffling around the house in the dark, trying to find your scent.'

'A girl died that night,' I said. 'She was murdered in the kitchen.'

'I know. I could almost believe that it was this sense of violence following me around that did it. I felt as though I was attracting it to you, then deflecting it away. Eve Baguley, a right old push-me-pull-you.'

I rescued my hand, but not before Eve thrust herself

against my retreating fingers. She wasn't wearing underwear and a streak of fluid painted my little finger.

'I want you, David,' she said. 'I feel sick with the need for you.'

Excited by her admission, I leant over to kiss her neck. I felt twisted and uncertain inside, an alien passion fuelled by the shock of the fire and her strange talk of stalking me in her unconscious. For the first time I saw Eve as a threat, but a vague one, without a specific agenda, powering through life with all the arbitrary destruction of weather.

She parked in virtually the same spot Seamus had chosen that first night we went out together and led me, at speed, up Moor Lane past the Dukes Playhouse and Cinema on to a narrow road. Thin sounds of a band tuning their instruments clung awkwardly to the air: the tattoo of a snare drum, the glissade of an electric guitar and a toad-like fart of bass.

'Their current single?' I asked and Eve kicked me gently.

We angled into a backstreet suffused with light. People were spilled on to the cobbles like strange litter, necking wine bottles and beer cans. A dog on a rope leash regarded the gathering with weary, cataract eyes. Everyone had remarkable hair, be it shaved (with or without pony-tail), dyed or teased into dreadlocks. I felt ridiculously conservative, settling my backside against a brood of wheelie bins while my eyes grew accustomed to the splintering light. We numbered perhaps a dozen but it seemed like many more.

'What *are* those things?' I asked Eve, whose face was bleached, free of any shadow. 'Arc lights? Isn't all this a bit over the top? The neighbours are going to go doolally, it's two in the morning!'

She shrugged then smiled and waved as a bearded figure emerged from the glare: Deep Pan. The chain between his nose and ear gleamed like a weeping scar.

He waved back before grasping the microphone which squealed its feedback protest. 'Shut the fuck up,' he growled, butting the mike, which sang even louder. 'We're The Front Bottoms. And *this* –' Deep Pan raised his arms as a chord vomited from the speakers (the vibrations of which were enough to spill an empty gallon can of Duckham's Hypergrade to the cobbles) '– is "My Fat Arse".'

'Oh my God.' The lights went down, replaced by a garish flood of purple. 'They've done a good job of it. But *The Front Bottoms*?' I said. 'My Fat *Arse*?'

But Eve couldn't hear me. The intro was coming to an end, Frank and Tonka suddenly statuesque as their chords reverberated to silence, arms raised, steel plectrums glinting. Then, over feeble harmonics:

What I lack in pitch
I make up for in punch
What I eat for breakfast
I bring back up for lunch
You might hate my haircut
You might think I suck
Well come and kiss my fat arse
'Cos I don't give a fuck

This last syllable was strung out for as long as Deep Pan's lungs could accommodate it. The song went on in a similar vein, ending abruptly. They went on to sing songs where only the titles seemed different: 'Prostitute You', 'Bone', 'Milk My Love Udder'. When the neighbours started howling complaints from upstairs windows and the police made their presence known at one end of the alleyway, The Front Bottoms turned to acoustic guitars and played a passable cover of an old Lou Reed song, Deep Pan's voice surprisingly melodic now it was devoid of any anger.

The floodlights killed, I sat with Eve towards the back of the alleyway, behind the modelled heads capped with vague light falling in from bathrooms and pale silvery streetlamps that had escaped a bricking. She leaned against me.

'You'll stay with me tonight, yes?' Eve asked, the words hot against my neck.

'I'd love to.' I felt her lips curl into a smile, her tongue press against my throat and move there. When she pulled away, cool air shaped the journey her tongue had made. She was looking directly at me. In this uncertain light her eyes were black.

I stared into them until nothing else mattered: the band became a meaningless dull constant; the people might as well be somewhere else. Eve's tattoo threatened to bloat and fall from the V of her bottle-green jumper. And then a scrape and a click and I was distracted from the kiss I was about to plant. I knew the noise – that scuff of boots with good, solid soles. She was walking away from the band, her half-length leather jacket catching the light poorly in its battered material where it gleamed like a skin of wax.

'I'm just going… for a piss,' I said, fighting to keep my voice even. Eve's hand took an age to free itself from mine; her nails clung to my cuticles with cattish tenacity.

I ran after the girl, who had already rounded the corner. The cobbles reduced my speed to an ungainly limp and threatened to send me sprawling into a bed of tired nettles running adjacent to the alleyway.

Our past keeps coming back, (sang Deep Pan)
You know she'll do for you.
His face is burning black,
There's nothing you can do.

I cast a glance back and Deep Pan was standing outside the garage, watching me. The audience were smothered in darkness but it seemed they were looking too: eyes glinting like chips of coal in a thick, black seam.

I could see Eve, wrestling with something that was spreading, stain-swift, across her chest. Or was she just dancing in and out of the shadows? The music seemed to cut off as soon as I put the corner between us. The girl was standing on the main road, looking up and down, as if checking for traffic. As I approached, she turned round and favoured me with a crooked smile. She looked just as I'd dreamed her, down to the shallow arch of her eyebrows, the burnished sheen of the buckles on her leather jacket. It was the woman who had died at the party. She showed me a number of deep wounds on her stomach and thighs. Out of her jacket pocket she pulled a claw hammer, which she buried, without ceremony, into the meat of her left eye. Then she – or rather, the driving force behind the illusion – came for me.

I ran back to the gig to find the audience vanished and a handful of people sitting on bins, smoking and sucking on bottles of beer. A cymbal shivered as it was put away.

'What took you?' asked Tonka, his eyes underlit by the orange rind of his cigarette.

'I went for a piss,' I said.

Eve lurched into me. She was thick with the smell of cider. 'David, where have you *been*? You were gone for an hour and a *half*.'

'Some piss,' said Tonka and shuffled away.

'Oh,' I said, trying not to display my shock. 'I ran into a friend and we got talking. You know.'

'Take me home, David.' She pushed a knot of keys into my palm.

'Just a sec,' I said, pushing past her. Deep Pan was alternating between fastening his mouth to a can of Red Stripe and the mouth of a girl in a catsuit.

'Pan?' I said. And then, 'Um, Deep Pan? Those lyrics, the line –'

Deep Pan's hand rolled like the closing slatted lid of a writing bureau over the jut of the girl's breast. He whispered something in her ear which made her nostrils flare and flatten as she snorted laughter.

'The line, Deep Pan, where you go –'

'Which song? Tell me the song.' His voice was oily and rough at the same time. Smooth bastard.

'Well, I don't know. I heard it as I went after… as I went off for a piss.'

'Deep Pan flicked something or nothing from my lapel. Either way, the gesture surprised me and then filled me with a kind of diluted panic; I was suddenly in the night club again, surrounded by threatening people with non-committal faces. 'What song? How can I tell you if I don't know the song, Daveness?'

'"She'll Do For You", or something like that. You sing a line that goes, "Our past is coming back", or something. And "You know she'll do for you".'

Deep Pan eyed me indulgently, smiling like a father watching his son achieve something almost impressive or worthy of comment. 'Me know no song of that description. It not in *my* repertoire, chumly.'

'But –'

'I. Said. No.' He squared up to me and his face screwed slo-mo into a moue of incredulity. 'You fucking hear me?'

Frank leaned over and touched Eve on the arm. 'Stick around. We're having a party. It wouldn't be the same.'

'I'll stay if David wants to stay.'

I shrugged, trying not to appear browbeaten by Deep Pan's swaggering. 'I'm easy.' Eve forced a look upon me. 'But I suppose I'm a little tired. It's been a long day.'

'So be it,' said Tonka. 'We'll catch up with the both of you soon.'

I led Eve back to the car park. She was very drunk. Once I'd strapped her into the passenger seat I stood a while, watching my breath mist and the curve of traffic as it sought the town centre or moved away towards Skerton Bridge. In a house somewhere near there, Seamus would be sitting with Helen, wondering why I hadn't come to visit them. Or maybe they'd be fucking each other senseless on the living room carpet. It wasn't a scenario that distressed me, perhaps because I was with Eve, perhaps because Seamus wouldn't be physically up to it.

I thought of the girl I'd dreamed – all of it; this clotted feeling that I was being pursued and the persistent threat of violence moving about beneath the surface of everything I felt or looked at. Increasingly, I believed something was trying to defeat my memory and remain hidden while my brain fought for it to be recognised. I was projecting all my suffering on to innocent objects – the nuts and bolts of it basically. It was doing my head in.

'Wake up Eve. You'll have to direct me.'

'Sorry,' she mumbled. Her eyes were all over the shop. 'I like you.'

'And I like you. Let's get you to bed, hey?'

We managed to get back to Eve's without too much trouble. 'Sweet,' she said, turning inside the circle I'd created with my arms and stepping closer. When she kissed me it was with an urgency that was almost frightening. I opened my eyes and saw hers screwed tightly shut, as if she were passing on something painful via our intimacy. 'You're so sweet,' she said, moving away.

We quested precariously through the caravan in the dark, guided by the thin light bleeding from the jamb of a door at the end.

Her room was lit by a pyramid candle resting in a tall, spiral bronze holder. A poster of a prison interior hung next to a circular mirror framed with chipped plaster, its glass misty and scarred. The ceiling, threaded with cracks and cobwebs, jerked away from us as the shadows messed with my perspective. I left her to slump on the bed and went in search of coffee. Waiting for the water to boil, I watched, through the cataract of grease and mist on the plastic window, night shift across the rooftops. In every new configuration of cloud I glimpsed a face but at the moment of recognition, they folded into something different. I poured water into two mugs of instant and carried them back to the bedroom. Eve was twisted into her duvet, in a posture only the intoxicated could find comfortable. Her legs were tucked underneath her so it seemed the knee marked her body's lower extremity. Her arms were pushed together into a Y-shape, wrists trapped between her thighs, forearms bared. Her head was pushed back into the pillow so that her throat made a rippled bridge between chest and chin. I sat on thin cushions beneath her window and looked out at the rooftops, dingy and matt in the moonless night. Drinking her coffee as well as mine, my backside growing ever more uncomfortable as it was chilled by the floor through the flimsy material, I let my focus blur and tried to tease out the last memories I could of school. There was a hazy area there, though I couldn't determine its origin – memory's capriciousness or drunken blackspot – whichever, I was stumped. I tried another avenue in: people with whom I had shared classes in the last year.

Lisa Strasser. A year or so younger than me. Her sibilants were juicy as I recall; I used to love hearing her introduce herself, as if she were salivating over the name.

Janine Gosden. Left a month before her exams because her boyfriend asked her to go to Alaska with him. She had a scar on her cheek in the shape of a key. Lovely beige skin.

And there's someone I know I'll not be able to remember, even as I tick off each of these names. Male – I know that much, but I can't conjure a face or a name. He sits in the corner of our sunlit seminar room, the yellow walls host to his shadow, so motionless it might have been painted there. Liz Bohanon. Mmmm. She wore halter tops after school. How did Seamus describe her bum now? Like two cocks fighting under a blanket? Something like that anyway. She was really nice. Boyfriend was previous year's Head Boy. Her dad was something big in toothpaste.

Iain Copestake. BO like a pan of boiled onions. His favourite word was eclectic – he certainly used it often enough. He liked to wear bandannas around his head. And sometimes circular-framed spectacles without lenses. The twat.

Daniel Hoth. Ginger hair. Hard bastard. Bit of a bully, but then, weren't we all? And a cunt when it comes to night clubs.

Me. Helen. Seamus. And… this other. Another mouthful of coffee. Cold. God I was tired. Quite why my hand should curl to a fist so readily is beyond me. And my breath thick, as though I'd just entered a sauna. I looked over to where Eve lay, contorted still, her chest now swollen, now flat. I remembered something.

The tattoo's tip, little more than a wisp of gold, writhed at the edge of her cleavage. I pulled back the hem of wool; the sweep of her breast was not enough to distract me.

I stared at the tattoo for a long time. Eve's eyes flicked open, no longer muddied with drink. She caught me by the wrist and eased me alongside her, reaching down with her other hand to unzip me. Her mouth locked on to mine and she sank the broad edge of her tongue between my teeth. Her free hand found another task and once her T-shirt was off, her bra unhooked, she moved away and swung over me, the shadows in their frenzy making unstable the geometry of her face. She dipped in to kiss me again, her breath fast and thrilling. I felt her cunt bounce against my balls and shift clear. She was still wet. I reached down to touch her and her thighs tightened and shook. She took me into her mouth and things started to go wrong. I couldn't look down at her because as she slowly moved up and down on me, her eyes were pinned on mine and I was suddenly certain that they weren't Eve's. She sidled around and I saw her heavy breasts trip across my stomach, her nipples snagging on my skin. The sight of the moth relaxed me a little as shadows descended.

I tried to enjoy myself and worked her energetically, hoping that exertion would get rid of my doubts. She perceived my athleticism as desperation and stopped sucking me.

'Not yet,' she said, and turned once more. Light flashed off her sweating back, giving the illusion of iridescent wings folded into their housing, delicate raphs spinning the light in cords of silver and green. A strange, chitinous rasp fled from her mouth as she descended on me with the precision of an insect craving nectar. Engulfed, I raised my hands to caress her breasts, trapped in the glare of those massive, compound eyes, fractured by the light. My hands mashed against her and she burst, covered me with billions of chirring spores. I was peaking, the nerves in the pit of my gut on fire. When I came, I realised that everything I'd seen had been a fiction, conjured from the splintered light ricocheting around the room. I was crying.

'Follow me towards the light,' Eve murmured, collapsing beside me and blowing out the candle. But not before I'd fallen for another trick: I appeared to be covered with gold dust from her body.

I dreamed immediately.

Eve was flying through a storm, her fragile wings struggling against the wind and the cargo she was hauling. I swung below her, knitted into a purse made from her spittle. We were travelling towards a coal of orange light. I was naked and vulnerable, but I felt protected because Eve was here. Behind me I could hear the awful, desperate noises of pursuit but couldn't twist in my net to see what was causing them. I looked up, following the spinning thread that connected me to Eve. Her wings were beating unsteadily, and every time a volley of rain drops impacted upon her soft body, a cloud of gold powder plumed out of her. I couldn't see her face to define the extent of her pain. I was as helpless as a babe but Eve radiated security and confidence with each stroke of her wings. She might have been ancient, such was her depth of wisdom, experience and control. She was my guiding light. Yet if she was trying to save me, she was likely to be my downfall too, because she was like a beacon, brilliant enough to attract others who weren't so benevolent.

The thrashing at my shoulder grew more pronounced. The heady reek of petrol suggested that the storm was formed of something more complex than rain. The coal flared before us, Eve drawn inexorably on, fascinated by its colours, its persistent chimeric dance. Awash in fuel, anaesthetised by the ignorance of dreams, I only realised I was burning when my skin turned black and shiny and the smell of my flesh cooking consumed me.

I walked most of the way back to Morecambe and managed to hail a taxi just as my feet were about to call it a day. My back was beginning to complain anyway, and, even though I could ill afford it, I felt I deserved spoiling in this way. The cabbie dropped me off on Regent Road just as a knackered yellow light staggered over the lip of the bay. Though I needed my bed, I decided to watch the sun come up. I felt compassion for our nearest star; one of those embarrassing, tender morning thoughts that would make me cringe later on. Reaching the barrier, I drew some of that semi-rotting sea air into my lungs and trawled the horizon for ships with eyes that weren't up to the task. The sea was pegged back, seemingly tucked under the leading edge of far-off land; the crenellated sand – where it wasn't bruised with oil – gave the impression it was shifting, dune-like, the longer I stared at it.

The stone jetty made itself known through a grey sleeve of mist at the end of which the lighthouse pulsed with a light so weak I was unconvinced as to its worth. I walked back to the guest house and closed the door of my room; picked up various phone messages that had been slipped under by my landlord on my way to the bed.

Helen called, 8pm
Helen called again, 8.30pm
And again! 9pm, 10pm Perhaps you should of left a mesage with us?

I tossed the sheaf of notes away and watched as one of them landed on the material which shrouded a stack of frames leaning against the wall beneath my sink. It reminded me of what I had to do. Guardedly, I pulled back the corner of paint-stained cloth and riffled through the canvases, wincing now and again when I saw a painting that had not come off. By the time I'd searched the pile I felt a bit depressed; nothing I'd created boasted any verve, any nerve. All of it was too safe and parochial. From there, I went to the older stuff I had stored in my suitcase down in the landlord's garage. He'd shoved the bag into an alcove above a shelf crammed with boxes of after-dinner mints, instant chocolate custard mix and sachets of ketchup. I unzipped the case and a painting fell into my hand. I knew it was the one even before I'd turned it over to look at the picture. A moth. I'd been quite proud of it at the time – I'd painted it while at school – but now I could see how poorly I'd executed the strokes: the paint was applied too thickly, the moth's anatomy was a joke and I'd tried to treat the wings to a little yellow and brown once my gold supply had run out. Still, the history of the painting was irrelevant. What mattered was the likeness of the moth, in shape, posture and tone to the tattoo on Eve's left breast. This was that, magnified. It seemed to swell and deflate even as I watched it, as if it was being powered by its own heart or that of another, like Eve's had been.

A sudden bark of static broke the quiet outside, followed by a voice foaming in its wake. The doorbell rang. I slipped downstairs and opened it on two police officers, their walkie-talkies chattering. I couldn't be sure if they were the same ones that had been trying to trace the car owner last night – this morning. They asked for Terry but I didn't need to fetch him; he appeared behind me, bleary-eyed, shambling. Maureen took up the rear, her arms folded around her chest. The policemen didn't say anything; they merely beckoned to Terry and Maureen and when I made to follow, they pointed at me and raised their eyebrows.

Seeing them there, in the street, looking up at Duncan's window – Terry's face creasing with concern and Maureen quickly looking away – I thought *fuck this*, shut the door and legged it upstairs. The police soon found their voices and shouted, imaginatively: 'Oi!'

'Duncan!' I shouted, slamming my palm flat against the door. I briefly thought about asking to see his socket spanners, that would get him moving, but there was no response. The door wasn't locked.

I had a look in the room and the next thing I knew I was answering questions in an interview booth in a Lancaster

166

police station. I was telling them what I'd seen and heard that night – including the coat behind the bathroom door, which I now realised wasn't a coat at all – while a small part of me had locked itself away and was combing through the detail of Duncan's bed asking itself again and again whether what it had seen was real. Whether it might be possible for him to still be able to breathe with his lungs externalised.

By the time they let me go, it was getting on for lunchtime. I hadn't eaten and I was ravenous. I was wondering what I should have: a sandwich, maybe, or a bowl of soup, and I couldn't make up my mind. I started panicking, knowing that if I didn't eat something I would die. The inability to think, the seemingly total lack of substantial difference between life and death drained me and I sank to my knees, gasping with fear, now conscious only of my heart and the minuscule lurches of horror when it paused between each beat.

I called Helen.

'I know what you're going to say, and yes, I probably am one.'

'You're a cunt too, while we're at it.' Her voice was hoarse, as though she'd been smoking too many cigarettes.

'Thank you. Did you have a productive meeting?'

'Fuck off.'

'Shall we have a productive conversation?' I oughtn't be so cocky but I couldn't help it. I was being pulled two ways over Eve and the other stuff; I didn't want Helen to lay claim to another part of me: I'd only just managed to jettison her.

'Will you come round tonight?' Now she sounded soft-spoken, almost afraid.

'To Seamus' house?'

'Yes. I'm still there. We didn't do anything last night other than watch a video.' She sounded like she was trying to reassure me. 'You made it very hard. I couldn't relax, David. I'd geared myself up for our talk and I kept expecting you to arrive so I couldn't get it out of my system.'

'So why didn't you talk to Seamus about it?'

'But I can't till you're here. It's what we agreed. There's no point unless you're here. Jesus, David. Don't you get it?'

'Okay. I'll be there tonight. What time?'

'Eight.'

'Fine. And how is Seamus?'

'He's okay. Gets me to run around after him. You?'

There was the suggestion of a hint of a trace of compassion in her voice. 'My back gets a bit painful if I walk too far. Otherwise, I'm comfortable.'

'And sleep? Do you sleep?'

I thought of myself arcing through the sky, chased by a wall of fire. I thought of Duncan, opened up like a strange, bloody flower. 'Like the dead.'

'I feel I know what's following us, David. I feel this close to it being given a name. I smell it constantly. I keep expecting it to walk straight through the door.'

Instead of agreeing with her, I said: 'What do you smell?'

'Oh, all kinds. Blackcurrant. And toffee. Children's things. Conkers. Do you smell anything?' Helen sounded dangerously close to tears.

'Petrol and smoke. And I see figures I can't recognise.' I didn't want her to psychoanalyse what I'd just divulged so I told her what I had been intending to keep mum about. 'Listen, I hope you don't mind but, well, I went to see Pol yesterday.'

She was quiet for a moment. 'You sneaky bastard. I haven't seen her for years. What right have you –'

'She told me you'd been involved in a drowning.'

'What?'

'I mean, that you'd tried to save a girl who'd fallen into the Lune. But she drowned. You never said anything.'

'You are talking shit, Munro. That is a bunch of shit.' Her voice was quaking, filled with knives.

'No. Pol was adamant.'

I heard her breathing as she tried to control her rage.

'Helen? What's wro –'

'Where did you go after you'd seen Pol?' Her voice was seeking normality but there was too much distress.

'I went to meet Eve.'

'Why?'

'Why not?'

'She's poisoning you.'

'There's a phrase involving a pot, a kettle and the colour black. Do you know it?'

'God David, you've become a vicious swine.'

'I've been taught by an expert.'

'I don't want to fight with you,' she sighed. Of course not, not when it seemed I was winning for once. 'I'll see you tonight. Please come.'

'What about this drowning?' But she'd hung up. I put the phone down. Once the receiver was cradled, it rang.

'Hello?' There was still a little gruffness about my manner so I hoped it was Helen calling back to rake over some more ashes.

'David, it's Eve. I missed you this morning. When did you leave?'

I felt instantly revitalised, more alive than I could understand. It was as instant and invigorating as ducking into a shower after the enervation of a sauna. Despite the fact that so many people expected of me and my fear that I was unequal to their demands, I was able to summon more cheer and optimism than I believed I owned. 'Eve, yes. I'm sorry but I left after making sure you were okay. I didn't feel too good myself. I didn't want to hang around and give you the breakfast-time spectacle of me with my head down the bog.'

'Okay.' But in that word I noticed an entire spectrum of suspicion and regret. 'Perhaps we should call this off. I mean, every time I talk to you, I see Helen in your eyes.'

A fat bubble of pain burst behind my eyes; my throat was sucked dry of moisture. Suddenly, everything looked dim and shaded, like the deep cross-hatchings in a cartoon by Robert Crumb. 'No,' I said. 'Not after last night. You made me happen last night. It was like cracking open a barrier and pulling out the real me…' I imagined myself saying this to Helen and almost barked laughter – Helen would have torn me apart. 'I need you. You… you're opening doors for me.'

I probably couldn't have admitted it then, but I don't think I'd have been able to carry on without Eve being there. Although she was now my lover, I found it difficult to see her as something other than my guardian.

nine
in vino veritas

We arranged to meet at lunchtime. 'By the light-house, why not?' Eve had said. The wind was up, as it always seemed to be whenever I got near the sea. The coastline opposite was teased from cast iron; burnished cavities, like those in a steel drum, were pitted with house-scars. Like a brief pencil scoring, smoke from a chimney linked hill with heaven. I strained to see people but other than the odd glint of light on a car window, there were none of the usual signs.

Fingers clasping the frigid railings at the pier end, I looked into the water. The sea worked like a muscle beneath my feet, clenching and squirting the water away in slow, massive spasms. I checked my watch. Eve was late and I was hungry. Leaning back against the railing, I watched the traffic hug the shopfronts. Funny how it remained constantly busy while the numbers of people shrank. Christmas was spreading across the awnings like slow fire but its promise seemed empty, all exterior, just like the shops its strange, tinsel ivy clung to. I took out a sketch book and opened it to the most recently used page, a quick drawing of Salcombe harbour choked with boats. I'd spent last summer there and though the weather had been sullen, seeing this representation was enough to fill me with a cloying, immediate nostalgia. It felt like a part of me so much more distant, like a holiday enjoyed as a child, shaped by the simplest of pleasures, like a scoot around an unremarkable funfair, an ice-cream on a freezing beach, flying a kite. I turned the page and pressed the stub of my pencil to the textured paper, waiting until their alien marriage felt less stifling. Quickly, I outlined the basic pattern of the street, growing bolder as my affinity with the graphite returned. The Midland Hotel looked suitably shoddy, as did the corrugated prow of the leisure centre. When I'd finished, I made a few notes about colour and turned my attention to the peeled boats gulping in the bay. I sketched them too, looking back down the pier to see if Eve was approaching. Sometimes the bay would be visited by scaups and bar-tailed godwits, plovers and whimbrels. But I'd never seen any. Perhaps because I didn't know what the hell they looked like. And Eve was forty minutes late. Well, fuck this for a game of soldiers. Moving alerted me to the force of the wind. It made my mouth misshapen and flapped my cheeks like astronauts pulling G. I looked down and felt my hair spread until the crown was bared. My suede boots were tanned with sand, blasted with craters of dried salt. Rain fell just as I walked on to the main road. I ran to the café and nestled into a chair, hanging my coat on its back and wiped my sketchbook free of water.

'Be?' asked the owner. His hair was lank with grease but then so was his café.

'Coffee, please. And a toasted tea-cake.' This he laboriously chiselled into his order-book with a constipated expression.

'Else?' he muttered, already turning away.

'No thanks.' I reached over to the next table and slid the abandoned tabloid towards me. For a moment, I thought I'd misread the date as five years previously. I caught the word 'faceless' and read about a male corpse found buried not a hundred yards from where he'd once shared a house with his lover. His face had been battered so badly, the features had turned to pulp. I turned to the sports pages, unable to shake off the image or why it bothered me so. Before my coffee came I'd grown jittery and in need for fresh air. My tea-cake landed shortly after, butter hardened like wax, napkin exten-

sively creased, as though someone had tried the origami
approach and given up.

'Joyamil,' said Mr Enthusiasm, though a tea-cake and
coffee hardly comprised something that substantial. I wolfed
the lot and hopped about at the till while he jabbed his finger
into the old-style cash register, offering a grunt of satisfaction
when it finally shot its tongue out and allowed him to
agonise over the change.

'Forget it,' I said. 'Stick it in the charity jar.' And out, and
out. Jesus, I felt pumped up with the need to scream or run for
ever. Once that option occurred to me I took off, sprinting as
fast as I could, and then flying faster, the whistling rain (as the
night often did) providing the illusion that I was running
more quickly than was credible.

Drenched, I ducked into a vacant phone booth and rang
Eve. No answer. My breath, amplified to something alarm-
ingly ragged, deflected back into my face, turning it cold.

Back at the guest house I scrubbed myself dry with a
towel and made a pot of tea while my landlord and landlady
went on about annual rainfall, grouting and how they
weren't racists, just culturalists.

In my room, I set the easel up by the window and slotted a
piece of paper beneath the clips. My paints looked dirty; the
bright colours tainted. I soaked a stiff brush in hot water and
worked out how I'd approach this from the sketch in my
book but then I thought, no rules, just do it. Ten minutes later,
I had a satisfying cobalt wash, steadily layered so that the
upper most part of the canvas was thinnest, barely touched.
This would do for the sky. I let it dry while I had lunch and
came back to it feeling enthusiastic, despite the stolid urban
nothingness it represented. In went the suggestion of buildings; I was pleased with the diminishing perspective, something which usually failed me. The lights I managed to turn
into fragmented stars, accentuating the presence of rain.

I called Eve. No answer.

Hills became ghosts in the background, so faint they
might have been made of the paper itself, rather than any of

the colour it had leached from my brush. I stopped when I felt I should start fiddling with what I had done.

I switched on the radio in time to hear the closing bars of the first Christmas carol of the year. Rather than make me feel mawkish, it infused me with warmth; I felt newly charitable towards Helen and Seamus. I would take some beer round tonight and try to fluff up the solemnity a little. As long as we were together and able to pool our knowledge, we'd be safe from whatever wanted to cause us any harm. If harm was what it wanted to mete out. And could we be really sure that this wasn't all one huge, shared nightmare, a *folie à trois* that we had infected each other with? I kept thinking of that face – so much like a thick, pale cake mix having something like cochineal folded into it. And the events that went on around me, seemingly pre-ordained so that they would occur whether or not I was around to witness them yet significant to me because they appeared to take place specifically so I would notice them. The tree falling in its forest: would there be a noise if nobody were there to hear it?

Mum was in when I called. I felt confident all this malarkey would be settled by Christmas and told her I'd be home to spend New Year with them. Inspiring to think that I'd be able to leave all this dross behind in a stale year that had promised little and delivered less. I told her my back felt fine when she asked, and after saying goodbye, went to check in the bathroom mirror. The skin looked very clean now that the scab had cleared; the scar was like a cut through a meat pudding: something black and encrusted welled in the gash, surrounded by pale and doughy flesh, still swollen. When I moved, the skin grew shiny and taut. Pain moved sluggishly inside, as though my nerves had forgotten how to work properly.

The afternoon was bruising. I called Eve. No answer.

'Shit.'

I thought about Duncan and had to get outside again. I felt wound-up, like a clockwork toy. I was desperate to relax but I didn't have any neutral zones. Every location I thought of

was a scene in the drama. I grabbed my sketch book and
walked.

The man in the gaberdine coat worked the far end of the
beach, tucked under the protective shadow of The Battery.
His dog lolloped around at his feet until, bored with the
ceaseless sweep of his master's detector, he lay down on a
rock and watched the seagulls.

I half-heartedly sketched the dog, keeping an eye on the
man's progress. What was he looking for? I must have seen
him every time I came anywhere near the beach but I had yet
to witness him digging anything up.

'I think,' Eve said, dipping her head to lick my ear, 'the
man in the gaberdine coat is a spy.'

'Oh really,' I said, turning to kiss her. 'Who's he spying
on?'

'You and me. He's recording this conversation too with an
ultra-sensitive microphone. Watch.' She wetted her lips and
whispered: 'Hey, man in the coat, I want to suck you off.'

The man jerked upright and looked in our direction. I
laughed, surprised by the coincidence and rested my head
against her leg. The anger I'd felt had vanished. It didn't
matter that she hadn't turned up on time or had left me spinning like a scrap of paper in the wind. It didn't matter how
panicked I'd become. She was here now. That's what
mattered. I looked up at her face, the strong chin and the
whorls of fair hair on her jawline. The broad mouth. The
pulse in her throat. A blue vein, fine as thread, worming
across her temples. I felt whole. I felt nourished.

'I wish I knew what he was looking for,' I said, shading,
without any great conviction, the dark areas beneath the
dog's body.

'Come on then,' Eve said, pushing me away. 'Let's find
out. Come on.'

I followed her down to the sand where she was trotting
towards the figure. The dog stopped panting and watched,
its body suddenly becoming more poised, as though scent-
ing prey.

When I caught up with her, she was finishing off a question. '– well known for that then?' was all I heard.

He shrugged. Guiltily regarding the worn handle of his metal detector, he stuck out a hand and I shook it. The skin was very cold and smooth as soap.

'David,' said Eve, 'this is Grainne Chawney. He's an archaeologist.'

'An archaeologist? In Morecambe? What are you expecting to find? Fossilised chip forks? Prehistoric Screwball cartons?'

'No, he's looking for bodies.'

'Fascinating,' I said, feeling a jolt as I wondered what might be under the sand. It sucked at my feet here, where it was gluey with water. I thought of the photograph Seamus had shown me of Dale Paris, taken just a matter of hours before his death. He had no clue, as he smiled into the lens, of what was to befall him. Or was there some kind of sign after all, some omen that one noticed but thought nothing of? Were dreams different, in the final, breathing sleep? Did animals shy away, smelling death? Dale Paris would be dressed as he was in that photograph still, but he'd be bones now.

'What's the range?' I asked, reaching for the detector, which he passed to me.

'Not great,' he said. He had a gentle American accent. 'Six, maybe eight feet.'

'Shallow graves,' I said. 'I wouldn't have thought that Morecambe Bay was a tipping site for corpses.'

'I'm here because of the chapel, really. There's a lot of stuff emerging in the cliff as the sea erodes it. We found a bone comb last week. Twelfth century.'

'Jesus, really?' I said. And then the detector went off.

I'd been ranging it around the sand by my feet. 'It must be one of the eyes in my boot,' I suggested.

Chawney's tongue spun around the tight O of his mouth.

'Ooh, exciting,' said Eve. 'Let's dig it up. Could be a fortune.'

'Could be a barrel of nuclear waste,' I said, cheerily.

Chawney took out a trowel and hacked at the sand. 'I've been up and down this beach for hours,' he spat, 'and you come along and hit pay dirt straight off.'

'Sorry,' I said, happy to leave him and his rusty old tins in peace.

'You never know what you'll find. There could be horses and carts down here. Lots of places in this bay where the sand is unstable. Suck you down quick as you like. I know – ah, shit. What's this?'

He surfaced, sand coating his knees and the cuffs of his shirt. He held a curved black mass in his hand; it was about the same size as his palm. He started scrubbing at it with an old toothbrush from his jacket pocket.

'Looks like a soap dish,' Eve said.

'I'm going to get this back to my room,' Chawney said. 'Got some stuff to clean it with there. Want to come? I can show you some of the other things I've found.'

I handed his detector back. I was going to decline but Eve was already pulling me after him. His dog, which he intro-duced as IQ, followed at a distance.

Chawney lived in a flat above the Gingham Café, on the seafront road amid dozens of guest houses, cheap markets and amusement arcades. His living room was bare but for a low table covered with audio tapes. *Vincent Price reads Edgar Allen Poe*, I saw. There was also a box of cheap paperbacks in a corner and a lurching futon, covered with a throw that looked as if it had done some time as a shroud. IQ sensibly ignored it and flopped down by the books. A plastic tray of cress on the windowsill wasn't up to much. Neither was Chawney, who was looking out at the sea.

'Would either of you like a drink? I've got banana Nesquik or Cup-a-Soup. Leek that is. With croutons.'

'Coffee please, doctor,' said Eve, falling into the futon and trading places with about ten pounds of dust.

'No coffee, I'm afraid. Ditto tea. I can't stand the stuff. And it's professor. But you can call me Grainne.' He was rotating the artefact in his hands, turning it this way and that in the

light. 'You know, I think I know what this is. Won't be a mo'.'
He stepped through a door and pulled it behind him. The
door failed to snick shut and swung back slightly into the
living room. Blue and white floor tiles, smeared with grime.
The end section of a melamine wall unit. A dried-up plant in
a pot on the floor.

I heard water rushing into a steel sink.

'Let's go, Eve,' I said. 'This bloke's a nutter. He doesn't like
tea.'

Eve pressed a finger to her lips and, glancing once at the
kitchen door, hitched up her skirt. She wasn't wearing any
knickers. She yawned wetly at me as she spread her legs.
Using the finger she'd hushed me with, she rubbed at herself
until she was red and my throat was dry. Even the dog's ears
pricked up.

'As I thought,' came Chawney's voice. 'I had to give it a bit
of a seeing-to but it's come up nice and clean now.'

Eve raised her eyebrows and I brayed laughter. She repo-
sitioned her skirt. As Chawney returned to the room, she
began sucking the tip of her finger. I found it difficult to sit
down.

'It's a palate,' he said. 'A human one, still attached to part
of the jawbone. Over thirty years old. Look, you can see some
of the teeth contain fillings.'

'Well,' I said. 'Shouldn't that go to the police?'

'I'm sure it should. But it isn't going anywhere. I'm having
it. Come and have a look at the rest of my stash. Most of this
is from Heysham –' he'd disappeared into the kitchen again
'– some pretty rich pickings in Heysham. But you've got to
watch out for the shit they pump into the sea from that
damned power station. You'll see me in waders most of the
time. And a mask. I'm not stupid.'

I followed him into the kitchen. There was an ironing
board set up in the corner with a heap of grey clothing on it.
He was digging around in a wicker basket, holding up trin-
kets that I couldn't identify. 'Bracelet, bronze. Bone comb I
was telling you about. Coins, last century. Pen inscribed *Willy*

loves Edna. Must be seventy years old at least. Bet I could get it working again.'

'Shouldn't all this stuff go to a museum?' I asked, not really caring one jot because I could now see that the clothing on the ironing board wasn't clothing after all. It was a great heap of skin, divested of bulk and bone, oily with some kind of moisturising unguent.

'I'm sure it should. But it isn't going anywhere. I'm having it,' he repeated.

I could see the shape of the arm, the hairs standing out on it. The hand was like an empty Marigold. A pale band indicated where a wedding ring had been. The light dimmed. I felt a hot flush at the base of my neck. Neither Eve nor Chawney were speaking. One of the fingers moved. I turned slightly and looked up through a sudden prickle of sweat. Eve was moving silently around the back of Chawney, who had become thinner, as though he was losing his substance to the heat of the room. Pain rippled into the centre of my skull and I retched. I didn't feel at all well.

'Okay?' asked Chawney, his head folding towards me.

Eve appeared through him, as he finally lost his solidity and I lurched towards the door which had somehow become just another section of wall.

'Watch out!' Eve yelled, scooping an arm beneath one of my flailing limbs.

Somehow I staggered outside without falling over. The sodden air revived me a little as I set off down the promenade, fearful of a return to my own room; it was too much like being in a cell and anyway, despite the cleaning-up that had been done, I was certain I could still smell the sour reek of fear and shit whenever I passed Duncan's door. I heard Eve behind me, and as her hand dropped on my arm there was a squeal of tyres as someone slammed on the brakes. I turned in time to see a small boy nudged slightly by a severely dipping Sierra at the pedestrian crossing. It tipped him over and the bag of aniseed balls he was holding scattered across the road.

'God –' I began.

'He's all right,' said Eve, tightening her grip although she hadn't bothered to look.

I allowed her to steer me back on course and we walked in silence while my body tingled with an unbearable itch. I felt that my surroundings – the people, the buildings, the seagulls – were stamped with some kind of mark, a potential. That at any moment they would reveal their true purpose instead of simply carrying on as they had been for however long their existence had lasted. It felt like the one time I had tried MDMA. Suddenly, the skin of everything around me had seemed transparent. I'd been afraid to look down at the ground in case I saw its hidden secrets.

'He's got his socket spanners,' I said.

'What?' she laughed.

'Duncan… when Duncan went off to that great Do-It-All in the sky, Terry the landlord was in there, pocketing his socket spanners. High-level wanker that he is. I'll spanner his fucking arse for him if he comes near me.'

'Come on,' she said, steering me into the unwelcoming dark of Davy Jones's Locker, a subterranean pub with a pool table and a constantly changing chalkboard menu of real ale. Witch's Biff was on sale today. 7.2 per cent. When Eve asked me what I was having I pointed at the menu.

'What is a biff, exactly?' I asked the barman. He shook his head.

'We took our drinks to the window which afforded a view of the little gulley by the access stairway and occasional shins. I put a song on the juke box – 'Seaweed' by Tindersticks.

'Cheery,' Eve said.

'Yeah. I was going to put on Nirvana's "Rape Me" but that would have been just too darned positive.'

'Are you okay now?' she soothed, rubbing the back of my hand with her fingers.

'I'm fine,' I said, a little too stridently. 'But that Chawney bloke? Jesus… he needs some attention…'

Eve pouted. 'He was interesting. He only wanted to show us what he was working on. Probably lonely.'

'He's a grave-robber. There must be laws against what he's doing. He's got a bloody morgue in his room. Above the Gingham Café, for God's sake. Bloody Ed Gein living above the Gingham Café! Papers'd have a field day.'

'Okay,' Eve said, holding up her hand to calm me. The barman looked over then went back to cultivating the smears on his beer glasses.

She said: 'I'm worried about you. There are things troubling you that should be out in the open. I can help you, David. You've such a sadness in you.'

'Stop it,' I barked, sloshing biff all over my T-shirt. 'I'm going to have another drink. Want one?'

She didn't give up on me but I couldn't work out what she was trying to do. It seemed she was trying to reach inside me with her words and dredge something from the silt of my past. I felt empty and cold, even though she was getting closer, sliding a leg over mine, pressing her lips to my throat as she spoke, as she worked at me.

I was drunk before long, but she continued to talk. When I was able, I concentrated on her mouth but I couldn't identify anything in the burble of her speech. Her rhythms and patterns meandered through my brain like a drug, pulling at my base emotions while a part of me was cold and distant, unable to key into their code.

'We've all got a skeleton to rattle,' she said, the first sentence I'd cottoned on to for a while.

It wasn't that she was being intrusive, like a partner who feels they have a claim over their lover's past and feels betrayed if the extent of their own disclosure isn't matched. She didn't dig for secrets like a pig rooting for truffles, unmoved by the hurt it might cause me. It was like being subtly frisked by a hand that would only go further if I subconsciously allowed it.

She said: 'It will kill you in the end.'

I pushed away from her and went to the gents. In the raw

striplight above the mirror, I travelled the blasted salt plains of my own face. The twin suns of my eyes, raging red and swollen, were sinking fast into a dusk I didn't want to rise from.

Eve barrelled in through the door and I caught her reflection a moment before I turned round. *It's because I'm pissed*, I thought as she slung an arm around me and manoeuvred me outside. *It's because I'm pissed that she appears not to have a head…*

'How far is it?' I wailed, trying to keep the border between the sea and the sky roughly horizontal. If we didn't get back to Eve's caravan soon, she was going to be wearing four pints of chunky biff.

'I've come to a decision about "biff",' I announced. 'It must be another word for "piss". Not that I've ever drunk piss, I hasten to add. And certainly not the witch variety. As undoubtedly that would possess magical qualities and would probably turn me into a badger. Or a small piece of earthenware pottery.'

'Are you going to shut up?' hissed Eve, buckling under the strain.

'That thing on his ironing board,' I said, to break the alcohol's spell, knowing exhaustedly that I was invoking another. 'That thing…'

'It was a pile of washing,' Eve said. 'Nothing to worry about.'

'He had a stack of bones –'

'Driftwood collected for his stove. David, you're shivering. You'll have to learn to relax.'

'How can I when you're near?' I said, rounding on her. 'Every time I see you I feel marked. I feel as though a sniper's drawing a bead on me. I don't know who the hell you are. When I see you I want to simultaneously fuck you until I'm knackered and run a mile. I want to crawl inside you and sleep for ever. You scare me to death and you thrill me.'

'Then you're ready,' she said, her voice losing its playfulness, her face now blanked into a serious sheet.

'Ready for what?' Her hand felt like the scrape of dry bone against my skin as she took hold of me.

'History lesson.'

We returned to the path and I noticed my line of vision had changed. It seemed as though I was looking the wrong way down a pair of binoculars. The periphery had become charred with shadow. The huge hotel on the corner of Broadway was a hulking suggestion; the homogeneous flats that took over from the guest houses as Morecambe's focus diminished were a series of flat blocks, like umber strokes from a broad brush. My back to the sea, I could have been anywhere. I saw the suggestion of a body to my left, struggling along the floor as it pulled itself along by its stumps. It flailed a vestigial limb at us as we came abreast of it. Eve kicked it away before I could see. The stink of rot filled my nostrils.

'What do you mean, history lesson?' I said, my tongue treacly with fatigue. I was sweating heavily. At one point it felt as though we were walking a field, the ground yielding beneath us. I could smell freshly cut grass and see goalposts. Ahead, a railway viaduct slunk across a brook like a series of giant stocks.

'There's a dead part in you. You know it well. You walk there often. You know its population. You know its roads. Before long –' her voice susurrant, a skein of dry leaves on a pavement, '– you'll be there for good, unless you *excise* it.'

Then the path swam back into view. We were at the tall, wrought-iron gates of the fun fair. Chains and locks looped around the struts like the preface to an escape act. The next moment, they were behind me but I couldn't remember climbing them. Whenever I glanced at Eve, I felt a bolt of fear and panic ride up between my balls, lacing my spine with dread. I'd stall but she'd gee me on, and I'd have to force myself to believe that the macerated, dribbling aspect to her face was due to my current fugue.

'I feel awful,' I gasped.

'That's because we're here now,' she said. 'The badlands of your head. You've allowed it to slip through the walls you've built around it all these years.'

A path led down the centre of the fun fair, bisecting a crude conglomeration of huts and turrets, stalls and tinsel pagodas. Eve's hand was a hot bundle eclipsing mine as we drew abreast of the first: a lifeless, splintered portacabin painted purple and done up to resemble a Romany grotto. The sign was gone, its ghost remained. *Fortunes told*, it might have said. I was beginning to feel a little better. My sight had returned and Eve no longer bore those hideous, unsettled scars.

'Have you ever crossed anybody's palm with silver?' Eve said. 'Ever been told what the future holds for you?' The sky was curdling, late afternoon greys gravitating to a point above the horizon like a sheet being tucked down the side of a bed.

'No, I've not,' I said, testily, still struggling with my tiredness and the threat of regression. 'I believe in making your own destiny. I don't think there's anything mapped out for me.'

'Really?' Eve gentled, sounding as though she knew better, sounding as though her mouth had a wry smile all over it. We went deeper into the park, taking in the silent, façade-like aspect of the various rides and sideshows. A doughnut and candy floss caravan lurched almost in defiance of gravity's laws; a child's ride – giant tea-cups and tiny helicopters – creaked in its immobility, the massive central bolt around which the seats spun broken in two. The ghost train seemed untouched by the damage, but only because its original cosmetics acted as camouflage. Scorch marks streaked across machinery and mouldings; burned oil created tarry scars in the grass. The cages of a lethal-looking ride hung from their supporting arms, melted by high temperatures into smooth, grotesque knots. The fire-hungry prizes arranged on one of the stalls offering dart challenges (*Score under 50 to win! No trebls, no doubls, evry dart must score in seperat beds. No argument*) had turned into a black cluster, like dirty, solidified detergent bubbles.

'I feel like a character in a Ray Bradbury story,' I said. Eve still had a curl to her lips. I kissed it away and when I moved back, I smelled woodsmoke. At first I thought I was having some terrible flashback linked to the awfulness of that night.

'Are you all right?' she asked. A plane of smoke drifted between us. It snagged against one of the scoops of her hair and twisted into her face, looping with it, once again making her seem insubstantial, of rather than in the smoke. Her eyes appeared in a pocket of calm but I couldn't see the flesh in which they must be cradled. I didn't want to lose her, or the grip on my fear, which was dwindling rapidly, so I clenched her hand even more tightly. 'Something is still burning here,' I said, relieved that there had to be something corporeal on fire, rather than the conviction of my eager imagination. I took a quick scan around, and my eye was caught by movement at the entrance. There was a figure standing there but it wouldn't remain constant in my line of vision. It kept dissolving and fading into the background colour, before morphing into some new shape. It was trying to make contact, I felt, but its vocal cords sounded blasted. A rasp lifted and lost itself to the wind. I was about to approach when I sensed movement behind me. Eve was gone. In my hand was a bunch of combusted sticks.

'Your history,' came her voice. 'It's on fire.'

'Where are you?' I called, my lungs filling up with what tasted like smoke from a barbecue. 'Jesus, Eve.' I staggered forward, choking on the meaty, greasy fumes. My eyes were streaming. I didn't know what I was going to do first: choke to death on my imminent vomitus or suffocate. I dragged a handkerchief from my pocket and covered my nose and mouth. My hand touched wood and I felt my way around what felt like a rickety fence until I was standing amid a crowd of trees. The smoke was thinner here, unable to develop itself among the divisive branches. Wads of smoke clung to the heights like strange nests.

Then there was movement, finally. Something drifting towards me through the blue mist. Slinking low and sinuous, a wind of muscle and fur. The cat sat a little distance away from me, observing me as I shivered and spluttered into my handkerchief. Catching my gaze, it hooked me and flung me twenty years into the past. I realised I hadn't thought of the cat on the school field in all that time, the way we'd lured it with little clicks and blown kisses. The way we'd scratched its head and listened for the purr. The way we twisted its head till the bone splintered and a red comma of blood flicked out from its mouth. Taking a Bic to its brilliant eyes.

And God, that wasn't all I was remembering…

Some time later I came up from a dream in which I was the perpetrator of every murder – real, screen or otherwise – that I had ever witnessed or read about. I dragged around the agony from every knifing, hail of bullets, garrote, drowning, explosion in a clear sac that was attached directly to my heart. It was a milky fluid that sloshed about. Different expressions of pain and suffering pressed against the membrane. 'Heaven marching,' they mouthed, before sinking back into the effluvia. Then I realised that it wasn't the physical pain that was my burden but the consequential torment that I visited on relatives and friends. I surfaced, sure I was suffocating, but the only thing that was stopping my breath was the scream that filled my throat.

Helen answered on the first ring.

'It's Seven Arches,' I said.

'Don't I know it.' She sounded hollow and tired.

'What happened?'

She told me. 'Fuck,' I said. 'What now?'

'Have you tried Shay?'

'No,' I replied. 'Do you want me to?'

'Forget it,' she said, her voice suddenly alert. 'I tried and there was no answer. Better we should just go round to see him. Can you borrow a car?'

'No problem,' I said, doubting that Terry would allow me the use of his Toyota.

'Pick me up. I'll be waiting outside the shop.'

I put the payphone receiver down and the ding from the bell echoed comfortably in the small alcoves of the ground floor. I sat back on the PVC pouffe and rubbed my eyes. Terry's footfalls made soft impacts above my head as he crossed the landing. 'Here's a bulb for you,' he said. 'Hundved watt, is that all vight?'

I heard Eiger's reply – 'Buggered if I know' – and a door snick shut.

The kitchen was empty but a pall of cigarette smoke hung above the dining table. The sound of a car starting up. I went to the window in time to see Maureen take off in her Peugeot. I returned to the door to their living quarters and tried it. It opened on a room struggling to be identified under a weight of clashing decor. Paisley wallpaper, striped corduroy sofa covers, a carpet like a map of the cosmos. There was a fish tank burbling away like a container of simmering soup. On top of the lid I hit gold. I snatched Terry's keys and slipped out the back, vaulting the gate and legging it along the alley to the car. I was in Heysham seven minutes later.

ten
seven arches

We said not a word on the journey back: a nightmare ride. Seamus' breath was a wet burbling in his chest which sounded inches from my ear. Helen drifted into the oncoming traffic on a few occasions and was rewarded with horns and flashed headlights. Luckily, the Marine Road was pretty quiet, though we had a panic when the snout of a police Rover quested into the road ahead of us. Helen seemed to get a grip of herself and guide the Mini more sedately past the dormant guest houses, in the windows of which sat mannequin-still people topped off with grey hair, perhaps sleeping, perhaps watching the sea as it filled the bay. A group of students nestled in the shade beneath the awning of the Gingham Café. And the lighthouse fastened all of this to the past, its beacon describing a line which bisected my eyes, filling my immediate world with light and snow. God, I was hammered. Seamus had been passing round a large hip flask of neat vodka – well, we had been passing it back and forth between ourselves; Helen was too busy building a hill of cigarette butts to join in.

Helen parked the car by the florist's off Heysham Road and we listened to the ticking of the engine as it cooled. I thought I could hear our own cogs and springs loosen a little, but it was just Seamus' leather jacket squeaking as he wormed his way to the side of the seat. The wind bound sweat to my face like a mask. I had to screw up my eyes to save them from a stinging. Through the barrier of lashes I looked up to Pol's window and saw a thin shadow slide across the ceiling away from me. Then the light went out.

'She's not going to answer,' I said to Helen as we slotted Seamus into his throne. She rang the doorbell regardless and we waited, watching each other's cheeks grow papery with the cold. I looked into the frosted, wire-grilled oblong of glass at the door's heart; it took a while to discern Pol's eye there, framed by the gaunt grey smudge of her face. She was looking directly at me, though she surely couldn't see anything.

'What do you want?' she spat and I saw her lower jaw squirm as it worked the words around in her mouth.

'Pol. Gran, it's me – Hel. Let us in. It's freez –'

The door slouched open and the hot breath from within was laced with almonds and oranges and age. She was something picked from the darkness behind: her skin grainy and softly cut off from the rest of her like something undeveloped on film. Of the masks I saw only an infrequent glint, as if their hollow eyes were shedding tears.

'Inside. Boneheads the lot of you. You're all thick with booze.' Her hand clung to the door's edge; the hook that was her blackened nail tapping frenetically against the wood. Its tip was encrusted with blood.

Helen and I dragged Seamus to the landing, preceded by Pol, who gusted ahead in a blowsy dress mottled with cigarette burns and stains. In one horrifying moment, as she was framed by the doorway, I saw her outline in the dress, etched as it was by the snow's luminance. It was like beholding an X-ray.

'Make a hot drink – I'm for a Bovril myself. Strong, mind, and don't go filching no stuff from me shelves. I'll have yer hands off.'

Seamus looked ready to protest but Helen pressed a finger to her lips.

Because I didn't want to be subject to any of her insidious little assaults, I went to the kitchen to make her drink, my hands unconsciously reaching for the kettle and the mugs. Instinctively, perhaps because I thought I'd catch another glimpse of him, I shot a glance out of the window, which was full of the bare lightbulb and my whey-faced reflection. It took a while to realise it wasn't mine at all, but something fly-blown and sagging, devoid of any features. After a stretch of determined staring, it faded, like frost on a heated wind-screen. Like a moth flitting from the flame.

Back in the living room, I handed Pol her drink while dili-gently avoiding her eyes. We were sitting in the soft clash of candles at the centre of the room. I looked at the painting above the fire (off – I could hear the wind thrashing about behind it like a trapped animal), at the picture of the woman and her grinning dog, and wondered why I thought there should be a bird in the picture too. Helen's hand rubbed up and down my spine. I realised how stiff I must feel and tried to relax.

'So,' said Pol, smugly, her voice deadened by the mug which hid her lower jaw. Steam turned her eyes into black olives. 'So. Why? Tell me that, Helen. *Why*?'

Helen kept her eyes on the fluid pattern of the hearth rug; its overlapping, busy strands of green and orange and blue. 'Why what?'

'Don't give me none of that smart chat, slammakin that you are. Christ, you come snuffling out of the shitey weather, dragging your touchy-feely fiddlers with you –'

I sneaked a glance at Seamus – suddenly we were part-ners in crime, our reputations defamed; I felt like a tyke sent to the headmaster for pissing in the sandpit. He, like Helen, was gazing elsewhere.

'You three. All of you shoddy and shabby. I'm grateful for the smell of the booze. God only knows –'

'Shut up! Fucking well shut up will you, you crabby old bat!'

'– what you reek of underneath.' But all the hostility was gone from Pol's voice. She stared at Helen in the way I imag-ined my mum would stare at me if I declared I wanted a sex-change.

'Get out!' barked Pol, her body bristling as though

covered with cockroaches. 'Get out of my house, you slut!' The words were painted with brittle blue streaks of sound; I never believed I'd hear such a screech.

Helen stood up. Pol actually snarled; a cat whose territory had been encroached. She pointed her crippled finger vaguely in the direction of the window. 'I said get out.' A thread of spittle fell from her mouth, weighted by a tiny sparkling bauble. I stared at it, wondering crazily if it would harden.

'I need something,' Helen's voice now conciliatory, its punch dissipated. I stood up, intending to leave them to it but she'd docked her lizard eyes with mine. Such a fury capered there though it was countered by a ponderousness that made her appear shocked, like a strung-out mental patient. Hadn't Helen mentioned something about Prozac in the past? If so, she'd stopped taking it.

'You sit down you groin-hungry bastid!' I complied, biting down on my desire to ask her to make up her mind about whether or not she wanted us to leave.

'What do you want?' Her hand was still flaying towards the window as if it were some freakish insect struggling to detach itself from her wrist. 'Obviously you don't need my help any more.'

Helen bridled. 'When have you ever given me any help?'

'The drowning.' Pol uttered the words with glutinous black relish: a linkman on TV introducing a horror film.

Though the words caused her to wince, I admired Helen's tenacity; she tilted her chin as though inviting a blow. 'You didn't help me. You just used it to fascinate those sad farts you call your friends. You used it as currency.'

'You'd have been nothing if it weren't for me. Ha! What am I saying? You've turned out rotten after all. You're a shite-hawk and a guttersnipe. You killed someone. You said so yourself!'

I was gnawing my bottom lip so voraciously that I hardly noticed the slow explosion of blood into my mouth. A rumour of cold crept through me. What we needed to discover seemed so close I thought I could pluck it from the end of my tongue. Helen's face had slackened, become as formless as kneaded dough.

'Photographs,' she said. 'I've come to collect some photographs.'

Pol's eyes narrowed. She knew Helen didn't need an escort just to pick up a few measly pictures but dutifully she shambled off to the bathroom, at last remembering to snatch her hand down to her side.

'Helen?' I tried to coax her out of her fugue. She looked hypnotised. Behind her face I could see Morecambe Bay's water-shy sand-flats stretched out and gleaming beneath the moon. I could make out hundreds of naked glistening bodies curled into the ground: all somnolent curves and hollows; any number of haunches and shoulders and shanks.

'Just leave me alone,' she said, in a voice that was fraught with distress yet resigned, the way someone sounds when they've been forced to accept a set of circumstances they didn't want. I wandered out to the landing, as close as I dared get to the bathroom, where Pol was scrabbling loudly. She was murmuring to herself, but the words were too flat and atonal to carry to me. I edged closer, ignoring the masks and a spray of pottery birds clinging to the wall, frozen in flight or spread out in modes of predacity. The door was a quarter of the way open; I could see the sink (complete with tide-mark) and a medicine cabinet above, which was closed, the mirror reflecting a print on the opposite wall that was all red and black squiggles. I still couldn't make out Pol's litany of madness. The scrabbling stopped; I began to sink back towards the threshold but not before she'd opened the cabinet and stung me with her eyes again. Her face filled the mirror, like a savagely cropped passport photograph. She smiled, putting me off balance for a beat until I realised it was more a rictus to show me what squirmed in her mouth, other than her tongue. I hurried back to the living room. Pol followed me and sat in the corner, face slashed into a raw harlequin pattern of light and shade. She was watching

Helen spread photographs around the floor while Seamus sagged impotently in his chair with all the submission of a dentist's patient. Pol looked at me with what could have been a knowing smile but I was unable to tell. I went back to the bathroom and splashed a little water on my face. The picture on the wall was of Half Moon Bay: a black and white photograph taken at dusk. I was trying to work out if the scratches were of the glass or of the photograph – figures walking the beach perhaps? – when I heard Helen call me.

Pol was still tucked into the fragmented angle of light, hands tirelessly rubbing at the hem of her dress. I thought of Miss Havisham and wondered if Pol had ever known any long-lasting love in her life, as I crossed the carpet to where Helen and Seamus were surrounded by photos. I leaned over, planting my hands on Helen's shoulders.

'Do you recognise him?' Helen said.

'I can't see,' Seamus complained, rubbing his eyes.

It was a group photo, taken when we were in our fourth year. One of those fish-eye camera jobs that pans around while you stay stock still. You have to stay stock still in order for the photograph to be taken properly. Move and you blur. Helen was pointing at one boy about ten feet away from me, his face smeared in the air as though he'd been shot in the head. I couldn't tell who it was, but I knew that he was wrapped up in what was happening to me.

'It's him,' I said, in a voice that was relieved and exhausted and scared to death.

The motorway was quieter than we'd hoped. I felt alienated from the few neighbouring cars and lorries as they powered south although I wondered at their freight both physical and otherwise. Who else was journeying towards a page break in the novel of their lives? I gripped the seat, fiercely wishing that whatever happened in the next few hours might deliver me from the desperation that had haunted me for as long as I could remember. Seamus and Helen were breathing dressmakers' dummies, Helen driving hunched over the wheel, peering through the waving windscreen wipers as they crammed snow into thick crusts at the edge of the frames. Her hands clenched and relaxed like dying spiders as she steered. A daisy ring made from green resin rose and fell on her little finger in time with her tension. I was too wired to take the wheel. Seamus' breath was a gargle rising from the back seat. I switched on the radio to drown him out but the poppy music that swam out seemed inappropriate and no other station had a signal sufficiently strong enough to beat the waves of static. I snapped it off and leaned back, allowing myself to be drawn into the pale cones spilling from the Mini's headlamps, and the destiny they etched for me on the flecked Tarmac.

I thought of what had happened at Helen's shop earlier that evening, when I'd rushed over to pick her up. Helen had been sitting in the centre of the floor, all of her water sculptures broken around her. A thin rash of sweat covered her face and her chest hitched as she took in breath. She'd trashed the lot. I picked up a flat, smooth disc of metal; one of several tears. Her initials were etched into its underside. I pocketed it, a souvenir: I wouldn't be back this way again.

Jared had turned up, early evening, drenched and shivering. She'd let him in and sat him by the fire. He hadn't said anything, he simply stared at her. Helen's voice was as flat as a newsreader's. We'd stood staring at the puddle in the centre of the room. Jared had disappeared when Helen went to call me. I say disappeared – he might well have just liquefied.

'Water was trickling out of the corner of his mouth. It didn't stop, just kept coming, making a pool on the floor. I got hysterical, thinking he was drowning, that he was in some kind of catatonia, drowning in my shop. And he smiled at me then, and there was a… David, I don't believe this, what I'm telling you. His teeth were rusting bars, like those on a drain, and there was a tiny figure, a girl, her wrists tied to the bars, her face bloated so much it was like a pink balloon. I couldn't see her eyes but I knew her. And he just kept getting wetter, like someone who'd just stepped out of a swimming pool. Streaming, he was.'

'It's over now,' I said, feeling as corny as the line. 'What are you feeling?'

'I don't feel relieved, if that's what you're getting at. I feel unresolved. Lost. I feel guilty as hell.'

'I know,' I said. 'Me too.'

We overtook a police car cruising in the left-hand lane, south of Bamber Bridge. I hoped they wouldn't notice Seamus' crumpled form in the back, pull us over, ask us what was going on, ask us: 'Is this your car, sir?'. I would have told them everything. But we weren't stopped and I waited for the relief that didn't come.

Helen swung the Mini off the M6 at Junction 22. The snow had stopped but I couldn't recall seeing the join. We sped past the traffic island at Winwick Hospital and joined the A49 towards Warrington town centre. We were minutes away now and I realised nobody had said a word since we picked Seamus up from Skerton.

But now: 'Home again, home again, jiggety-jig'. Seamus' song hung like a black veil, partitioning the two halves of the car.

On Lilford Avenue I sighed and the sound whined through my teeth. Nobody seemed to hear: we were all concentrating on the clump of black at the end of the road that heralded the woods. I saw a thin streak of light. A train, passing over the Arches?

'What do we do, when we get there?' asked Helen. Her mouth sounded tight and dry.

I didn't know and Seamus wasn't imparting any great wisdoms either. The question remained unanswered although I was certain our immediate future would be more a matter of what we'd find rather than what we would do. It was out of our hands.

'Park the car,' I said, picking up the torch and checking the batteries. The beam blazed in my eyes: when I closed them I saw bloated red shapes. Helen did not look as though she was dealing with this very well, which was upsetting because we had always relied upon her in the past; she was the unflappable one who basked in the vicarious thrill that hearing other people's problems gave her.

As I applied the handbrake, I took a sidelong glance at her. I was quite sure that since leaving Pol's house (with her pouring scorn upon us from the landing and promising us our lives would be sorry, barren affairs) I hadn't seen her blink. Seamus seemed much heavier but I couldn't decide if this was because we'd been stuffing him into and freeing him from the car all night or he'd chosen to make himself more difficult to manoeuvre due to the shock we'd suffered and his reluctance to take any further blows to his enfeebled constitution.

'How the fuck are we going to wheel him up there?' Helen asked, nodding her head towards the fence surrounding the field and the sharp incline immediately beyond it.

'I don't know, but we'll have to find a way.' I checked up and down the fence's reach and found a gap that would accommodate Seamus, if not his chair also at the same time.

'I'll manage to walk, if you could stand my arm around your shoulder.'

And so it was. We stumbled up the path, pausing to deal clumsily with the fence (I tore my jeans – and part of my thigh – open on a hook of metal). We bundled through and I half-carried, half-dragged him up the incline, our grunts competing with each other until we reached the top. The criss-cross structure of branches above looked like fractures in the sky. I had a feeling this was the last place the three of us had converged before we were blown apart like seeds from a dandelion clock.

I had to leave Seamus on his own while I helped Helen with the awkward wheelchair. I unfolded it and wrestled him in, holding him steady by the shoulders and looking down at his wasted shape, huddled into his old greatcoat. 'Chins up, fatty,' I said, and he found a smile from somewhere. I was fit for nothing now and flopped down on the snow.

'Oh come on, you fanny,' chided Helen. 'I know from personal experience that you have more stamina than that.'

'That was a long time ago,' I said. 'I can only manage the odd five-minute shag these days.'

'Instead of the marathon seven minuters when you were in your prime?' coughed Seamus.

'Fuck your mother,' I said, good-humouredly, 'if you can find the rock she crawled under.'

Helen said: 'Look.'

At the field's far end, where it began to dip towards the canal, soft, ochre light danced. I tensed, waiting for the sound of MacCreadle's bike or the percussive effect of half a dozen cans of Bastard Brew being opened at the same time. It took us twenty minutes to cross the field, as Seamus' chair kept getting trapped in the snow or clashing against a frozen divot in the earth, threatening to spill him out.

'You never said, Seamus,' I began, glad that I'd found something to talk about, something to fill the silence that wouldn't have sounded as twattish or desperate as a comment upon how brutal the weather had been recently. 'You never said what happened to your lady friend, Chicken Little, the one who thought the sky was falling in on her.'

We'd reached the Arches; a pall of relief and affection swamped me, despite the blind panic fuelling our journey here. Someone had lit a candle for us, it seemed; it shivered, a pathetic thing, as much use as an umbrella made of salt.

'A welcoming party?' asked Helen. It would have been a relief to see Juckes and Smoac swing down from the embankment, whooping abuse and threatening to kill and eat what they couldn't fuck. But all I could think of was MacCreadle, reclining in the dirt, being force-fed the souls of all the children he'd precluded from life. I half-expected to see his nemesis – that headless, mummified Siren – come tumbling out of the shadows, offering us titbits from the folds of her shroud-shawl.

'She wasn't my lady friend,' murmured Seamus, jolting me. 'You've got it wrong. Dawn was anything but.'

I knew what we were going to hear. Perhaps at that moment I understood exactly what was happening to us all; how we were linked, how we were so tightly knotted together in more than just friendship and nastiness. They were devilish knots and something foul lay at their heart. Eve, Jared and Dawn understood that and had been busy unpicking them. Maybe they understood that because they were the same person, or mirrors of the same person. Mirrors of us. The thought jolted me because we never saw them together and none of us ever met the other's 'friend'. I don't really know who they were, but I suspect they'd been a part of our make-up for many years. I also had a feeling that we would never see them again.

Why else would I paint a golden moth if not in anticipation of the woman who wore it on her breast? Certainly not because of any bow to creativity; my paintings were second-hand, passed down, left behind. Streets, houses, punched-in cars, starving dogs pissing against dead trees. I remember the day I drew the moth. I'd spent a day with my dad in the garden. He'd been having one of his bonfires and I was standing well back; fires always gave me a headache. I'd had to sit in the grass because I felt so dizzy. Part of me was being totally attentive to what Dad was saying, some harmless old guff about scouts and fire and, 'What's the best way to get rid of stuff, David? Doesn't matter what it is. The best way? Burn it.'

But I was also keeping an eye on the fire; that series of frozen orange leaps through the air, like watching a zoetrope spill its magic. I found myself attuned to its blurring speed and able to take visual snapshots as the flames distorted and dissolved in a wink. The moth was one of them, and it kept coming back. I dreamed of it for days after, only managing to kick it into my back brain by giving it some life on a canvas.

'Dawn locked herself in the loft,' said Seamus. 'She wouldn't come down. I was sending up food for her to eat every morning; she'd pull it up in a bucket tied to a piece of string. At night, when I was trying to sleep, she whispered to me through the floorboards. Most of the words I couldn't hear but now and then I'd pick out a few such as "pressure" and "suffocation" and "crushed".'

An aeroplane limped overhead, engines protesting against the black weather. Once it had disappeared, Seamus went on.

'She infected my dreams but I panicked if I closed my eyes and couldn't hear her. It's like I needed her around to feel safe. I'd go to sleep and have these long, hot dreams of smothering. People without faces forcing food into my mouth until I could take no more. But it wasn't food. It became soil, packed into my lungs, my mouth splitting with the effort. Jesus.'

'Where's Dawn now?' I asked, settling Seamus' chair by the embankment. I started picking up bits of litter, careful not to prick myself on one of the rusting syringes lying around. A fire would do us the world of good.

'She's gone. I was sitting in the living room, looking out of the window. I heard the trap door swing open and she came down. I didn't... I couldn't look round. I heard soil trickling to the floor as she moved towards the door. I wanted to beg her to stay and scream at her to fuck off. And this fucking soil kept falling. I didn't know what it was but I couldn't turn round. And then she said goodbye and her voice was full of grit. Just as she shut the door she said something else but I couldn't make out what it was.'

Seamus looked around in his chair at me scrabbling on the floor. His eye was a swivelling bearing, catching the candle-light and spitting it around. 'I think she said: "Mercy". What the fuck was she on about?'

Helen leaned across and rubbed his hands, murmured assurances, smiled. I took my collection of damp sticks, empty crisp packets and dead leaves to the candle and managed to get them ignited. Bitter smoke lifted, spreading when it met the underside of the arch. 'Get him near this,' I called to Helen, who began forcing the wheelchair over the unstable ground. She arched her eyebrows and pointed out the wooden chair, smashed and soiled, lurching in the nettles behind me. I clapped my hands and retrieved it, placing the lengths of wood in a pyramid over the heart of the fire.

'This should warm us up,' I said, too cheerily.

'Who's got the fucking sandwiches and Vimto then?' Seamus sneered, shivering under his blanket.

We settled ourselves around the flames, listening to the small explosions as the heat met pockets of air, or insects in the wood. Shadows sparred on the ceiling.

We didn't say anything for about half an hour, simply watching the flames gorge on the fuel, reach their peak then begin to dwindle. Time became something ductile, pulled out of its usual linear state and knotted up into something confusing. It was as if, while the shadows cavorted and shuddered, we gradually powered down, until we were dormant. I felt so relaxed I might not have been there. Sensory impingement was at a minimum. No cold, no heat. I could no longer smell the smoke or hear the crackle as the chair was consumed. Seamus and Helen were indistinct shapes filling my periphery. And I was conscious of the shadows. I knew we were all conscious of the shadows. But now they no longer seemed to be originated by the fire; they were of the arch's ceiling, their energy spent. Meandering across the failing brickwork like molten tar, I watched my past unfolded before me, creating a montage in black as the sour core of me cracked open like a rotten gourd, defining me in a moment more acutely than any passage of experience I had absorbed since. One moment, one act that I had buried and was now exhumed to caper, brilliant and rank, in my thoughts for the rest of my life.

We used to bully Tim Ashbery. At first it was all pretty harmless stuff, rugby-tackling him as he walked to school over the field; sticking worms in his pencil case. Like you have to be courteous, get to know them before you really lay into them. He had ginger hair, so he had no chance really.

And smelled like some cat's latrine. At first he took it all in his stride – thought it was a big joke. Rough and tumble. All lads together. That kind of bollocks. But then it got serious. One winter day, we decided we were going to rip his trousers off. One of the boys suggested ramming an icicle up his shitter. We were going to go for it. Tim was standing by the all-weather basketball court, shuffling about in the snow with his white NASA cap. The pitiable fuck. We came at him, five of us I think, from the top of the rise, where the school canteens were. And then he did the weirdest thing. Took off his clothes. He started beating himself up, pulling his hair out. Screamed something awful. It was almost funny until he started to bleed. Soon as he turned the snow pink, we legged it. We left it a few weeks and then started up again. Because of what he'd done, we felt we had to teach him a lesson. How dare he bully himself? – that was the insane line we took. That was our justification. Up until the spring we were giving him grief. Around that time I was playing cricket non-stop, trying to make the county schools side. I was never without a cricket ball. My nickname was Corky.

We were thinking of new ways to get to him and someone suggested killing the stupid cat that hung around on the field for him every day. I wasn't too keen. We had a cat called Hovis around that time – Loot's mother – and I was pretty keen on the things. But I was overruled.

We killed the cat in the morning and left it for Tim to find when he walked across the field. The bastard set fire to his own head. I went to help, to put out the flames but it was too late. His skin was black and one of his eyes had cooked like a poached egg. He was mewling pathetically, writhing around in the grass. I looked behind me but the others had scarpered; the only other figures were two hundred yard away, kicking a tennis ball around the quad.

He wouldn't shut up. He would not shut up.

I rammed the cricket ball into his mouth, stamping it down until I heard his jaw crack and the ball lodged deep in his throat. I ran when his body started arcing. The smell of lighter fuel stayed with me for days, throughout the enquiries and questioning, but I couldn't remember where it had come from. I didn't understand why I was being questioned. When school got back to normality, I couldn't work out why there was an empty seat next to Benny Lawson. And then I couldn't recall what I was bothered about: the layers of my forgetting had begun to settle.

There were still shadows swelling against the ceiling, even though the fire had burned down to a rubble of ash and embers. I was aware of Seamus, out of his wheelchair, scrabbling through the snow to the embankment. I hoped the grinding noise I could hear were his boots on the gravel and not his fractured bones scraping against each other. I'd subsumed his secrets too, during the unfolding of my own. Helen's too. It was hard for me to apportion any kind of weight to them (Seamus trying to give Evan Foley a hand-job as he lay, trapped, dying underground before plunging an ice-pick through the back of his head) because they were my friends and I could understand their motives for doing what they did (Helen abandoning her mouth-to-mouth when all she could hear was water gurgling in the girl's lungs, braining her with a half-brick while her eyes bulged in suffocation).

I wanted to ask Seamus where he was going but I was frozen, my limbs stiff and unresponsive. I slurred a few words of warning but I could barely speak. Helen was staring into the fire, paralysed by her own epiphany. The snow had started again, measured and heavy. I could hear every single impact.

A train hooter sounded. The Liverpool/Manchester Sprinter. Maybe the last of the night although I didn't know what time it was.

I heard Seamus whimpering as he scaled the embankment with its loosely packed gravel and ineffective barbed wire barriers. I couldn't move. Bonded by Seven Arches as we might have been, our collective dawning had produced a kind of fission. It was as though my heart had split into three, chilling me and grinding all the energy from my body. Seven Arches was feeling it too, the old mortar that kept it together, along with all the sordid hopes and sullied dreams that had fed its dank recesses over the years, weakened by the sudden suck of the present.

The train sounded its horn again, closer now. I could hear the metallic whine of the rails signalling the train's imminent passing.

'Seamus!' I called. I could no longer hear him, although occasional pebbles bouncing down the embankment marked his progress. He didn't answer me.

Helen's eyeballs had rolled back into their sockets. Shock was painting her mouth blue. The only part of her that was moving was her foot, twitching spastically at the edge of the fire, scuffing up small clouds of ash.

I struggled to my feet and lurched towards her. She reared up, holding her hands in front of her face as if warding off a blow.

The train's clamour looped in and out of the arches; an enormous sound. Great nets of dust dropped from the ceiling. I heard a loud crack and then, just as the viaduct collapsed and I hurled myself out of the way of the plunging tonnage of brick, I heard a soft, percussive punch, followed by a wetness, similar to the sound of a flurry of snow hitting a tent.

I just wanted to get away as the entire sky seemed to fall into the hole of my head, a symphony of rending metal and shattered glass. I felt as if I was at the centre of a black hole, dragging matter into the nagative vacuum of my heart.

I was wrong about Eve and the others. They weren't mirrors of us. They were... God, I don't know. Glue. Some form of adhesive providing a bond between the living and the dead. Just as Eve had been my protector and nemesis, she had been guardian angel to Tim Ashbery. She, Jared and Dawn drew death to them. The bodies strewn across my path were botched jobs, enforced dress rehearsals. It was me who was meant to die. Because deep down I wanted to die – the only way I could atone for what had happened. There were no reprisals from beyond the grave. Ashbery's corpse wouldn't rest because I couldn't allow it to. It was festering deep inside me, fruiting with terrible profligacy, filling out every niche of my being with rot. Ditto Helen and Seamus. We were lost souls because the events that should have destroyed us had merely clouted us senseless. Any hint of those monstrous acts welling up inside were swiftly broadsided by the subconscious, and the results of that were for us to become a little bit darker, a little bit more unstable. We were walking comas, safely ensconced in a fictional past of our own making; black pearls sealed inside dead oysters.

I lifted myself up out of the snow, leaving a cartoon outline, a freakish portal that might have allowed me access to a nowhere where I could blank everything from my mind. I was breathing heavily and I'd pissed myself. Blood squirted from the tip of my tongue in a bright, coppery fizz.

The Arches were concealed behind a low bank of brick dust. The train had collapsed into the void where our arch had disintegrated creating a tiny universe filled with pockets of chaos and calm. Miraculously, the candle continued to burn, shining through the fug like the birth of a new star. Those arches had been steeped in our moral decay. Our shock was the detonation that brought about their demolition.

The train was empty; at least the carriages that had jack-knifed into the viaduct were. I picked my way down to the embankment, trying to ignore the great fan of blood and clothing that surrounded the accident site. The driver was dead, but intact, his head crushed against the glass of his windscreen, which had withstood the impact. I could hear a stertorous hissing noise, and welcomed it. The silences that fell when it paused were horrible. I could smell the brick dust now, as it layered me with all its historical accumulations: ancient spray paint, stale piss, soiled rain from the bilious cooling towers of the power station. Into one of these lacunae I called a name – Helen or Seamus – I don't know which.

Neither responded. The high-pitched rasp of MacCreadle's bike as it whistled down Lovely Lane spurred me into action. I was standing there, holding my dick like a baby while my friends lay in the wreckage, needing my help. I approached cautiously lest the mangled tower of train should settle further. I could see a figure pinned beneath the twisted metal but couldn't discern who it was. It was naked. I called again. Helen's name this time. No answer.

Skirting the debris, I found a path to the body that was relatively clear. I edged towards the curl of flesh and began to get very cold. Shock was kicking into my system, fuzzing my head so it seemed I was viewing everything though crumpled cellophane. I could tell now that the body belonged to Seamus; his bald head poked from the intersections of steel in a grotesque representation of birth. His face was thrust skywards, the patch gone, displaying a chalky nugget in his eye socket. A pool of blood surrounded him, mixing with oil. One of his arms hung from the edge of a warped door frame. Only when my mouth filled did I realise I was gagging. He looked peaceful. He looked unreal. I knew I was still alive when I realised that my tears weren't freezing on my cheeks.

The air was fresh. My mind felt as clean and as cold as a gum from which a bad tooth has been wrenched. A few minutes later, backing away from the weight of his death, I saw Helen. She'd fallen into the canal and was face down in a broth of oil, her arm twisted behind her back. I could see the resin flower on her finger. A great bloom of red had blossomed at the small of her back. I waded in and fished her out, knowing she was already dead. I touched the blood. It wrinkled, much like the sugar test my mum used to perform on a saucer when making strawberry jam. As I flipped her over, I knew that the set of her face would be a constant with me for as long as I lived; as permanent as a tattoo. Maybe that's why I looked at her, to damn me for eternity, for what I did.

This was where it ended for us – our unstable (but compulsive) friendship torn asunder on the exposed skeleton of the train, the collapsed waste land of sandstone.

I didn't fully appreciate how ingrained Seamus' presence had been upon my own. He might have been anathema to me in many ways but he was also irresistible. That it should end so bloodily here, in the one place where we had felt so alive and involved with each other made it doubly traumatic. My tenancy of Seven Arches was over. Nothing beckoned at me from beyond its seedy confines.

Trying to keep my eye from dwelling too long on the new configurations of Seamus' head, I rooted around for something to cover Helen and found a partially burned blanket in a bed of nettles. I pressed my hand against her breast for the last time, where her flesh was so white and smooth. Then I fastened the buttons at the top of her dress and stood up straight, closing my eyes to a bout of dizziness.

Through the ticking of the train as it cooled and the various creaks and wails as it discovered new stresses and alien alignments, I heard a sound, as of beating wings. I couldn't see anything that authored the flapping, but I was growing more jittery by the second. I wanted to be away. Especially as I now realised that it wasn't MacCreadle's bike I could hear, but a siren.

I tramped back through the snow, intending to return to the car and drive it until the petrol ran out. Maybe head north, find some mountains in which to lose myself.

The night thinned; I watched the puke-stained morning soil the horizon. I was so cold I couldn't feel my mouth.

The compulsion to go home, to hug my mum and dad and tell them I loved them, was unbearably intense, especially as I could see their house from here. They would be sitting up in bed with cups of coffee, sleepy and warm. Still holding hands after all this time. I wished I knew them better. Loot fled through my mind; a sinuous loop of jet. I could almost smell home and the simple, massive love of my family. Dad's silly little sayings such as: 'Well, David – what do you know?' and 'Do you want to buy a battleship?' Stuff I'd grown up on with Kim and would no doubt bewilder my own children with one day. I thought of Mum attacking the Russian vine in the garden or folding herself into the sofa the way only mums can. I wanted someone to put a plaster on my knee and to sweep hair from my eyes when I was sick in bed with a cold. I wanted that little clump of dependent years back – just for a short while.

The flapping had increased, the sound of loose clothes on a washing line, frisked by the wind. In my pocket, my fingers moved against something sharp. I pulled the metal tear out and brought it up to my face, trying to see it in the poor light. The flapping stopped just as the sirens cut out. Blue light spat across the field. Bursts of static. People calling, their voices frantic. The clatter of an approaching helicopter.

In the moment before the tear turned to water and trickled between my fingertips, above the clamour of disaster teams as survivors were sought, I heard the desperate, clotted shriek of a newborn.

I closed my eyes, turned around and opened my mouth.

FRONTLINES
The future of fiction

SONG OF THE SUBURBS by SIMON SKINNER

Born in a suburban English New Town and with a family constantly on the move (Essex to Kent to New York to the South of France to Surrey), who can wonder that Slim Manti feels rootless with a burning desire to take fun where he can find it? His solution is to keep on moving. And move he does: from girl to girl, town to town and country to country. He criss-crosses Europe looking for inspiration, circumnavigates America searching for a girl and drives to Tintagel for Arthur's Stone... Sometimes brutal, often hilarious, *Song of the Suburbs* is a Road Novel with a difference. Told in ever-more revealing episodes, it marks the published début of one of Britain's most exciting new writers. ISBN 1 899 344 37 3

HEAD INJURIES by CONRAD WILLIAMS

It's winter and the English seaside town of Morecambe is dead. David knows exactly how it feels. Empty for as long as he can remember, he depends too much on a past filled with the excitements of drink, drugs and cold sex. The friends that sustained him then – Helen and Seamus – are here now and together they aim to pinpoint the source of the violence that has suddenly exploded into their lives.

"I loved it. The observation has the freshness and vividness of lived experience, and the supernatural manifestations are just as arrestingly original. The portraits of everyday loneliness are brilliant. Altogether I though it was one of the finest and most haunting modern spectral novels I've read." — RAMSEY CAMPBELL   ISBN 1 899 344 36 5

THE LONG SNAKE TATTOO by FRANK DOWNES

Ted Hamilton's new job as night porter at the down-at-heel Eagle Hotel propels him into a world of seedy nocturnal goings-on and bizarre characters. These range from the pompous and near-efficient Mr Butterthwaite to bigoted old soldier Harry, via Claudia the harassed chambermaid and Alf Speed, a removals man with a penchant for uninvited naps in strange beds.

But then Ted begins to notice that something sinister is lurking beneath the surface. ISBN 1 899 344 35 7

B-format PAPERBACK ORIGINALS – only £5

Available at all good bookshops

The Do-Not Press
Fiercely Independent Publishing

Keep in touch with what's happening at the cutting edge of independent British publishing.

Join The Do-Not Press Information Service and receive advance information of all our new titles, as well as news of events and launches in your area, and the occasional free gift and special offer.

Simply send your name and address to:
The Do-Not Press (Dept. HI)
PO Box 4215
London
SE23 2QD
or email us: thedonotpress@zoo.co.uk

There is no obligation to purchase and no salesman will call.

Visit our regularly-updated Internet site:
http://www.thedonotpress.co.uk

Mail Order

All our titles are available from good bookshops, or (in case of difficulty) direct from The Do-Not Press at the address above. There is no charge for post and packing. (NB: A postman may call.)